MEET THE FORCE RECON TEAM . . .

JACK SWAYNE

The leader of the team. A brilliant tactician and superb soldier. For him, failure is not an option . . . ever.

GUNNY POTTS

A giant of a man. Loyalty to his team comes first, the mission comes second . . . and nothing else comes close.

NIGHT RUNNER

A full-blooded American Indian. Even with the cutting-edge technology used by the team, the deadliest thing about him is his senses.

FRIEL

An ex–street thug turned disciplined Marine. A natural-born killer with no remorse. Possibly the deadliest shot in the world.

FORCE RECON

The explosive new series by
James V. Smith, Jr.

By James V. Smith, Jr.

FORCE RECON
FORCE RECON: DEATH WIND

FORCE RECON

DEATH WIND

James V. Smith, Jr.

BERKLEY BOOKS, NEW YORK

This is a work of fiction. Names, characters, places, and incidents are
either the product of the author's imagination or are used fictitiously,
and any resemblance to actual persons, living or dead, business
establishments, events, or locales is entirely coincidental.

FORCE RECON: DEATH WIND

A Berkley Book / published by arrangement with
the author

PRINTING HISTORY
Berkley edition / April 2000

The Penguin Putnam Inc. World Wide Web site address is
http://www.penguinputnam.com

ISBN: 0-425-17406-9

BERKLEY®
Berkley Books are published by The Berkley Publishing Group,
a division of Penguin Putnam Inc.,
375 Hudson Street, New York, New York 10014.
BERKLEY and the ''B'' logo
are trademarks belonging to Penguin Putnam Inc.

PRINTED IN THE UNITED STATES OF AMERICA

10   9   8   7   6   5   4   3   2   1

For Chris

The Spartans don't ask how many the enemy are
but where the enemy are.

FORCE RECON

DEATH WIND

EVENT SCENARIO 14—DAY 1

"BINGO BRUTUS." Jack Swayne spat the words at the boom mike at his lips. Two words to set off the kill phase of his Force Recon Team's mission. The perfect mission too, so far.

From Iraq's no-fly zone to the south, the lead pilot of two F-117 Stealth fighters was to say—

"Spartan One, this is Pave Nail Six-Two, confirm you have a visual on Brutus."

Leave it to the Air Force to get chatty when the two words would work just as well. So much for perfection.

"Bingo Brutus," Swayne said. He let his tone add, *Damn you, listen up.*

Bingo meant Swayne was eyeballing the target of Event 14. *Brutus* stood for Imani Abboud Dahni. Why didn't the guy just say *Bingo Brutus* to confirm he'd heard?

Would the weenies in cockpits and ops centers never get it? A dirt-eating grunt in spitball range of the bad guys didn't want to spill his guts after every fart and giggle. And he didn't like some console commando "going Alvin" in his ears either, to use Friel's words for it.

But this pilot just had to go chipmunk: "Pave Nail Six-Two," he said. "Roger Brutus. Stand by for E-mail."

"Roger." In his mind's eye, Swayne saw the jets streak up at sixty degrees and pass through Mach Two. As the pilots hit their time hacks they would jerk their jets vertical. And cut loose two bombs apiece at once. The high-G toss would fling the winged bombs into an arc a half mile high. The arc would ease into a glide of thirty miles right to Swayne's team.

"Spartan One, this is Pave Nail Six-Two, be advised as to *bombs-away* in five ticks. Stand by to paint Brutus and his boys in thirty ticks, on my mark." A pause of three seconds. "Mark. You have E-mail, and Pave Nail is on the way home to the barn. Good luck and good night."

Swayne ground his teeth. *Fine and dandy. And what do you hear from the little lady? Want to fill me in on your plans for the night? How much wine to suck down? How many two-stars to suck up?* Why was it the combat troops did their talking at the mission debrief? While the armchair grunts did theirs on the radios and in their chat rooms, bars, and beds—and all their fighting in their dreams?

Swayne kept quiet. Why bother with more talk? The four smart bombs were away, now in free fall. The law of gravity had taken over. It would hand off the bombs to the team once they lit up their laser beams in—Swayne checked the LED digits of his stop watch—two-four seconds. The brain in each bomb would ID its own lasers and fire onboard jets to make final course changes. Each would home to a kill. Swayne's IR laser would direct two of the bombs, both at Abboud Dahni. To be on the side of certainty, the idea was to kill him twice. It wasn't enough for Swayne.

Abboud Dahni's boys had set off car bombs on Wall Street, Fleet Street, and the Champs Elysee. All on the same day less than a week ago, killing more than five hundred and setting a packed school bus on fire. Payback time was now only—one-niner seconds away.

Swayne kept his mind on Abboud Dahni's bearded face. One finger on the right barrel of his binoculars started the clock in his field of view. He waited for the team to sound off. On his left, Friel growled into his mike, "Roger, mark." Night Runner, to his right, grunted his thumbs-up. Each of them took time to ram a foam plug deep into the ear canal that wasn't already filled with his radio receiver.

Nothing left to do but wait. And in—ten seconds—give the order to paint laser spots on their targets. Then wait for the *flash-bang-thank-you, ma'am.* End of mission. Event Scenario 14, except for the extraction, would be history. Ditto the summer camp of half the world's worst terrorists. And Mr. Terrorist himself, Imani Abboud Dahni, would have had one bomb driven through his heart like a stake. The other would scatter his remains.

Blender-ized, martyr-ized, and vaporized. The perfect end to a perfect blood-sucker. Compliments of the United States, the Marine Corps, Team Midnight, Force Recon, Captain Jack Swayne, and his men.

The perfect mission.

Too perfect to Swayne's way of thinking. No matter how he sliced and diced it. No matter how many times he did the math. No matter how hard he played the devil's advocate. It kept coming out the same—flawless. *Aces,* as Friel would put it. *Smooth as Granny's apple butter,* as Gunny Potts might say. *Fine with me,* as Sergeant Night Runner might say with a nod of his head. If he said anything at all. Maybe just the nod.

THEY HAD JUMPED into the heart of Iraq, sixty-three miles south and east of Baghdad, just two hours ago. All four touched down within ten meters of the briefed LZ. Unlike Event 13, a perfect HALO drop. Four stand-up landings. No lost weapons, gear, or commo. No sprains, no splinters, no sweat. Swayne's report to the Operational Mission Command Center took all of a nanosecond, a touch of a button on his Personal Locator Beacon. The PERLOBE signaled a satellite that sent his location and mission status to

OMCC. Nobody in the center had given in to the urge of all staff weenies since the invention of radios: to flap their lips at grunts in the field. All Swayne heard in the tiny speaker planted deep inside his left ear canal was a simple "Roger, Spartan One."

No wonder Swayne felt herds of roaches mill about his gut.

He had shucked his harness and tossed his para-wing into a heap. By then Night Runner and Friel had swept east and west of the LZ looking to shut any stray eyes that might have seen them drop. Potts dug a hole big enough for all four chutes. By the time Swayne oriented his palm-sized GPS to the march route, Night Runner had slipped into his line of sight at the point. *How did he do that?* Swayne wondered. *No gadgets, not even a compass. Still, he found the march route.*

A "wagons-ho!" gesture by Swayne set the Blackfeet-warrior-turned-Marine into liquid motion, floating like a fog across the moonscape of Iraq, silent and fuzzy. By the time the sergeant melted into the night ink, Friel, the team's sniper and special weapons expert, had trudged into the two spot. Friel shuffled across the landscape, rattling stones and crunching sand lumps. But at least he kept his mouth shut, and Swayne shook his head in dismay. He had never known Henry to stifle the smart-ass for longer than five minutes. Ever. If this was not perfection, what was?

Swayne, a leftie, took up the three spot ten meters behind Friel, a rightie, so their weapons covered the flanks. Potts fell into file, watching their six. Swayne had briefed them to clear the LZ in two minutes. They did it in one.

Night Runner led them to their attack positions in forty-five minutes, half what Swayne had allotted. The ridge they found on the ground looked exactly like the one in the J-2's aerial pix. Night Runner took time to un-stack a pile of three stones so nobody would kick them into the valley below, tipping off the enemy. The sergeant had said he would do so in the briefing.

Friel had scoffed at that back in the ready room at Quantico. "That's what I call going hemorrhoidal, Chief." It was Friel's term for anal-retentive. After Night Runner set the stones aside, Friel shook his head in awe. But kept his mouth shut. Now that was too much for Swayne to believe.

He hated to peek over the crest of the ridge. A mission like this could not have gone like clockwork so far. Not unless CIA had blown it where it really counted. He knew damned well that once he bellied up to scan the valley with his night-vision, laser-designating, camera-equipped, ranging binoculars, there would be no enemy. Not even the goatherds CIA photo-analysts had ID'd as advance men for Imani Abboud Dahni. Nothing below but boulders and brush, even the goats gone, having grazed out the sparse vegetation in the nine hours since Swayne had pored over the photos. Hell, there was a better chance of finding the Chinese embassy down in that gulch than a bunch of bad-asses planning to car-bomb their way to heaven.

Like a lot of other missions he'd been on, this one would be a bust. Zilch bad guys, zip BDA.

Nothing to do but slink out of Iraq and chalk up one more mission to failed intel. Which, by his count, undid at least fifty percent of all missions anyhow.

Before going over the top, Swayne checked left and right. Night Runner had crept to the north. The clump of darkness Swayne spotted against the hillside might be a sandstone outcropping. Or it might be an Ivy League–educated Indian brave from Heart Butte, Montana. Swayne blinked. The clump of night vanished, and he knew which. Friel moved south, lurching across the slope, setting off tiny gravel slides until he found his ready position. He worked his butt into the sand, forming a chair seat for himself. Potts wedged his own huge form into position among the boulders along their back trail. And Swayne began his low crawl toward Camp Fiasco.

Event Scenario 13 had rattled the team's nerves six months ago. The Spartans had pulled off their mission. Technically anyhow. They'd rescued the Commandant of the Marine Corps from French separatists in Canada. But along the way they had gotten into shootouts with both the Army and the Navy. Friel and Potts had taken hits. The Marines had smoked out a mole at the Pentagon, but not before she had set back at least one top-secret program. PERLOBEs had already found their way into special ops units of France. Meaning that, sooner rather than later, any terrorist with ready cash and a grudge against Walt Disney's homeland would have them too.

Even so, the team had sharpened up. As far as any unit can hone itself in training. Even the toughest exercise could not mimic battle conditions, to Swayne's way of thinking. What they needed to put them into top shape was a mission in Operation Desert Fox. But back then Friel still jogged with a limp. Gunny Potts had not shed the twenty pounds he had picked up in his hospital stay. Gen. Harley V. Masterson himself had offered the team first choice of combat ops. Swayne had declined. Too reckless to put his team in harm's way at less than a hundred percent.

But by now Team 2400 had reached its peak. Too bad they weren't going to be able to use their skills on a live enemy force, Swayne thought. He reached the top of the ridge and propped himself on his elbows. He brought his night-vision binos to bear on the spot where the terrorist camp should be. Bare brush and goat manure and—

"Son of a bitch," he hissed aloud, breaking his own rule against idle chatter. For less than a hundred meters away— 93.762 meters, by the digital readout in his NVBs—stood Imani Abboud Dahni, radical Saudi prince, target of Event 14. At eighteen-power, he looked close enough to take out with a fixed bayonet. The prissy playboy who killed Westerners for grins, blaming it all on dicta issued by his God.

There stood the killer, baby-faced even with the beard— Pretty Boy Lloyd, Potts called him. Swayne could even see gravy stains down the front of his sheets.

First Swayne snapped several time-captioned, digital photos for the record. Then he backed down and out of sight behind the ridge. He ordered Night Runner and Friel up so they could scope out the camp and find their targets.

Then he made the report that signaled the bomb-toss: "Bingo Brutus."

EVENT SCENARIO 14 now stood at fifteen seconds until laser-painting time. Fourteen. Thirteen. Counting down. The perfect end to a perfect evening. Enough to make Swayne queasy.

IMANI ABBOUD DAHNI admired his work. A crowd circled the cooking fire, where a kid roasted on a spit. His dream had come true. Freedom fighters from Africa, Asia, Mexico, the Pacific Rim, India, Pakistan, Canada, and Northern Ireland had joined him. Yes, there were some odd characters— the animal lovers from Britain and the neo-Nazis from Idaho.

But his vision of a unified *jihad* had materialized. Two Western journalists had come. Rival Western journalists at that, one from *The New York Times,* the other from the *Washington Post.* Before midnight a camera crew and reporter from CNN would arrive. Escorted by Abboud Dahni's prize catch: Hassein Khali Bin Gahli. The Death Wind himself.

The mere mention of Bin Gahli's name stopped conversations in this camp. Assassins of presidents and schoolchildren alike chewed their lips in silence.

Legend had it that Saddam had once quipped that Bin Gahli must have learned from the Devil himself. Bin Gahli had scowled and said he had yet to teach the Devil all his tricks.

Abboud Dahni smiled. With the arrival of the CNN crew, he would have it all in place. First the speeches. Then the interviews.

Then he would send teams to the four corners of the world.

And stand by to tally the wreckage.

LANCE CORPORAL HENRY Friel counted down as he lay on his belly. At ten he finished scoping out the valley. At nine he slipped his finger through the slit in the goatskin glove on his right hand so he could feel the buttons and trigger of his 20-millimeter smart gun. *Skin on steel.* A master-blaster had to have the touch.

At five, he reviewed his part in the mission: Use the invisible IR laser dot in the scope of the gun he called *Blowpipe* to paint the biggest group of men. Give the smart bomb twenty seconds to capture his beam. At twenty-one in the count-up, shut off the laser. At twenty-two, duck behind the ridge. At twenty-three, put his head between his legs and kiss his ass good-bye.

Even a ridgeline between them and the target zone wasn't enough, for shit's sake. Four tons of boom-boom launched at oh-dark-thirty from Bumstuck, Egypt, by some bluebonnet preppy jet jockey off a glorified Sega platform like they was hand grenades out of a slingshot? Friel didn't care what the captain said about direct lines of sight, laser captures, and such bullshit as that. A two-thousand-pounder wasn't going to be undone with an *Oops!* and *I'm sorry about that shit.* When the smart bombs turned moron, and the friendly fire got jiggy—

His mental countdown reached one. Friel grew as serious as he knew how—*serious as a corpsman giving hisself a vasectomy,* the gunny would say. He put his doubts out of his head. *This was killing time.* And he had no room for nonlethal thinking.

SERGEANT ROBERT NIGHT Runner's stopwatch would vibrate when it was time to turn on his laser and escort his smart bomb to the east end of the camp. Unlike the other laser flashlights in the team, his projected a visible dot. He looked down on supplies and pack animals: mules, horses, and camels. Night Runner didn't like the idea of hurting animals. So he picked a tent city as his target.

The stopwatch tickled his wrist just as Swayne's command buzzed in his ear: "Begin painting."

Night Runner directed a red spot onto a section of canvas near the peak of a tent. Half a dozen men had gone in only seconds ago. He counted to himself, bunching his warrior's muscles to spring backward off the ridge at twenty.

SWAYNE PAINTED AN IR laser dot on Abboud Dahni's gravy stain where it ran into the folds of his sheet below the belt. Hell, the bastard wouldn't care whether he was struck in the face or the foot with the two thousand pounds of explosives. Either way there wouldn't be enough left of him at ground zero for maggot brunch. Swayne split the difference. So the bomb would hit him where it hurt the worst. Even if it didn't go off.

This one's for you, Brutus. From the mothers of all those children.

QUANTICO, VIRGINIA—1104 HOURS LOCAL

MARINE COLONEL KARL ZAVELLO, listening for a "Mission complete" report from Force Recon Team 2400 out of Iraq, hardly dared to breathe. He knew the Air Force had launched their smart bombs. The only thing left was impact and BDA—

He waved off the radio operator coming his way brandishing a handset.

"Not now," Zavello said, his one good eye flashing behind black wraparound sunglasses.

The operator's hand shook as if she had palsy. "White House on the landline, sir."

Zavello peeled back his lips, baring gapped, rounded teeth like that of a killer whale. "What'd I say?"

"Sir, I—"

"Not now, dammit. Take a message."

"Sir." Caught between two jousting bulls, the buck sergeant felt her eyes well with tears. "It's the National Security Adviser. He won't be put off. Sir. Please." She held her hand over the mouthpiece as Zavello vented a stream of filth into the air. Only when he had run out of breath did she hand over the phone.

The colonel snatched it as if he were catching flies. He clapped the phone to his ear. "Zavello," he growled. As he listened, the skin above the frames of his sun shades rumpled. "Are you nuts? Calling off a mission after it's already in progress?"

He held the telephone away from his ear. The OMCC staff froze as if seeing a vision of the paranormal—somebody on the planet could yell louder and curse worse than Zavello. As the volume grew and the obscenities flew, Zavello glanced at the control center clock. A twisted smile crept across his crooked lips. Finally the tone in the telephone turned to demanding an answer.

"Yes, sir," Zavello said. "Uh-huh. I see. . . . Yes, yes, I'm clear on that. As soon as you finish here, I will get on the horn and call off the fighters." The voice broke in. Zavello said, "*Mmmmm?* Yes, sir, I'd be happy to repeat it. I'm to call off the fighters and direct the team on the ground to clear the area without incident." Zavello smiled and nodded. "And if the ordnance has been launched, do not paint targets. Yes, uh-huh, yes, sir. Just let the bombs fall where they may. Fine, sir." He remembered one of the hick phrases he had heard one of Swayne's men use. "Fine as frog hair on a baby's behind, sir," he said, his voice smooth as twelve-year-old Scotch whiskey. He bared his whale's teeth in a pale imitation of a smile, letting the voice lecture on until it ran down and cut itself off in mid-curse.

Zavello tossed the phone to the sergeant. He hawked in his throat, as if to spit. "Senior field-grade duty officer on deck," he barked.

A crisp major jumped to his feet, dancing as if he had to pee. "Yes, sir. Major Burke, sir, yes, sir," he said.

"Contact the United States Air Force liaison officer for this mission and direct him to call back the two sorties before they drop their ordnance," Zavello ordered.

The major blinked as if sending Morse code. "But sir—"

Zavello skinned his lips away from his Orca teeth once more. "Do as I say, Major. The National Command Authority has directed us to call off this mission because, without the knowledge of or consultation with our State Department, some twink at the United Nations has directed the United Nations Special Commission, or as Americans know it, UNSCOM—and we here like to call it *SCUM-SCUM*—to return to Iraq for inspection of that country concerning weapons of mass destruction. If you had the ears to hear, you would have deduced that from the telephone conversation that I just received. In addition, it has come to the attention of the White House that at least three journalists from United States news organizations have infiltrated into Iraq and may be at this very moment in harm's way if that bombing mission should be allowed to continue unabated."

The light of comprehension dawned in the major's eyes. Zavello was playing a game of his own. He nodded and glanced at the clock on a wall. Some political pimp in the White House wanted his orders followed. And dammit, Zavello was going to follow orders. To the letter. The whole speech, the big words, the—

"Major, get your ass in gear."

The major found a phone far, far from his boss.

Zavello stood at attention like a maestro calling his choir to order. His hands churned the air, sketching a mushroom cloud. "Ba-da-bing, ba-da-*BOOM*!" he bellowed three times, each time louder than the last. Each time he sent the cloud churning higher and wider as he stood on his toes. Finally he fell red-faced into a chair and broke into spitting, hacking guffaws. This created high anxiety in the OMCC staff. Nobody among them—if this was laughing—had ever seen him laugh.

THE IRAQI DESERT—2105 HOURS LOCAL

IMANI ABBOUD DAHNI FELT BLESSED, as if he'd been chosen a prophet. He wanted to embrace all that he had wrought. So he spread out his arms, accepting God's blessings, throwing back his head to the sky. For a moment he thought he saw a shooting star, which had always meant good luck to him. Then the nose of a two-thousand-pound bomb struck him in the pelvis, the impact alone killing him even before he could hear or feel the explosion going off at the juncture of his legs.

NONE OF THE Spartans saw the strike. Seconds before the blasts, the three Marines on the ridge slid down the slope to put as much earth as possible between themselves and the explosions. After turning off their voice-activated mikes to save them from the shock wave, they braced for a pounding. Each had picked a spot clear of rock slides. Each clutched his weapon and buried his face into the crook of one arm to save his night vision. Each spent his next few seconds alone with his soul.

NIGHT RUNNER FELT the earth move. It slapped his back like an old friend after a clean kill of a five-point buck in deer season. Even with earplugs he could hear the shrapnel singing by overhead. The concussion sucked his lungs empty. His skin prickled, both from the shock in the air and in his thoughts. On the other side of the ridge behind him lay a cauldron of hell he had helped create. He had turned his enemy to ash and dust. Worse yet, he'd killed the enemy's animals. At times like this he worried for mankind. He wished high-tech had not come to this. For by making the killing impersonal, new weapons had shrouded the face of death. What if men had to kill each other face-to-face with knife and fist instead? The raw intimacy of such murder might make men shrink from it. He weighed the idea a moment.

Nah. They'd always killed each other well enough before the smart bombs and nukes. And would still.

GUNNERY SERGEANT DELMONT Potts reckoned it a square deal that men who lived by the bomb died by the bomb. You put your biscuit hooks into the fire and start playing around, you better damn well expect to have your ass blistered now and again. Thing was, this was way better all the way around anyway. Better than a kangaroo trial where the only ones that get anything out of it were the lawyers sucking at the angel tit of the taxpayers' money tree. Better than a firefight, where a decent Marine might get hurt.

This way was clean. One minute a gaggle of terrorists is diddling around a campfire like a bunch of Girl Scouts roasting marshmallows. Next minute they are the marshmallows, vanishing like a fart in a tornado, flying straight up to terrorist heaven like they're always ranting and chanting they want to do.

So he could go home to a goober pie and a Coca-Cola.

Yeah. Sounded to him like a good deal all the way around.

FRIEL WISHED HE could watch. Just once he'd like to see the last look on one of the cheese-eating bastards that had killed sixty-three kids in city streets not so long ago. He came off the streets himself. Could have been him in another time. Or one of his family any day now.

But the captain had shot him down when he asked to watch the impact at the briefing. Which pissed him off. Later on the chief had told him to check out the story of Lot's wife in the Bible next time he wanted to get up close and personal with fire and brimstone. He didn't remember too many Bible stories, no matter how hard the Jesuits had tried to bongo them into his head. But he remembered the ones where God kicked ass like he was a Force Recon Marine his own self. And he remembered the chick that didn't listen and got her own ass turned to a block of Morton's best.

Okay, so it could give you a case of bad karma to watch a bomb go off. Still. He'd heard about the sheep test, and he wanted to see for himself. Maybe he could invent a bomb-proof mask and try it next time out.

Just one little peekaboo. It'd be better'n Wile E. Coyote handing over a stick of TNT to the Road Runner. And what he wouldn't give to see that.

But the captain says nooo-uh!
Officers. He'd never met one that didn't need an enema.

SWAYNE WAITED FOR his second wave of ordnance. A cluster bomb had homed on his laser behind the high-explosive.
At a thousand feet it had deployed a set of air brakes,
keeping it clear of the first three bomb blasts. Even with
ears plugged he could hear the shriek of wind through the
open tail fins. A sequence of doors was to open on the main
bomb casing at one-second intervals. Then 1,432 bomblets
would rain from the sky, each a half pound of space-age
explosives as powerful as ten sticks of dynamite. They each
had their own fins that made them spin and drift like little
helicopters. They would spread out and carpet the area of
the valley from one end to the other, drifting downwind a
quarter mile. Any second now—
    There. A rolling explosion worked its way across the
sky behind them. Swayne had seen ultra-secret videos of a
test on a herd of eight hundred unshorn sheep staked out
over most of a mile. He knew the sickening stats. Even
through four inches of wool, 98 percent of the animals suf-
fered wounds, 87 percent disabling, 73 percent mortal. Had
any terrorists not been killed outright by the first three
bombs, the bomblets would mop up. Anybody idiot enough
to stand up to be counted would be counted among the
dead.
    When the explosions had sputtered out like the last ker-
nels of popcorn in the pan, Swayne turned his mike on and
directed his team back up the hill for bomb damage as-
sessment: "BDA time."

BIN GAHLI MISSED Abboud Dahni's barbecue by less than
a mile. The pair of laggard mules packing the CNN gear
saved his life by slowing him down.
    Television.
    Bin Gahli had seldom seen it and had no use for it. Nor
propaganda. Nor winning the hearts and minds of people—
not Arabs, Iraqis, or even his own men. When he wanted

somebody's heart or mind (or ear or tongue or head or hand
or sex organ, for that matter), he took it. At the point of a
knife. Not even Allah impressed him all that much. If Saddam could declare himself a god, then gods weren't worth
two dinars, now going at a thousand dinars to the dollar.

Better to trust his own instincts. So when he sensed
something in the sky above them, Bin Gahli leapt off the
faint track they had been following. He threw himself flat
in the sand and covered his head.

He didn't care about the two men and the woman of the
CNN crew caught in the open. They could worry about
themselves. But they did not. As the earth belched smoke
and fire, they stood bedazzled. Only their mules reacted, to
shy.

Evans, the sound man, key grip, best boy, and all-around
techno-wizard, had wrapped one of the lead ropes around
his wrist. When the mule took off into the scrub, it first
jerked him off his feet, then broiled his skin with a rope
burn as it galloped off, kicking and braying. Watson, the
shooter, editor, and producer, finally realized what had happened. He dropped to his knees, whining a prayer salted
with curse words.

Nina Chase, the face, or on-camera talent, saw it unfold
like a play staged just for her. Funny how Watson dropped
out of sight when he went down. Even funnier when the
mule jerked Evans off his feet and dragged him off, leaving
nothing but a trail of dust. But she loved the fireworks best
of all. First the three explosions, a heartbeat apart. Then
columns of smoke rising in the strobe-light show that followed. As she turned around in place, she saw the men of
her escort diving off the trail into the bushes and boulders.
The strobing lights put everything into stop-action. Each
dive jittered across her field of view like a hundred flash-
frozen images, a flip-and-see photo-motion booklet come
to life. She should have been afraid.

But no. What luck. A no-shit baptism of fire her first
time in the field since leaving the *Washington Promoter* for

the Atlanta-based network a month ago. On her first CNN outing? *Imagine!*

Seconds later the show ended. By now Nina chided herself for not taking cover. She knew she might have strong news instincts, but her survival skills in the past six years had leaned toward the social and political. Next time, she would play it safe. Dictate her notes lying flat on the ground. Rehearse a ten-second blurb from behind the rocks.

Speaking of rocks, Evans kept howling about his arm being torn off.

"Shut up, Dale, I can't hear myself think."

Evans shrieked, "Up yours, bitch."

Nina wasn't in the mood for a fight. She patted down the pockets of her safari jacket and came up with her tape recorder. She dusted it off. She thought she should capture rough notes for her first story. Lead with the vivid stuff. The lights. The dazzle. The mules. Oh, and the flip-and-see images, the—

"Hey, people," she said. "I'm about to put some notes on tape here. A moment of silence would be nice."

But no. Evans still felt sorry for himself. "Hey, yourself. I'm bleeding here. Come see."

"What am I, your mother? I don't kiss ouchies, Dale." Or anything else. "Come on, Watson, hold it down. Why don't you track down the gear so we can get pictures if we get some more fireworks."

But Watson had not finished praying his obscenities. He asked God to work impossible sex acts between the editors and producers who had sent him out here to die. And he had a few ideas about what the mules could do to Nina too if she told him to shut up again.

The guy was a million laughs. Or would be when she told the crew back in Atlanta about his antics. So he was scared. Fine with her. But did be have to be so damned loud about it?

"You men shut up." She made the sound of a spitting cat. "Men. I should say babies—damn tape player!" She shook it and tapped it. No use. It sounded like a tiny mill, grinding sand to talc. Evans and Watson had begun a duet that sounded worse than a pair of 1940's country singers. Or maybe cats in heat. Yeah, cats. The tape died with a final crunch of gears and the smell of hot plastic. She threw it away and blessed it with a few curses of her own.

Too bad. How she'd love to have these crybabies on tape for—

The two came at her. She could see them only as shadows, but with shadows of balled fists. *"Dale? What the—?"*

She realized that Evans and Watson thought she'd been cursing them out. "Wait, wait. I was talking about my tape player, boys. Now don't you lose your heads—"

But they did lose their heads. The sound man, to a short, crescent-shaped sword wielded by a shadow that melded with his. The cameraman lost his to a shorter curved knife. Nina saw a flash of the blade before it disappeared into Watson's skin and circled his throat to the bone. A bare, muscular arm twisted the head, separating the neck, letting the body drop.

Nina heard a cough rattle from the corpse. A single huge form came toward her. She couldn't take her eyes from the apparition that took shape in faint moonlight. The guy held Watson's head under his arm like a sack of corn. Watson's open mouth still kept trying to scream in her face. She closed her eyes. She said the closest thing to a prayer that came to mind, not much improved over Watson's cussing: "Sheeze Louise almighty God."

FROM THE CREST of the ridge, Swayne, Night Runner, and Friel looked down on the damage. Black smoke mingled with creamy dust like swirled ice cream. The pall ebbed and flowed between the valley walls like sloshing water, forming eddies and billows. But in slow motion. This was more a dream than a body count.

Swayne had seen death scenes many times over. But not like this eerie, vacant hole where more than ninety men had camped just seconds ago. Revulsion set his mind loose. He thought he saw a Death Angel at a hover, wings spread over the feast of blood as admired his work, deciding where to start feeding.

Swayne tried to shake off the vision, but a chill settled over his shoulders.

"Inferno City," Friel said. "Runner? Your guy Dante? If he'da seen this, he'da wrote his pome all over again."

Swayne did not get on him for talking out of turn. Inferno didn't do justice to this slaughter. Which grew worse when he turned on the thermal imager of his NVBs. For now the radiation of body heat could show him through the cloud what he could not see using the starlight alone. Four large glowing hot spots showed up like green diffuse beacons right out of a Steven Spielberg movie. One was the campfire ring. Three marked ground zero of the two-thousand-pounders. Several hundred other, smaller, hot spots told where bomblets had detonated. Beyond that, on the valley floor, strewn body parts glowed a dim green in his NVBs. Somebody had taken life-sized, green-tinted pictures of men and animals, put them through a Ronco vegetable chopper, and scattered the pieces like a ghastly jigsaw puzzle.

Pointless to try counting single terrorists—no bodies were whole. So he did the next best thing, switching on the digital IR camera in the NVBs. He snapped photos from one end of the valley to the other. Compared to the before-pictures, these might well be from the moon. The bombs had knocked down slabs of the valley walls, filling in low spots, burying corpses and carcasses. Near the rope corrals, the cliff wall shimmered in green ooze, proof that pureed men and animals had splattered against the stone. No matter how many times he had seen devastation like this—especially destruction he had helped create—it always got to him.

He thought the cloud might settle by now. Or drift away. But no. The Angel of Death had looked up from his feast. He stared at the three members of the team. He smiled broadly. And winked. *At him*? No, beyond him.

A shudder swept over Swayne. This was crap, he told

himself. No Death Angel lifting his head, just a billow of the cloud. No smile, but a streak of black smoke. No wink, but a blur in his own eye. One second an angel, the next a donkey, the next a bunny. *Yeah, a bunny is all.*

Rather than give in to his revulsion and bonehead ideas like Angels of Death, Swayne forced himself to focus on the mission. They had stayed in this area too long. Men always survived strikes from the air, even one as bad as this. He didn't want to deal with crazed, armed survivors out of their heads with pain and rage. Or with reaction forces seeking revenge.

"Mission control," Swayne said into his microphone, "Mission complete."

Zavello's voice crackled in Swayne's earpiece. "Can you confirm Brutus's dead body visually."

"Negative," Swayne said. "There's a fifteen-meter crater where he was standing three seconds before the strike. Not enough left of him to constitute a dead body."

Zavello growled, "Then I want pictures—"

"I have movement across the valley," Night Runner said, cutting off Zavello. In one of the simplest yet most elegant technological advances of the modern warfare, the voice-activated radios of each team member had a priority. A higher priority could override any transmission of a lower priority. And marvel of marvels, the lowest priority of any member in the field could suppress any radio transmission from a headquarters weenie, presumably even the President.

"A casualty?" asked Swayne. He liked that Zavello had shut his mouth rather than trying to jump in. Zavello might be a hard-ass staff weenie now, but he had once been a field soldier in combat. With that empty eye socket to prove it. He knew enough to eat his vomit when his field Marines were in contact.

"He's not been hit," Night Runner said. "He's too fast, too deliberate. Neither stunned nor struck."

"I got the Mook in my sights," said Friel. "Popping up like a gopher at one of them Coney Island shooting galleries. Want me to de-cap him?"

"Negative," said Swayne, feeling his first surge of anger at Friel. The kid knew damned well this was a ghost mission. They were to stay below enemy radar, out of sight and out of fights. Move in silently. Paint the target. Move out like mice, not rhinos. Avoid contact at any cost.

"Rally. Now."

The three Marines slid backward off the crest of the ridge, keeping out of sight of enemy eyes across the valley. They regrouped at the pile of boulders that included Gunny Potts. Swayne patted down his own body, moving from his chest to his thighs. This action told each team member to check himself out too. To be sure they'd left no weapons or clues behind. The instant four thumbs came up, Swayne pointed out the egress route. He regretted it immediately. Night Runner needed no compass, let alone directions. Class act that he was, Runner moved out briskly, without even raising an eyebrow at his leader.

As he ran, Swayne gave the mission a tough critique. No matter how he nitpicked, he could find no fault of substance. A few excess words on the radio. And Friel's wanting to pop a cap. And that dumb-ass thing about the Angel of Death. (*Dammit*! Why couldn't he get that image out of his head?) He didn't believe in omens. (Did he?)

The mission. Focus on the mission.

As world-class athletes do, Swayne had taught himself and his men to visualize. They had sat in a dark room, their eyes closed, playing in their minds how each would perform his own role and how the team's overall action should come off. Sometimes for hours, letting the mission unfold in real time. This one had turned out as well as any ideal Swayne had ever pictured.

So why it was it that he felt so uneasy? Was it perfection itself? Maybe perfect execution wasn't the heavenly ideal that it was cut out to be. Swayne decided he would have felt more comfortable with a little bit of hell to contend with—as long as it wasn't *too much* hell. He'd rather not deal with angels from either place.

• • •

NINA FOUND HERSELF face-to-face with Watson, both George's head and her own held up by the hair. She stood on tiptoes to ease the pull. She knew she was lucky, so far. Look at Watson. He hadn't a leg to stand on.

She wanted to scream, to cry, to reason, to blubber, to beg. But what had that gained for Dale and George? If Bin Gahli planned to kill her anyhow, why not go out with a little class?

She patted down the pockets of her new jacket—she had shopped at Eddie Bauer for one of those high-powered Dan Rather safari things—and finally found a packet of Camels in a sleeve pouch. (Did they have to make the damned jackets so difficult? Why all the loops and tags and buttons and slits and Velcro? Should you need a goddamned instruction book just to operate a jacket?)

She pulled at the corner of her mouth with one end of the cigarette so it stuck out the side of her face. She glanced at Bin Gahli, his ugly mug more a sore than a face. He had been radiating hatred on high beams since she met him. In the light of her flickering Bic, he gave her a look of wonder now. What did she have to lose? She jammed a second smoke into the center of his slack-jawed, slimy-lipped puss and lit it up.

Still, George Watson's slack face gaped at her from only a foot away. So she stuck a third cigarette to his drooling tongue and lit it as well. Then she locked eyes with the terrorist whom she'd never heard of before this afternoon.

"What? You think my sense of humor is too broad?" she asked.

Bin Gahli's furious dismay turned into a furious smile. "You dat boosht crazy broad, all right." He released his grip on her hair, and Watson's as well, tossing the head aside, sending it rolling. It came to rest looking like any other rock on the desert.

She dragged deeply and—*What the hell?*—spray-painted him with a stream of smoke. "What now, salami face?"

"You boosht," he snarled. It dawned on her what he was saying.

"Bullshit yourself," she said. Amazing how some words held up across the language barriers.

Bin Gahli flared his nostrils and lowered his head until his broad flat nose was within an inch of hers. "Maybe I rake you and killed you. How be dat boosht?"

"Dat bullshit be fine by me, but do me a favor," she growled. "Killed me first, then rake me all you want. How be dat?"

Bin Gahli may not have gotten the irony, but did seem taken by her nonchalance in staring into his face of death.

"You spoken dat English?"

She lifted one side of her upper lip, giving him the universal body language for *Duh!*

"Maybe you talk dat English by me."

"You want me to be your translator?"

He nodded.

Nina pursed her lips. How about *that*? Maybe she was the prima donna everybody said she was. The minute she acted as if she didn't want something—in this case her life—somebody was there, just dying to hand it to her. She shrugged, hoping that she would not push Bin Gahli too far. For if she could get out of this situation alive, she'd have the story of a lifetime. Pulitzers. Emmys. Book deals. The works—even if this *was* a nobody terrorist. Maybe a few choice words by her could elevate him to a glittering infamy. And the more infamous he became, the more prominent she would be in the circles that mattered to her.

Bin Gahli said, "Maybe I not want killed you yet."

She closed her eyes and waved her hand between their noses. "Then stop hosing me down with the donkey breath, will you?"

When she opened her eyes, Bin Gahli had vanished. She heard the footsteps of sandals and boots grinding in the dirt from others of the group around her. Somehow this band of men had developed ways of communicating without words. If these guys were as good at killing people as they were at flitting around the desert like zephyrs, they might well be the next terrorist celebrities. All they needed was a good publicity man—or woman. But—

A rush of feet and the sound of bodies hitting the ground.

The last time this group started licking ants off the desert, the earth had opened up and belched fire. Heads had rolled. She ought not stand around thinking about fame and fortune. She lay down and inched off the trail.

A soft step rattled the pebbles three feet from her face.

"Niner Jays? Where be dat Niner Jays?"

She recognized the voice. Bin Gahli. She realized he was calling her name. He needed an interpreter and English lessons besides.

"Mr. Bin Gahli," she murmured. "It's me, Nina Chase. I'm down here." She got to her feet and stepped onto the trail to find Bin Gahli with a second man, whom she had not seen before. And she certainly had not heard him approach. Bin Gahli might be one to walk softly and carry a short knife, but this new guy, whose profile looked like that of a weasel, was quieter than settling dust.

In his broken English, Bin Gahli tried to introduce her. But he spoke too fast, and it came off as noise. Pots and pans falling out of the cupboard maybe? She glanced at the sky and tried to paste the grunts and belches as words on the layer of thin clouds up there. Sounded as if he said: *The guy's name was Al the fur dealer, an independent operator who told Saddam Hussein where to place his neon signs to attract inventions of the illegal hospitals of the great Satan, America.*

Huh?

This interpreter stuff wasn't going to be so easy after all.

"I didn't catch that," she said, looking down from the heavens. But Bin Gahli and his ferret had vanished again. She cursed to herself.

Half a dozen men she had thought were tree trunks and boulders came to life and ran toward the spot on the horizon where the explosions had gone off. Two other men grasped her by the elbows, one on each side, and began leading her after them along the faint trail.

"Where are we going now?" she asked. But these two were not the linguistic wizards that Bin Gahli was, and they didn't even bother to grunt at her in answer.

NIGHT RUNNER LED the team at a brisk trot for more than a half hour across the trackless desert toward the pickup point. He felt more than secure. Even cocky. Of course, he kept off the roads and trails, but they wouldn't meet up with Iraqi troops anyhow. Saddam's Guards, if they sent a reaction force at all, would barrel-ass across the desert, lights on at full speed, guns blazing at even the sight of a herd of goats. At least that was how the dim bulbs ran their field drills. In any case, Night Runner was running point for the team, his eyes and ears running point for him. Not to be immodest about it, but his warrior's senses could put most high-tech weapons and any Iraqi regular to shame.

Only when they had moved to within a quarter mile of a secondary track not used since the Iran-Iraq war did Night Runner call a halt. Each man knew they had more than an hour to kill before setting out to meet their pickup bird, a stealth-equipped Night Hawk. And each man had his own job until it was time to start the thirty-minute trek on a zigzag route to the pickup zone.

Friel moved up to cover the road. Potts shifted north twenty meters to watch up a blind gully. Swayne and Night Runner huddled. Swayne snipped two fingers between their faces, and they turned off their mikes.

"How long?" asked Night Runner, who would now backtrack beside their escape route to see if anybody had followed. Swayne would send an update to Zavello.

Swayne checked his watch. "Take fifty minutes."

Night Runner drifted away, making himself part of the black of night in only five steps, two forward and three to the oblique. Then he fell to his knees and waited. He had practiced this move many times over. Still, it always made him grin to think how he could vanish before the very eyes of anybody watching him go. Such a simple trick too. The eyes tried to follow him, but he dropped below line of sight and the horizon. Thus, no silhouette. A man staring right at him could not see in the dead spot at the center of his night vision. And the longer the man stared, the less he could see.

He watched Swayne shake his head and turn away. Only then did Night Runner move out. And too softly to give himself away. Even to his own team.

QUANTICO—1117 HOURS LOCAL

COLONEL ZAVELLO RELAYED SWAYNE'S REPORT. It landed at the White House like a flaming bag of dog crap on the doorstep—plenty scary but too tricky to stamp out. Three times Zavello had to explain that the smart bombs had been launched before anybody could stop the mission. The White House foreign policy adviser didn't buy it. He demanded proof. The Marine colonel might have only one eye, but he wasn't blind to the rules of the Beltway blame game. He pointed a finger at one of his staffers, who, in turn, pointed a finger at his fax machine, already loaded with proof, the time-annotated transcript of the duty log.

Zavello knew that the faxes had hit home when the foreign policy twink on the phone sputtered, then fizzled to silence. Zavello smiled. He could picture the geek cupping its paw over the phone to ask what the hell was going on.

Zavello even heard somebody tell him the time-captioned video tapes of the logs were already en route by courier.

When the geek came back on the line, its demeanor had changed. It was still pissed but it had no way to blame the Marines.

Zavello let the geek speak. He said his *uh-huhs* and *mmmms* in all the right places.

"You understand the United Nations acted rashly, so eager to get arms inspectors back inside Iraq that the Secretary General did not fully coordinate, *damn him*."

Uh-huh.

"The United States Ambassador had not been forceful enough in recommending a delay in sending SCUM-SCUM on its way. *Pissant*."

Uh-huh.

"Of course, nobody—not even the limp-dicks in the State Department—would be so stupid as to reveal the secret strike against Abboud Dahni."

Mmmmm?

"To whisper a secret into U.N. is the same as dropping leaflets at the *Washington Post* and other newspapers, as well as all the terrorist capitals of the world, for chrissakes."

Uh-huh.

"The White House now has a new mission for your Force Recon team inside Iraq."

"Sir?"

THE DESERT—2121 HOURS LOCAL

BIN GAHLI JOGGED behind his ferret-scout, Jaffari, the best of all the Men of the Sand. From toe-cracking experience Bin Gahli had found it more useful to watch the man than try to see where his own feet landed. When Jaffari zigged, Bin Gahli took two more strides and zigged himself. When Jaffari leaped, Bin Gahli compensated for the distance between them and leaped in turn. When Jaffari came to a stop halfway down the slope into the valley where he was to have met Abboud Dahni, Bin Gahli jammed on the brakes and threw the butt of his rifle to the rear, catching the man behind him in the sternum before he could run into his back.

"A man's body," Jaffari said. He bent over, took a medallion off the corpse, held it up to the light, and amended his report: "Half a body. One of Abboud Dahni's people."

Bin Gahli spat, making a noise that had the effect of three commands: Forget about Abboud Dahni, who was useless as camel shit anyhow; get a move on; and be quick about it.

Smells and sounds mingled with an air of danger, filling the valley of death. The heady fragrance of explosives mixed with the scent of roasted goat, blended with the aroma of charred human flesh—Bin Gahli had been the author of those smells often enough to know them. From dark places rose up the squeals of horses and men, groaning, keening, wailing, praying, cursing. The mud he had slipped in was likely made of blood and guts.

None of this moved Bin Gahli. A bigger concern was that one of the wounded might hear them. A casualty might fire at them, mistaking them for an enemy patrol. Even calling out in Arabic wasn't a good idea, in case the injured men could hear the sound but not the words through shredded eardrums. Only strict silence might save them from being shot by the victims of this bombing.

Now. If only one of his own idiots did not step on a dud bomblet and kill them all. Bin Gahli was glad when he began climbing the far slope of the valley.

Once he was atop the ridge, a touch on the shoulder by Jaffari told Bin Gahli he should stay put while the scout searched the area for sign. Bin Gahli sat on a boulder and brazenly lit a cigarette. Any enemy here would have long ago left.

Bin Gahli thought about his new status in the galaxy of blood. Even on a good day, terrorism was a jackal-eat-jackal business, and Bin Gahli never knew when one of the glory hounds like Abboud Dahni might try to cut the field to one, himself. But now the pretty little goat turd had gone to heaven. Leaving Bin Gahli alone at the top of his world.

He dragged deeply on his cigarette. At his feet, scrambling on hands and knees, muttering and cursing, five strag-

glers in his second unit came up the steep slope. Making
too much noise. Bin Gahli cleared his throat. The five scattered like a herd of desert goats at the attack of a wildcat,
leaving Nina alone at Bin Gahli's feet.

Bin Gahli debated: Should he kill the woman, then rape
her, as she had as much as suggested? Or the other way?
First the rape, then the killing? Perhaps it would be more
diverting to turn her over to his men and let them decide.
Certainly, he had no need of her. Who needed a translator
when the only messages you sent to English-speakers
would come from the barrel of a gun? And who needed
sex, when there might be nearby Americans or Israelis to
track down and kill?

Still, she did amuse him. He pulled his knife. Kill her.
Not kill her. Which would be her fate? He decided to let
her decide. He flashed the blade of his knife so she might
see it. If she cried, she died.

SWAYNE COULDN'T BELIEVE his ears. Event Scenario 15?
Before they had extracted from 14? It was one thing for
Zavello to modify a mission on the fly. He had always
trained his team to stay loose. To adapt to fluid situations
was part of the game. But to throw a new exercise at them
without so much as a briefing was almost too extreme. Even
for a Force Recon team.

Zavello didn't cut him any slack. "If your team is unable
to persuade the UNSCOM inspectors to turn around and
proceed back toward Jordan," the colonel rasped, "you are
to direct the U.S. members of that team to detach themselves from UNSCOM and evacuate with your team. Do
not give U.S. members the option to decline your offer. If
necessary, remove them from the country against their
wishes. Acknowledge code Echo-Mike-Echo-One-Zulu."

"Shit," Swayne said into his open mike.

"That ain't it," Zavello bellowed, and Swayne cringed.
He had once again let down his guard in the field. He'd
come off no better than Friel. He cursed himself—this time

silently—as he entered Zavello's code into his handheld computer.

He heard a snicker through an open mike.

Friel, damn him.

DAY 2—0001 HOURS LOCAL

NINA ARRIVED AT Bin Gahli's feet with two fresh discoveries about herself.

First, she didn't feel so tough anymore. The smells in that cauldron of horrors had turned her stomach. Falling to her knees in mud that should not have existed in the desert had finished the job. She had grabbed an arm to help herself up, an arm with no body attached. She had hacked and gagged all the way across the valley.

The second realization dawned with the glint of Bin Gahli's crescent-shaped blade, which he held against his leg. Suddenly her mouth didn't seem the weapon she had thought it was. No amount of smart-ass banter would bail her out now. Her CNN star flamed out. Her awards crashed. Her fame died. Just as she was about to.

She saw Bin Gahli's muscles tense, and decided to use the only weapon left to a woman armed with nothing but guile and a belt-buckle knife too short to do her any good. She decided to rip open her safari jacket and flip up the front of her sports bra. With Bin Gahli distracted by her bare breasts, she would leap at him, scratch out his eyes, and try to bite through his throat. Maybe get at her belt buckle and put the one-inch blade to his jugular.

Screw it, she decided. Forget the cheap thrill and go right for the throat. She made two fists with straightened thumbs and poised to plunge them through Bin Gahli's eyes. She would ram them right through to the back of his Neanderthal skull. She saw him draw the knife back to his hip. She drew a breath. A scream might give him a second's pause, just long enough to bury her thumbnails.

She dove and screeched. Before her thumbs could penetrate his eye sockets, he turned his body and stepped back. Shrieking, she flew by him, her right fist striking him in the jaw, her left hitting something else, sharp and solid. She hit the ground thinking that she might have punched a stone. No, a man, all elbows and angles, squirmed beneath her. The wiry shadow of the weasel who had popped into her life moments after the bombing had become skin and mostly bones. Too late now. For him as well as for her. If she couldn't kill Bin Gahli, she'd shred this son of a bitch. She grabbed for his ratty face, scratching and clawing, drawing breath for a second scream and a killing bite to his neck, waiting for the blade of Bin Gahli's little steak knife to slice off her head.

SWAYNE SENT THE code the computer told him to send. He followed up by voice: "Acknowledge Sierra-Hotel-India-Tango-Two-Uniform."

"Acknowledgment correct." Zavello handed Swayne off to one of his staff weenies, who gave him the details. Eight-digit coordinates of the UNSCOM team—this came from a CIA PERLOBE transmitter planted in the heel of one American's boot. A digital map came up on Swayne's computer screen. It showed Swayne's position, the UNSCOM team's location, the team's original helicopter pickup point, and an air route to intercept the moving convoy of three white-painted vehicles. GMC Suburbans, the staffer told him for all the good that would do to know.

Swayne shook his head. If only it were that easy—draw

some lines on a map, lines calculated by a computer. Then
expect people more than a hundred miles apart to link up.
ID three trucks by make, model, and year and think that'll
help men execute a rescue. Plunk down eight map digits
and tell them to meet a helicopter and vanish like a good
intention at the crap tables. Shit.

And if things go wrong, what? Maybe just punch Pause,
the way a video player puts his game on hold to take a
pee?

SURE ENOUGH, NINA felt a hand tighten into a fist in her
hair. Bin Gahli yanked her head back before she could bite
into the weasel's neck. Next would come the slice to the
throat. After that, she hoped, nothing. *Did you have any
feeling with your head off?* she wondered. Who knew?
Watson had not made a dying declaration on the topic.
Should she?

No need. Bin Gahli did not kill her. He laughed, maybe
amused that she had beaten his man down, reducing him
to spit and sputter. To Nina the little guy did come off as
Deputy Barney Fife. She wondered if Bin Gahli ever
watched the Mayberry gang in action.

She began laughing too. Not in humor, but only because
she felt giddy. It felt so weird to be alive when she had no
right to be.

Bin Gahli's laughter infected his men. They yukked it
up until Bin Gahli went sober. Then they clammed up. So
did Nina.

"You beeg catfight lady," Bin Gahli said. "Beat my Jaffari down like dat much boosht." He held up a thumb and
forefinger, barely visible in the moonlight.

Before she could think of what to say that wouldn't give
offense, Bin Gahli turned to Jaffari and spoke in his gargle.
The weasel responded in mild tones. Nina wondered that
he could be so calm. During Jaffari's report, Bin Gahli
began nodding, and to Nina's relief, made his knife dis-
appear with a flick of his hand. He turned to Nina and
began flapping his lips, spraying her down with spit.

"Jaffari find four Merry-can. I been taken dat Merry-can home. Given heem boosht-sombeets-bashtad Merry-can dat Saddam."

Bin Gahli wanted to capture the Americans and hand them over to his cuz? But—"How can he be so sure they're Americans?" she wanted to know.

Bin Gahli had never heard a funnier question. He roared with laughter. Nina wondered if her words translated into low Arab humor. The terrorist sputtered at Jaffari and went hysterical again. Jaffari did not. He gave Nina the stink-eye, and a chill crept up her spine. She had insulted him in the worst way. First by beating his ass. Then by doubting his report. She vowed never to be alone with the guy.

Finally Bin Gahli collected himself and gave her a lame-ass explanation, all gibberish.

But not so Nina couldn't interpret snatches of the blather.

Four Mah-yeens meant four Marines.

One righty-han seedy Mah-yeen been dat beeg gone became, "One right-handed city Marine with a big gun."

Two righty-han Mah-yeen Bedouin sounded like, "The second right-handed Marine was a Bedouin." She couldn't be sure what the hell *that* meant.

Turd leffy-han Mah-yeen offshore been tall affaleet stopped her heart: "The third, a left-handed Marine officer, tall and athletic." *Yikes! Jack Swayne, six-three, a former basketball player, was left-handed.*

Bin Gahli saw more than passing interest in the details about the Marine officer. "Sheerush," he added, "been berry sheerush."

She blinked rapidly. *And Jack was very serious indeed.*

"Been berry hanshom," Bin Gahli said.

"Handsome? You're telling me this guy can tell if somebody's handsome by their footprint? Come on." Nina faked a laugh as best as she could. "You're putting me on," she said. "What'd you do? Find their wallets and driver's licenses?"

Bin Gahli gave her a blank stare. He didn't get it. Fine.

But the terrorist leader hadn't finished. "Four been dat neegarow Mah-yeen," he said. "Berry beeg. Righty-han fahm neegarow."

Nina remembered the black gunnery sergeant in Jack's unit, a man the size of Rhode Island. Astonished, she turned to the one called Jaffari, but he had disappeared. Again. And again Bin Gahli took off on the run with his squad at his heels. Somebody shoved her, and she stumbled down the ridgeline after them, running more quickly than she thought safe. The man behind her prodded her with the barrel of his rifle if she lagged even a step.

She hardly felt the abuse. So shocked was she at the weasel's little psychic stunt.

Four Americans? And Marines? she thought. Was it possible? Could it be the same Marines? Jack Swayne's team? She hoped so. She had seen Swayne and his group in action before. In Canada. They could save her. Or nobody could.

Then again. Bin Gahli's band seemed just as deadly. And ruthless besides. Utterly without scruples besides, besides.

No, she assured herself. It couldn't be Jack. Probably half the teams in Force Recon had city boys of all races led by handsome officers and noncoms. Hell, to her ninety percent of Marines were drop-dead gorgeous.

She remembered Sergeant Night Runner, the Indian brave in combat boots. He was otherworldly in the way he walked and read information in the snow. Could he be the Bedouin they were talking about?

But this Jaffari. He had supernatural qualities too. And the satanic nature of a terrorist to boot.

No, it'd be better if Night Runner didn't come up against Jaffari. And best that Jack never faced Bin Gahli either.

NIGHT RUNNER HAD backtracked almost to ground zero when he saw them. Six—no, seven—men coming over the ridge. Survivors of the killing zone? No. The blast would have left its victims too dazed to move as these men. They were too organized, too steady. His warrior's heart leapt.

They trotted as if they had a purpose. Could they be following a trail that a scout had given them? Somebody Night Runner had not spotted?

A glance through the nightscope of his rifle told him what he did not want to believe. Night Runner found a switch with his thumb and turned the night-viewing device into a recorder so he could capture the face of the man leading the squad. His head swiveled up and down, side to side, shadowing the Spartans as if tracking in broad daylight instead of only a quarter moon. *He was tracking them? In this light? How could that be? No way.*

At the team's rally point among the boulders, the tracker stopped for a second, turned to the huge Arab behind him, made a circle-the-wagons gesture in the air, and took off along the same path that Night Runner had led the team on, jogging almost as fast as the Marines had.

This was serious. Night Runner slipped the safety. He might not take out all of the terrorists—they were too well dispersed and armed to the eyebrows. But he might stop the tracker and bring down the big man, obviously the leader. That would gain time for the team. As he put the aiming point on the left shoulder of the tracker, now bent over to read sign where Night Runner had changed direction, and just as his finger began to take the slack out of the trigger, a new noise froze his shooting finger. Night Runner swung his scope back to the right and saw a second group of terrorists coming over the ridgeline. This sent the price of poker up. And the odds of his team down. He swung the rifle back to his pair of targets in time to see them slipping into a wadi out of sight. Night Runner had led Swayne and the others into the very dry streambed. He knew their tracks in the flat bottom would be easy to follow for the next four hundred meters.

Night Runner cursed himself twice. First, for not shooting the tracker when he had the bead on him, and second, for feeling so fearful about the man. Then again, if he had started a firefight, the two groups might have overrun him from opposite flanks in no time. Then, all they would have had to do was wait for Swayne and the others to respond. They would know, as every fighting man in the world knew, that Force Recon Marines never left one of their comrades in a jam.

No matter now. The chance was gone. Night Runner dropped into a wadi that paralleled the original track. He took off at a full sprint, thankful for one tiny edge—at least he knew where he was going. He cursed himself anyhow for a third time in the last minute for having made one other error. One that could be fatal.

He slapped at the button beside his ear, reactivating his mike.

EVEN BEFORE NIGHT Runner had uttered his one-word report, a stab of high anxiety ran through Swayne and the others. Running flat out had made Runner grunt into his mike before the word "Alligator" cracked in their headsets.

For simplicity the team ID'd three levels of potential danger, indicated by words starting with the letters A, B, and C. Code words such as Canary or Chipmunk would indicate all clear, minimal danger at most. A code word like Badger would mean an increased danger from an enemy but nothing the team could not either evade or take on. Alligator meant imminent, lethal danger, a force strong enough to overcome the team and one aware of the team's presence. The code had nothing to do with radio security— high-tech electronic scramblers took care of that. Their code simply let a man give a one-word danger signal when he had neither time nor words to explain.

Swayne picked up the cue. "Spartan Three, are you able to report?"

"Negative."

"Should we move out?"

"ASAP."

"Rally at the LZ?"

"Roger."

Swayne wanted details, but he knew better than to be the weenie at the other end of the radio contact. So he directed the team to rush in line across the road so an en-

emy gunner could not pick them off one at a time. They
dropped into a ravine, grouped up, and moved out. Potts
led, and Swayne brought up the rear, glancing over the
shoulder. Night Runner had developed the egress plan himself. Even if he hadn't, there would be no danger of him
getting lost.

That danger fell on the rest of the team, which did not
have Night Runner's skills in the wild.

Still. Swayne's mouth went dry. Like every Marine in
Force Recon, he and his men could navigate day or night
with the help of digital compasses and a global positioning
system accurate to within a meter. They could find their
LZ without Runner.

But maps and gadgets were one thing. The actual ground
was another. Nobody ever broke his ankle falling into a
badger burrow in the middle of a map. And no snake had
ever crawled out of a GPS screen to bite somebody. But
plenty of Marines had been hurt by those things in the field.
A picture might be worth a thousand words, but the dirt
underfoot spoke ten thousand words more. That was where
the warrior skills of Night Runner had come into play so
often and so well. Better than any computer, he could crank
a thousand variables into his head and come up with a
coherent picture that translated into a plan. Better yet, he
could lead you across the dirt. He would point out the
badger holes so you could pass by them. And he would use
the barrel of his rifle to set the snakes aside so nobody—
man or reptile—would get hurt. Without Night Runner,
Swayne and his team might as well be naked. And blind.
Swayne promised himself that he would learn more about
Runner's skills in their next training cycle. He hated the
feeling of emptiness that hung over him—

The idea of a void brought Nina Chase to mind, for
some reason, and he put her aside. Where the hell had *that
thought* come from?

NIGHT RUNNER FELT so odd. Sure, he was in a foreign
country. And yes, he faced an enemy of a different culture.

But the oddity went deeper. He felt so . . . primitive. Being alone like this made him recall things. Not things in his memory. But things in his genes.

He saw himself as an Indian scout, alone, dashing across a wild, strange land. The scout had seen a fierce enemy from another Indian band that outnumbered him many times over. So he ran full out. Not *from* his enemy, but *at* him.

Night Runner. Blackfeet scout.

He carried a high-powered, flat-trajectory rifle with exotic sights and a grenade launcher beneath the rifle barrel. But the scout carried a lance. He wore combat boots. The scout went unshod. He wore cammies, he wore a breechclout. He—

He was no longer a Marine sergeant.

For that matter, he was no longer Night Runner.

He became that heroic warrior ancestor of his, Heavy Runner.

His soul turned hard. He had felt panic when he saw the Iraqi tracker bent over the trail, showing skills he had never seen outside the Blackfeet Nation. Now he felt angry. Moments ago he was a northern plains warrior and a Marine Corps warrior all in one package. He was better than either. And either one could rub out the Iraqi.

Now he was Heavy Runner, more fierce than any.

He ransacked his mind for a way to use the ground against his enemy. He remembered. He turned right at full sprint and climbed the tallest bit of high ground in the area. Below the crest of the butte, he collected himself. He forced his lungs to take slow, measured breaths. Then he low-crawled to the top, certain that he would be able to see down into the wadi.

His eyes picked up shadows moving among shadows, and he pointed his rifle sight at the first squad, now four hundred meters away. He picked out the lead man. They had moved more quickly than he had expected. His respect for them climbed a notch. But that would not stop him from taking out the tracker with his first—

Then he saw something that caused his heartbeat to trip, caused him to remember he was a mere mortal. Night Runner was his name, not Heavy Runner. He was nothing but a man, not the spirit of a warrior. And subject to mistakes like any other man.

JAFFARI KEPT UP a pace that Bin Gahli had seen him sustain for hours, on the hottest of days. So when he stopped in the wadi, Bin Gahli chafed at the delay. Even *he* could track the four American intruders without the Bedouin. Why, he found the trail so obvious that any one of the morons guarding the woman could have followed it. By Allah, even she could have followed this track.

Then he saw that Jaffari wasn't checking tracks. He had laid back his head and directed his nose like radar, collecting scent from the air. He'd never done that before. To be on the near side of safety, Bin Gahli crouched among a bed of stones the size of stew pots. He looked around. The five other men in this first squad dove for cover. Maybe they weren't as dumb as they looked.

He kept his tongue. Jaffari had gone to that world that Bin Gahli could never penetrate. The animal world. Jaffari could see, hear, and smell in a range beyond that of normal humans, beyond even Bin Gahli's own superb instincts. Better to be silent and wait for him to return.

Finally, when Jaffari made eye contact with him, Bin Gahli grunted.

"Most assuredly an American," Jaffari said in his language. "They have a distinctive smell, you know. An hour ago." He stepped off the trail into the wind, crooking one finger behind him so Bin Gahli would follow.

Jaffari darted from one bit of cover to another for fifty meters, then bent to one knee and swept a hand across the hard ground. Bin Gahli could see nothing.

"Here. Look closer. One man, very stealthy," said Jaffari.

"Tracking the Americans?" asked Bin Gahli.

Jaffari snorted. "No. Backtracking. A typical trick by

some forces. More often the Israelis than the Americans. But this American. He is not typical. He is the one who walks with soft feet. Like a Bedouin Man of the Sand. I'm puzzled. This set of tracks goes back toward Abboud Dahni's camp. No tracks show his return. Did I miss him?"

Bin Gahli spat. "Soft feet. What boosht is—?" He threw himself behind a sand dune to his left, a reaction to Jaffari's dive to his right.

As a spatter of sand stung him. As bullets tore up the ground where they had stood. Followed by the sound of three bursts of gunfire.

Bin Gahli's men fired back at the sound and sight of muzzle flashes.

Bin Gahli flapped his arms at his men. The shooting stopped so he could listen.

When no other shots came from a high ground, he muttered to Jaffari, "One man?"

"Yes."

"Your backtracker with the soft feet?"

"Yes."

"Follow him or return to the main track?"

Jaffari took a deep breath.

This surprised Bin Gahli. Jaffari nervous? Jaffari hesitant? Who was this man with the soft feet?

"Jaffari? We sit. But time goes by."

"The wadi. Both tracks lead to the same place. But down there is less danger of an ambush."

Jaffari afraid of an ambush? Who was this American?

SWAYNE HAD JUST finished checking his GPS, trying to pinpoint the spot where the team should turn north toward the LZ. Just finished missing Night Runner again—he would have known where to veer without using a computer. And just as he shut down the backlit LED screen, he heard the gunfire. The seconds until he heard Night Runner's voice became hours. Finally:

"Spartan One, this is Three. Engaged a squad of seven,

negative BDA. Keep moving. I'll rally with you at the pickup point."

The stunned Swayne said, "Wilco out?" his response in the tone of a question. *A squad of seven?* That was the reason Night Runner had used the Alligator code? *Seven lousy men? Against a Force Recon team? That was something to sweat?*

FRIEL FELT A sudden sweat in his kid gloves. Night Runner throwing down on a whole squad of camel jockeys and coming up bolo? Night Runner? Next to Friel himself the best master-blaster in the Marine Corps? Zip for seven? *What'd they have? Force shields or what?*

A FEELING OF bad luck struck Potts in the gut. This mission had started out so good but now started to stink bad as yesterday's beans and cabbage. That note in Night Runner's voice? The chief nervous as an alley cat at a dog show? Dang that to hell. Time they saddled up their mother ship and beamed themselves the hell out of Dodge.

WHEN NINA HEARD the gunfire, she hit the ground before her escort did. She snuggled into the biting gravel and listened to the footsteps. Some of the men ran to the left, others to the right of the trail, branching out as two fighting squads.

She might not know much about warfare, but she knew three short bursts, answered by a brief volley, did not a major battle make. She hoped it was battle enough to give Bin Gahli a bullet to the brain. Before she could long reflect on the joy of such lead implants, her escort dragged her to her feet and made her run again.

THE GLORY OF Night Runner's out-of-body experience as a Blackfeet warrior had indeed burst like a snot bubble. Even as he pulled the trigger he saw the slugs pepper bare ground. No tracker. No band leader. No joy.

And now he did what his name told him to do: run at

full speed by night. He didn't like to flee from a fight. But he knew he must rejoin the team and lead them out of Iraq safely. Forget counting coup on the enemy, as legend said Heavy Runner had done. This was no dick dance, to use one of Colonel Z's terms, no contest to see who had the longest tool. This was a mission to kill and not be killed. They'd done half of that. Time to do the rest.

After making his reluctant report to Swayne that he had failed to take out any of the Iraqis, he reran events through his head. What could he learn from the fiasco? Clearly, the tracker had picked up his scent. Not once, but twice. First the smell lingering from his pass while backtracking. The second time, a hot scent. His body odor had wafted over three hundred-plus meters, alerting the scout to leap before he looked. A mere fragment of a second before Night Runner pulled the trigger at that.

A part of him told Night Runner he'd best get out of Iraq tonight. Take time to get back to warrior basics. Sharpen skills grown dull from lack of use. Regain a humble spirit. Suppress his arrogance in believing he had no equal. It had cost him a kill and exposed the team to peril.

Such a basic error too. How could he have been so lazy as to backtrack on the upwind side of the Spartans' egress route? Just because the terrain made for easy travel? Face it, he'd gone to fat in the brain department.

Only a heavy regimen could trim that fat. Fasting. Time in the sweat lodge. A spell in the wilderness in survival mode—not so much as a knife. To hone his senses. And dampen his pride.

Damn! He couldn't get it out of his head. How could he have been so cocky as to believe that no soldier in the world could match him in stealth? That Arab tracker had shown him up like a beast of beasts. Skills keen as a hawk's cry. Night eyes of the owl. Legs of the pronghorn. Nose of the wolf.

Night Runner felt something creep up his spine. A feeling he had not felt since he'd left the rez to enter the Ivy League, a foreign world within the already foreign white man's world. The feeling was an F-word with a capital F. One far more obscene than the Anglo-Saxon curse word.

The very idea of Fear spurred him to run even faster.

It was his only edge, this ability to run full out. The terrorists would have to move with care, to guard against ambush.

He crossed the road and picked up the track of his mates. They had used a trick he'd taught them, moving in file, stepping in each other's tracks. Not that it mattered. A tracker like the one on their trail would have made his count by now. In fact, would have had any number of insights about his team.

There was the obvious, of course: that they were Marines. The Spartans wore boots with tread patterns that mimicked those of the military in the target country. So the prints were not a giveaway. But only Force Recon Marines operated in teams of four. Nobody else in the world—not counting amateur freelancers—worked with fewer than twice that.

This tracker would pick up on many less obvious signs too.

He would ID Swayne as a southpaw because his right-to-right stride went half an inch longer than his left-to-left stride. Likewise, the tracker could ID the others as right-handers because of the longer length of their left-to-lefts. But there was more.

Item: Friel's wound hadn't healed fully, as the captain thought. Every time the kid stood up after a rest, he limped a bit for the first hundred meters or so. From the stiffness left over from the injury on Event 13. That showed as a shorter-than-normal stride with more weight on the good leg. After the gimp limbered up, his gait betrayed him as a Yucky—young urban cock of the walk. City folk grew up walking on concrete. Which gave their track a pattern—the heels hit hard, toes out. They often scuffed their feet. On softer ground, this walking style made them prone to lose balance. Friel's in-your-face stroll, weight back, chin thrust forward, made him stumble at times.

The tracker would read even more in Friel's track. He often carried his smart gun in one hand, usually his right, making the footprint slightly deeper on that side. That told the tracker he carried a large weapon. The lance corporal showed his give-a-shit attitude in the irregular, herky-jerky pattern of his footsteps. Night Runner could read his mood of the moment: bored, tired, angry, distracted, exulted—any of these—by the character and distance of the stride, the drag marks (the longer the toe drags, the more tired he was), and the disturbances around each print. And so could the terrorist tracker.

Item: Potts walked with his weight forward, flat-footed and balanced. As did most farmers, ranchers, and hunters used to moving in the outdoors but without stealth. His boot soles showed a strong push-off, which meant he had done heavy work in the fields, including football fields. He lifted his legs with the thigh muscles, and high-stepped, again like a football lineman. The gunny also carried a heavier pack than the others, crammed with spare ammo for the Brat. This load made him top-heavy, subject to the sway a tracker would read in the fissures around his tracks. The wear pattern of his boots tended to give away his race, showing a broad, triangular foot without the usual high arch of a Caucasian. The regular pattern of his steps indicated an older, more mature, and deliberate soldier. In sharp contrast to the reckless Friel.

Item: Swayne was clearly a white man, and an athlete in one of the finesse sports like tennis. He was likely a sprinter as well as a basketball player. This showed in the grace and balance of his stride. (Night Runner knew the captain had played point guard in college from his bio, not his prints.) Unlike Potts and Friel, Swayne did not a plod like a thigh-walker. He used his calf muscles and flexed his ankles. This gave him more spring and greater speed over short distances. His self-assured gait was confident but cautious, definitely serious. A sharp tracker would know that he was the leader of the team because his frequent hand signals to members of the team and turning to check on his men often put his body out of balance. Again the tracker could read this in the track fissures and pressure points his prints made on the earth.

Night Runner knew his own track would give him away as a stalker. Even while jogging, he tended to put one foot directly ahead of the other like a fox. He left a light trail at a walk because his foot hit the earth with the outside of the sole and rolled flat. He kept his weight forward, putting the heel down last. When stalking, he walked with an even more pronounced fox-walk. He kept erect, his weight balanced, his feet lifted high to avoid pebbles and twigs. He stepped down on the outside of the ball of a foot. And rolled the foot flat slowly before putting his full weight on it and lowering the heel. That which gave him his stealth would betray him to any tracker worthy of the name. His Indian heritage could not have been more obvious to the Iraqi tracker if he'd dropped copies of his bio on his trail.

Even so. None of it would matter. Not if they lifted off the ground in the next twenty minutes and left Iraq and its star tracker behind.

Funny thing. The idea of escape did not comfort him. This night would nag him for all time. He'd found somebody as good as himself.

Finally Night Runner came to a spot where the team's tracks ended. He checked the rocks beside the trail and saw that the Spartans had done a passable job of hiding their tracks across the boulders. Still, they would not fool the man following them. When the tracker came to the end of the trail, he would also find the white dust of pressure marks on the sandstone grit. Night Runner had to fix the situation.

So he imitated Potts's flat-footed-stride interval to extend the trail. He walked down the wadi a hundred yards to hard ground. Then, without turning around, he walked backward herky-jerky, not quite in the same steps. This would mimic Friel's bounce, too often too careless to step into Potts's prints. Back at the start of the ruse, he sprinted forward, making his own catch-up track beside the one he

had faked. At the end of the false trail, he retraced his steps
backward again, this time making a sure set of tracks for
the captain. He didn't try to inject too much identity into
the tracks. Like most counterfeiters, he would rely more
on the dark and sleight of hand—or foot, in this case—to
carry off the sham.

Once again at the start, he stepped off the false trail onto
the sandstone and used his cap to brush away the grit powder. He sprinkled a fist full of sand over the scuff marks.
Then he leaned down, putting his face close to the stone.
He envisioned himself as the wind and blew at the sand.
Once he had doctored all sign across the stone for two
meters, he tossed away the last of his sand and took off,
following the real trail of the Spartans. By day a tracker
with the terrorist's gifts would not take the fake. But at
night he might stick to Night Runner's false trail and follow
it past the turnoff point. That would earn the Spartans two
minutes. After the end of the track, he'd see through the
hoax at once. He'd backtrack and read clues in the sand
that Night Runner did not have time to hide. Namely, that
he had changed his stride moments before creating the false
trail. But the team would gain two more minutes, maybe
three.

The tracker would make a quick circle. He would find
the actual trail in another two minutes.

The fakery didn't need to be flawless. Night Runner
needed only to buy enough time for him and the team to
climb aboard that helicopter and, as the gunny might say,
beam themselves the hell out of Dodge. Five to six minutes.
That ought to do it.

SWAYNE SCANNED THE terrain below through his NVBs
and saw Night Runner dart up the hill. He wished for a
report. A bit of good news, if you please.

Finally Night Runner slipped into the night shadow of
a boulder. Only his voice emerged from cover: "Two
groups of bad guys. Not regulars, but two bands of terrorists. One a squad-minus, the other a platoon-minus."

At last Swayne knew why Night Runner had called the Alligator. A force too big and too dispersed for four men to engage, let alone one.

Swayne had a question. Before he could ask, Night Runner answered. "Maybe ten minutes behind us."

Swayne spoke his next to the OMCC. "Request ETA on the pickup bird."

The tremble in the comeback told Swayne the call came from the cockpit of a helicopter. "Roger, this is Night Hawk Three-Seven. ETA niner minutes."

Swayne bit his lip, then called to Night Runner: "Three, this is One. Is it enough time?"

"Will advise."

NINE MINUTES, THOUGHT Night Runner.

If it wasn't enough, the team would have him to blame for not taking out the Tracker—he had begun to think of him as Tracker with a capital T.

Night Runner stopped at the military crest of the hill, the last vantage point that allowed him to check their back trail all the way to the base of the slope. A quick scan of the wadis through his nightscope told him the terrorists had not caught up yet. Now as he crouched against the cool stone, he tried to decide what he would like to see in the next few minutes. Nothing? Or the sight picture of the Tracker, the front post of his sights glued to the center of his chest?

Wishing for a choice was not to be. Even as he thought about them, the first group of seven hit the start of his false trail. The scout broke stride. Not good.

The Tracker put up a hand. The others held their ground. The Tracker jogged down the counterfeit tracks in a crouch. Night Runner knew—he just *knew*—the man was not going to take the bait. He wondered. Would his trick have fooled himself? He shook off the self-doubt.

And slipped his rifle's safety to off. This time he knew his target. He would not try to split his gunfire between the Tracker and his leader. He would drain an entire clip on the gravest danger to his team. The Tracker. Spray at his feet and let the recoil lift the muzzle. If the man threw himself down, it would be into the beaten zone of his fire.

Sure enough, the knot of men milled about. Through their midst, reverse-marching, came the rat-faced Tracker. He jogged back to the spot where the Force Recon team had left the wadi for the hardpan slopes.

So much for the five or six minutes.

Night Runner figured the range: five hundred meters.

The Tracker pointed upslope and held both arms out to his sides. To Night Runner it seemed as if he were offering himself for crucifixion. Daring the Indian to try killing him. But his arms pumped and dropped. Before the Marine could lay his bead and fire, he vanished behind the spine of a ragged ridge with the others.

Night Runner knew it hadn't been a dare at all. He cursed himself for thinking so. Stop trying to put this down to a personal level, he told himself. Of course it wasn't a dare. Since the first cavemen had organized for battle the hand signal had been the same: *Spread out and move out— on the double.*

The second band of Arabs joined up with their brothers. They swarmed up the rock garden in a long rank.

If the Tracker had taken the false trail, the Spartans might have gained enough time to lift off. A close call, but at least even odds. Now, he reasoned, they might have less than five minutes when they needed—he checked his watch—at least seven. Too close a call unless he could pin down these guys.

Night Runner scanned left and right along the line of advance. He updated the count of twenty-six to Swayne and added, "Permission to take them under fire."

"Roger," Swayne said. "Night Hawk Three-Seven, re-vised ETA?"

"Night Hawk Three-Seven, six minutes at . . . mark."

"Roger. Spartans fire at will."

Potts opened up, hosing down the landscape with his Brat.

Swayne asked Night Runner, "Three, do you need backup?"

"Neg—" Night Runner saw the Tracker stand up to wave one arm in a circle over his head. Night Runner threw down on him, but the Iraqi ducked out of sight again, popping up in yet another position, making the same signal. Night Runner could see that he was shouting. The wave of Iraqis abandoned caution and scrambled up the rocks. Night Runner then heard the noise. The sound of helicopter blades. Muffled, yes, because the craft was flying low-level and with blades built to minimize flap as the craft dipped and turned. But there it was. He had never known any man to have better hearing than himself, even among the Blackfeet. This was too much. He must kill the Tracker. ASAP. Forget the reasons: ego, pride, motherhood, tribal loyalty, huckleberry pie. Any or all would do. He had to rub out the man.

If only the man would stand still long enough.

The Tracker dodged from cover to cover, springing into the open in spots that Night Runner didn't anticipate. Night Runner swept his scope left and right to gauge the situation. The terrorist leader had schooled his men in small-unit tactics. They took the hill, not in one wave as he had thought, but in lapping lines. One rank held ready to give fire support as the other rank moved through and set up in turn.

Then he saw something that caused his pulse to flutter. One of the Arabs pulled at a fence post draped over his shoulder, held it at his chest, and telescoped its barrel. *Red-eye*! They had a Red-eye. *Damn*, the heat-seeking, shoulder-fired, surface-to-air missile came out of the Vietnam era, father of the more modern Stinger. But they still had life enough for war in the 21st century. Red-eyes homed on turbine exhaust. In flight at top speed, a stealthy Night Hawk diffused its hot exhaust and deflected it upward so a Red-eye could not lock on. But on the ground or at a hover, forget it. To the missile's heat-seeker, the craft would look like a house afire.

Runner had no time to think about the Tracker or ego

or his Indian family tree or spears and arrows. He had to
report the Red-eye.

THE TERSE MESSAGE struck Swayne like the snap of a wet
towel. *The bastards had Red-eyes?* He thought first of the
pilot. "Did you catch that, Night Hawk?"

"Three-Seven, Roger, three minutes out. Turning to final," the pilot said, his voice flat as boiled beer. Runner
might have told him to expect coffee and donuts instead of
the risk of a missile up the tailpipe.

Swayne liked his courage. "Spartan Three, recover."
Swayne said.

"Roger," Night Runner said. "I threw out boomers set
on thirty-second delay. Get set for three flash-bangs in . . .
ten seconds, Night Hawk."

"Three-Seven, Roger."

Night Runner burst through the Spartan line and kept
running. Friel followed him thirty yards up the hill, where
they set up fire support. Potts and Swayne would move up
in turn. After the—

A series of flashes erased the night for three nanosec-
onds.

Swayne opened his eyes and glimpsed the helicopter on
final. The pilots, warned against night blindness, would
have shut their eyes until the three grenade flashes. That
had to be scary—landing with your eyes shut. Now. If only
the boomers could hold off the Iraqis.

NINA HAD HIT the ground along with Bin Gahli's men at
the sound of metal on stone. In the pale moonlight she saw
one man cover his ears. She did the same. One of her
guards tried to crawl over her feet. She kicked him away.
He kicked back at her. She kicked him on the hip, just
missing her aiming point. He got to his knees and fumbled
with his rifle.

"Hey, Einstein," she yelped. "Didn't you get the word
about plugging your ears?" He aimed his rifle at her face
and strained some kind of Arab F-word through his teeth.

She closed her eyes. "Sheeze Louise almighty God." The guy was going to kill—

A blast from upslope drove the thought from her head. Although she lay behind a stone the size of her Lexus, she thought the Iraqi might have shot her, perhaps with a shotgun, so much did her body sting. She dared to open her eyes in time to see the man being thrown into the rocks below. He tumbled like the corpse she hoped he was. Two more explosions rocked the night, triggering gravel slides. The cries of men filled the air—she could hear the shrieks through her hands.

She rolled onto her stomach and elbows. She opened her eyes to slits. Pockets of men rose all over the hillside. She watched them sprint up the slope, silhouettes against the sky. Some of them limped. More than a dazed few stumbled. One poor guy attacked the wrong way, downhill, staggering and shooting, chanting in Arabic. Until he fell flat on his dentures. But most of Bin Gahli's men attacked into the teeth of the fire from above, leaning toward the slope as if walking into a driving rain.

So that was what they meant by a suicide attack.

So this was hell.

"NIGHT HAWK THREE-SEVEN, ten seconds from touchdown." The pilot didn't have to say so, but he and the Spartans knew this was a vulnerable moment. Stealthy or no, the helicopter made noise. Enough so that that most sophisticated of weapons-detection systems, the human soldier, could pick it up. Hell, a monkey firing blind at the hushed buzz might bring down the bird with a stray shot.

Swayne told his team, "Pick your targets well. Four, use proximity fuses so they keep their heads down."

"Done that already," said Friel in a tone of *Whattinahellayouthink?*

Swayne let the attitude pass. Now was not the time.

He visualized the way this battle ought to come off. His team had the firepower to hold off a force two or three times the number they faced. A lot of points in the Spartans' favor.

To his far left, Friel would suppress the Iraqis with the smart gun, his Blowpipe. The eight-pound, unwieldy weapon held only six rounds in each clip. But what rounds they were, each a twenty-millimeter missile with a self-contained guidance system, each on a discrete frequency. Friel could designate a target either by a visible laser or IR beam. When he fired, a charge of compressed gas launched the tiny missile at subsonic speed, with no muzzle flash and little noise. Then a tiny rocket motor ignited and propelled the round to a high speed, and quickly. A homing device in the nose of the round would pick up the laser beam, then the target selected by Friel. It would recognize the target on its own by digital imaging.

The missile locked on with the tenacity of a pit bull. It could follow the digital signature moving at sixty miles an hour. Even if the target changed profile. If a walking man sank into a crouch, the round's memory would recognize it and compensate for the change in shape. In tests, Swayne had seen the device fired at target silhouettes that shifted from left profile, to a running man, to a diving man, to a prone, head-on image. The missile adjusted each time until it struck home. The only instance in which he had seen it go awry was when the man-target went behind a tree and disappeared from digital sight. So the missile had remained on point at the spot where the image had vanished. The armor-piercing sabot round punched a hole through the foot-thick hickory, slashed through the target, and buried itself twenty inches deep in solid limestone behind.

As the first round locked on, Friel could redesignate a second target. The gun would apply a new frequency to its laser, and a second missile could be fired before the first had struck its target. And a third, and so on.

The projectile had several features. Swayne had called for proximity fuse. Radar returns told the round to blow before it struck its target. The explosive would throw a lethal blast of shrapnel a good fifteen meters in all directions. That made it an area weapon, which could maim a dozen unprotected men at once.

Chalk up one very big point to the good guys.

To his far right, Potts was armed with the Brat machine gun, so called because of the noise it made when fired on automatic. The gun was a 5.56-millimeter knockoff of the workhorse of conventional forces since the Vietnam, the M-60 machine gun. With a few innovations, such as adjustable rate of fire and mounted ammunition drums instead of clips. A reliable weapon, and in Potts's hands as deadly as spraying bullets from a fire hose.

One more point for the good guys.

Night Runner carried a modified M-16, with a 40-millimeter grenade launcher attached below the barrel and a sophisticated television camera on board. It allowed the sergeant not only to see at night, but also to point the gun blindly around a corner and, while watching a miniature video monitor suspended from his helmet, to shoot at targets covered by a dot on screen. All the while remaining behind cover.

Up to three points now.

Friel was the primary sniper, calling himself the DK, designated killer. And it was no boast. What he fired at, he hit. Night Runner, the second-best shooter in the team, could be depended on to acquire targets and kill them anywhere within range—and that was what made his earlier no-kill report so astonishing.

For this mission, Swayne had armed himself with a CAR-15, the 5.56-millimeter version of the M-16 rifle, except with a shorter barrel and telescoping steel stock. Not terribly accurate at ranges beyond three hundred meters by day, the carbine was capable of putting out a respectable spray.

While Friel shot off his first magazine of missiles, Potts laid down a curtain of fire. Night Runner should have been firing by now, but wasn't. *What the hell was he waiting for?*

Swayne swept the slope with his NVBs.

He saw three Iraqis creep across a flat rock an instant before a twenty-millimeter projo went off in front of them. A *crack!* followed by the screams of one man. Two others lay limp and silent, green pools flowing out of each across the rock.

Potts doused the hillside with tracers. Two terrorists took three tracers apiece. Five solid ball rounds flew unseen between each streak of red. As many as twenty-three slugs might have ripped and tumbled through the pair. The men fell backward off the slope and rolled, dead before they hit the ground.

Behind him, Swayne was aware that the helicopter's rotors had stopped slapping the air. The bird had landed.

Crunch time. Subtract a point or two for the precarious situation. Almost even odds. A toss-up.

"Make them keep their heads down," he called over his radio. In short order, Friel fired off three more missiles. Whether they killed, maimed, or just created noise, did not matter. As long as the Arabs lay too low to peek at the LZ.

Night Runner had *still* to fire his first round. What was the holdup with him? This was not the Night Runner he knew. What had happened out there on the back trail? What had changed him?

NIGHT RUNNER KEPT up his scan of the Iraqi line. Potts and Friel could lay down enough fire without him. But each time they fired, they had to back off and move to the side to take up new firing positions. That he did not want to do. He dared not be in mid-jump from one boulder to the next when that shooter stuck his ugly Red-eye out from behind cover. He needed to spot the man and stitch him before he could fire. If not, then at least bore a few holes into his missile tube.

Night Runner too heard the helicopter touch down. His gut tensed. This was it.

The pilot called out, "Night Hawk is down." For the first time, a note of stress cracked his voice.

Swayne said, "Five seconds of mad-minute fire and we're out of here. On my command."

A blur. Night Runner focused his scope. Finally. He saw the Red-eye, the cap off its business end. The tube poked out from behind a boulder and waved about as its shooter shifted his body. Getting ready to raise up and fire, Night Runner thought. But the Iraqi kept his head down. He would know he could outwait the team. The Marines would have to get aboard the ship. For a few seconds their fire would be unaimed. Then the craft would slosh around on the LZ, raising dust, wind, noise. The shaking would affect the Spartans' aim. As the bird hovered and took off, the Red-eye shooter would be safe. He could stand up for a clean shot, right up the twin tailpipes of the extraction bird. Even if the missile only went off in the heat cloud above the helicopter, it would do its job all too well.

Night Runner heard Potts and Friel slinging all they had at the Iraqis. He could almost hear Friel: *No point in taking ammo back to the crib when I can fire it up a few terrorist asses.*

Runner felt dizzy. He realized he'd been holding his breath. He told himself to breathe. *Deep and slow. Long on the exhale. Listen for your heartbeat. Be ready, Marine.*

The pilot called out, his voice strained, "Spartan, this is Three-Seven, let's move it, dammit."

Swayne gave the command. "Mount up. We're out of here."

The Spartans knew the drill. They'd practiced it often enough. Friel and Swayne would move out first. When they had set up near the LZ, Runner and Potts would leapfrog past. One sniper and one super-gun to each wave.

With Swayne and Friel on the move, Potts stopped firing to change drums. In that brief pause, Night Runner caught his break. The Red-eye shooter raised up to peek around his boulder. Only half his face emerged, but half was enough. Night Runner could not wait for more. But neither could he give in to the urge to rush. He covered the man's right eye with his aiming dot and went through his sharpshooter's checklist. *One deep inhale. Release and hold. Take out the slack. And feel the pulse. Between the beats . . . a burst of six.*

EVER SINCE THE grenades had gone off, Bin Gahli had kept on the move up the slope. The ferret stayed at his side. He had to admire the man. Never did he fight long-range, but always up close, with steel, not copper-coated lead. Yet he showed no fear of advancing under fire.

To Bin Gahli's mind Jaffari was the best soldier not in Saddam's army. He never bellyached. He did not vary his temper with the weather, hot or cold. He might smile when they had meat, but he could grin just as wide after a week's fast. In the desert Bin Gahli had seen him drink wine, water, blood, and more than once, urine—his face showed no change in taste between one drink and the next.

Bin Gahli kept to low ground and crept to within a hundred meters of his enemy. Amid the noise of the combat, he could barely keep track of the helicopter. But he did not fire. Not yet. He knew he would have his time when the helicopter lifted off, a time when one well-placed bullet might kill all the Americans at once. Or one missile.

Somma could rise up with his Red-eye, take aim—

At the thought of Somma, he glanced back and saw the idiot peer around his boulder. Bin Gahli yelled, "Down, fool. Get down until—"

Half of Somma's face splattered to pulp. Bin Gahli didn't care so much about the man. *But the missile.* He bunched for a dash. *He had to have that Red-eye.* Before he could leap, he saw the tube dance across the ground, pushed and torn by bullets. He buried his face against the stone. The missile blew in its tube.

SWAYNE KNEW THE fire pattern. The burst of gunfire had come from Night Runner. Finally. He listened as two more bursts and the explosion followed. *Ahhh! That was it.* Night Runner had held his fire so he might take out the Red-eye.

Leave it to Night Runner. Swayne felt a twinge of shame for doubting the man.

Friel shot off three quick rounds to keep the enemy cheek-to-sand, then turned to sprint upslope. From the flank Brat tracers streaked down the sky. Potts didn't need sights. He just moved the stream of red around as if watering the garden with bullets. Bits of fire spun off into the sky like sparks from an arc welder.

Swayne turned and sprinted past Potts to where the ground dropped into a channel that circled the last slope before the LZ. He had fought this very battle on the map in case they had to escape under fire. The first two men into the channel would lay down fire for those following after. When he leaped into the ditch, Swayne saw Friel had made it first. Then Potts flew by, diving to safety.

Swayne could do little to add to the fire of those two. Better to get to the top of the hill and give the next round of fire support. Rather than put his back to the Iraqis, Swayne circled left so he could gain the LZ from cover. On the move with Friel and Potts firing—and no return fire—Swayne took up doing what he did best. He put his mind to work on the next two minutes, figuring the best course of action for the rest of their escape. He glanced back and saw Night Runner roll over the sandbank too. In the next second all three guns worked over the Iraqis.

They'd soon be home free. Swayne dared to think it.

Despite their stress, the pilots kept tight mouths. What else? These were not just pilots but *Marine* pilots.

His mind raced. The enemy had his respect. They kept pressing the Spartans, even with heavy losses. He had fought regular battalions that did no better than spray the air with bullets, making all the noise of a Chinese holiday. Not so with this group. They showed strict fire discipline, perhaps too strict. Fine with him. The less they used their weapons, the better the team's odds of getting out of there.

Swayne gained the hilltop. And he had his plan.

He shot off two clips of thirty rounds each, keeping his aim low. He knew the sound of tumbling bullets twanging in the face of a soldier would scare him even worse than rounds snapping by an ear.

In turn, Potts and Friel counted off as they had made the hilltop. The three of them put down fire until Night Runner called himself clear. Swayne couldn't believe the lack of return fire. *What the hell were the Iraqis waiting for? A UN cease-fire?*

A comet tail of sparks streaked overhead.

"Son of a bitch!" Friel said.

The very words running through Swayne's mind.

DAY 2—0100 HOURS LOCAL

NINA CHASE, STAR reporter, had yet to file her first story. But she saw this battle as her big chance, one most reporters would not get after even years in the field—since most overseas news jocks mostly got their news from each other, mostly in hotel bars. Not her. She had this backseat driver's view of a top-secret mission of U.S. forces. The government would never admit to such a thing on the record. But she had proof of it. She could see it unfold with her own eyes. And from the point of view of the terrorists at that. *Sheeze.*

Not that she'd done all that much gawking. She'd seen more of the ground in front of her face than anything else, a point of view tainted by a river of blood rolling toward her from up the hill. She shifted two or three times to avoid getting wet from it, but each time the scarlet stream found a new channel under her friend, the rock shielding her from the American bullets. Finally she gave up moving around and lay in the blood. That beat the hell out of getting shot and spilling her own precious plasma.

Sure, it was a brief battle. But lethal. Iraqis had fallen all around her. But she didn't feel good about her captors dying. She wished the whole war would just stop. She'd seen enough. She already knew more about combat than she ever wanted to. Combat was nothing like the movies. No trumpets playing brassy fanfares, no drums beating courage into the hearts of G.I. Joes (or CNN Janes). No splendor, no glory, no glamor, no glitz. She found nothing to feel good about in any of it. Once she'd thought that nothing could be more dangerous than covering D.C. politics. Not now. This was worse. Compared to this, politics really was a game.

She felt nothing but fear. Scratch that, she felt misery too. She had to urinate, and urgently. The feeling was made worse because she lay on her belly, trying to flatten her body against the ground. Soon the idea of wetting herself did not seem so embarrassing. Far better to die of shame than to be torn up like some of the Iraqis she'd seen hit.

Odd. She'd never expected to feel such sharp hunger pains. She wished she had a Chicago-style dog. Although she knew it would come back up, so nauseating was the taste and smell of gunfire and explosive powders hanging in the air. Not to mention the blood-goo on her nice new Dan Rather safari shirt.

If only she could cut her thirst. Swallowing felt as if she'd taken out her own tonsils with a pickle fork. She wanted a gallon of root beer, right from the jug. Then again, she'd have had to deal with that urge to pee if she drank anything.

Maybe she could relax, have a cigarette. No. The second she lit up, somebody on one side or the other would shoot her in the face. She—

The noise!

More than anything she wanted earplugs.

The racket of battle might be its worst aspect. It pounded in her ears with the report of every rifle and explosion of everything the Americans aimed her way, as if they had singled her out for execution. At first the shooting seemed merely a jackhammer in her ears. Then her eardrums went numb, and her head recoiled with each gunshot, as if the muzzle of every gun was going on beside her ear. Until eventually her whole body flinched and jerked with each report.

A part of her wanted to bury her face and hide, maybe even cry. While another part wanted to run down the hill screaming—anything to escape the noise.

All that kept her from doing either was curiosity, a perverse sense of wonder at the obscenity of it all.

Then came a hiss from somewhere above. She glimpsed the shower of sparks cutting across the sky, leaving a trail of golden, flaky embers in the night. It seemed to her no worse than a bottle rocket.

The streak of gold caused a distinct lull in the fighting. She raised her head.

An innocent pop made her flinch. Then a bright white light floated above them. When she squinted she could see a parachute above the light. A flare? All those bangs and bullets shut down by a flare?

What was the big deal?

NOTHING IN THE age of high-tech warfare could have chilled Swayne's heart more than the crude flare that hung over their heads. The team, in gray-puddled camo, stood out like roaches on the kitchen tile. The Night Hawk, painted black, sat like a beached whale on the alkali-white LZ.

"Spartan, this is Night Hawk," the helicopter pilot said, his tone shot through with stress. "Getting a little antsy here."

"Roger. Spartan Four, can you take out the flare?"

"That's a neg," Friel said. "The light washes out my scope, and I got no IR projos."

"No joy," Night Runner said before Swayne could ask.

Potts's voice boomed in his ear. "I'll give her a—"

The *bra-a-a-a-t* of the Brat drowned out the rest of his words.

"Lay down a base of fire," Swayne told the others. He sprayed most of a clip at a blur farther to the left flank than he would have thought. So. That was why there had been so little return fire from below. The Iraqis who could move at all had slithered away laterally to get outside the fan of fire from the team. Swayne shook his head in grim respect. This group was smart. Very smart. Some of them had climbed high enough on adjacent slopes to be level with or above them.

Bad. Very bad.

In this light—

The Night Hawk, big as a bus—

He didn't want to think about it. But he did have to act.

"Watch the flanks," he said, and fired to their right. He heard a man's cry. Rather than giving Swayne satisfaction, the kill made him more anxious. Runner drew a similar cry from the far left. *The bastards nearly had them in the bag.*

Potts had spent most of a drum on the flare, to little effect. The barrel of the Brat began to glow coal-red as the rounds streamed out. Any number of slugs hit the flare, knocking off burning fragments in brilliant meteor showers.

Still they lay exposed to its glare.

The terrorists began firing from the flanks. Slugs plowed the ground around the Spartans and spanged off the Night Hawk's skin.

Swayne gave the order, and he, Runner, and Friel rolled off the hilltop to regain cover in that channel down the slope.

The blades of the Night Hawk began biting into the air even before the pilot called out his takeoff.

He was about to leave the Spartans on their own.

Swayne had no problem with that. It was the right thing—

All at once shadows raced across the battlefield.

Potts had raised his stream of fire from the burning white phosphorus of the flare to cut the cords above it. The light fell from the sky, its parachute trailing like a rag, and sailed out of sight. That was what had sent the shadows streaking.

Now the flare burned on the ground, casting an eerie glow from a ravine off to the west. One of the Iraqis, exposed on that flank, tried to find cover. Running crouched, he nearly made it. But a round fired from Friel's smart gun exploded in his abdomen, tossing body parts in all directions. Overkill, maybe, thought Swayne, but they now needed every casualty they could wring out of this fight.

"Mount up," Swayne hollered.

Friel broke away first, as the team had planned. Once inside the helicopter, he would scan the landscape and pick his targets. He was the best man for holding steady aim inside a vibrating helicopter. Night Runner was to board second, Swayne third. Potts would wait until last because his gun made the most noise and sprayed the most fire. By the time he'd be ready to mount up, the others could put out almost as much fire as he could.

And fire they did, Runner and Swayne shooting left and right of the great bulk of the gunny as he dashed their way. Friel fired out the far door.

Swayne lay across the deck of the craft, his elbows over the edge of the deck, shooting at muzzle flashes. To his mind, the pilot was too nervous. Swayne didn't blame him for keeping the craft light on its wheels—he needed to be ready to yank them to safety once Potts got on. But he let the Night Hawk dance around. Which cut down the effect of the team's fire.

The helicopter's nose lifted a foot off the ground.

"Hold it," said Swayne. He looked down and saw the aircraft balancing on its rear wheel. "Last man will be aboard in two seconds," he said. "Hold what you got."

Potts dived to Swayne's left, his weight bringing the helicopter down to earth.

"We're up," Swayne said. "Let's get out of here. Move it, *move* it."

The helicopter's nose rose again, and the Night Hawk danced on its tail like a dragonfly.

Swayne was no pilot, but he'd flown in the back enough to know that didn't add up. On takeoff, the nose should go down as the tail lifted. By now they should be sailing off the hilltop.

"Watch it," Swayne called out as the helicopter wallowed in the air. "I say again, the Spartans are all aboard. Move out to the north, low-level. Move it, move it, *move it, move it, move it, move it*—"

Friel cursed in Swayne's earpiece.

"Shut up, Henry," Swayne said, his anger flaring as he turned to give him hell.

"Un-ass the bird!" Friel shouted. "Both pilots are head-shot."

Swayne saw a lot on one glimpse. Frosted holes in the windshield. Slumped heads in the cockpit. Friel crouched, ready to jump. But he would not bail until Swayne gave the okay.

As if Swayne had a choice.

"Abandon ship," he yelled. "Get the hell out of here."

As he lost his balance and fell out on his face.

QUANTICO—1515 HOURS LOCAL

ZAVELLO SAT STARING at the radio speaker as if he expected it to begin broadcasting video to go with the radio transmissions he'd just heard. He had seen too many helicopters shot up in LZs already, in his own war. So he knew what the pictures would look like.

In his mind's eye, he saw torque bucking the aircraft up and to the left, its nose tilting until the rotor blades slapped the earth, wrenching the Night Hawk into pieces. He saw lethal fragments fly in every direction as next the tail rotor disintegrated, then the turbine fans.

Fire-resistant fuel tanks or no, most crashes that involved gunfire would overcome the self-sealing capability of the cells. JP-4 aircraft fuel would splatter in every direction, atomizing at first, then vaporizing. A spark or chunk of hot metal would touch off the vapors. Torching anybody within twenty meters. Killing the lucky ones outright.

Zavello keyed his microphone. But did not transmit. He knew Team Midnight didn't have time to listen, let alone talk. What could he tell them? They'd soon know more than they'd ever want to about a chopper fire. All too soon.

THE DESERT—0116 HOURS LOCAL

NIGHT RUNNER SCRAMBLED OUT the high side of the Night Hawk as it listed in the air. By the time he jumped, he'd risen ten feet. He hit weight-forward, tucked his shoulder, rolled, and came up running. He found speed he did not know he had. In only a few strides, he shot past the captain. At the crest of the hill, the helicopter blew. A flash of super-hot air hit him in the back, throwing him into the cold of night beneath the lip of the LZ.

FRIEL BAILED, THE same as Night Runner, but he did not hit with him. The sling of the Blowpipe snagged on a door catch of the Night Hawk. He hung in the air, thinking stupid ideas. That maybe the gun would break loose. Or the door handle would give. Nuts with that, he thought. That wasn't going to happen. Maybe if he could jump up and jerk the gun free. But how was he going to get leverage to jump when he was hung up by the gun?

All the while he kept going up, up, and away with the Night Hawk. God, he hated them damn things. *Goddamn Iraq. Goddamn—*

Forget that. Only one thing to do. Something no Marine ever dared do.

He let go of his rifle.

He fell, but only a foot. His pack harness caught on the landing gear, and could not fight free. He heard the swipe of rotor blades. The damn thing was about to crash. The Night Hawk was going to grind him into the ground like the butt of an unLucky Strike.

Then a force stronger than gravity lifted him off the gear. He felt his shoulders crunch and saw the huge hands of Potts grasping him. Friel looked up into the face of Gunny. Gunny had lost his jacket. And he looked pissed.

Did he know Friel had dropped the Blowpipe? Was that why he—

Potts pitched him backward without a word.

Friel hit the ground with his heels, fell back, and skidded on his butt. First thing through his head was: *Jeez, Gunny, don't let the cap'n court-martial my ass for losing the Blowpipe.* Second thing was: *Thanks Gunny, for saving my ass.* Third: *Gunny! For chrissakes get your ass outta there.*

The blades slapped the earth as he rolled over and out of the way. He saw Night Runner pass by the captain. He got to his feet and ran. Two strides into it, something struck him in the ear like a ball bat—he knew from the streets what that felt like.

Not three steps later the fireball erupted.

Friel felt himself flying, frying, lifting, and soaring. *Wild.* The feeling might have been okay most days. Except his head was on fire.

His body tumbled. Then his face felt like a hot shower after a sunburn. As his back chilled in cold air.

Then came the fall.

Like falling in a dream. Only he didn't wake up. He hit the ground, flat on his back, like a WCW wrestler on the wrong end of a body slam. He lost his breath, lost his sight, lost feeling in his legs. Maybe he lost his mind. Or maybe he was dreaming. Or else just dead.

Dead. Friel bet on dead.

He fought for breath.

No, If this is life, better gimme dead.

POTTS HAD GONE out the left side of the Night Hawk just behind the captain. But a snag on the nose of the craft caught his jacket as he ran by the cockpit. It raked him along the ribs, wadding up the cloth, hoisting him back into the sky.

Like gigging frogs down in the Georgia swamps. Except for being on the wrong end of the gig. Potts knew he was no damn psychic, but he could see what was about to happen well enough. The Night Hawk was going to pitch him over like a fork of hay, then land on top of him like a ton of pancake mix. So he threw the Brat away, shucked his coat, and hauled himself up onto the side of the Night Hawk. As he was about to jump clear, he saw Friel hooked on the gear.

In theory he could have jumped over the infantile delinquent to save himself. But that thought could not even occur to Potts. One of his men was about to pay the ultimate price. As Night Runner would say: *So morons all over America would have the freedom to go on the Jerry Springer Show and shame the species.*

Potts acted in the only way he knew how. He pulled his boot knife—his Georgia toothpick—slashed the man's straps, lifted him out of his harness, and threw him clear.

Potts lost his footing when the first rotor blade hit the ground, pitching the Night Hawk into a spasm like a stuck hog. He held on to the landing strut and braced for a vault over the belly of the rolling craft. He never saw the second blade except as a blur in front of this face. He felt it, though, as pain in his forearms. He looked down to see that his hands—*botha them, for the luvva Granny's sweet potato pie*—had been cut off. They clung to the strut tube still. He tried to shift his grip, but—

Hell, them biscuit hooks ain't going to do what I tell them.

Hell of a note. But the enemy could not defeat him so easily. He was a Marine, damnit! A Force Recon Marine!

In the next instant a blow to the face struck him blind.

Funny thing. The pain in his head made him forget about his hands, even the agony of knowing he had no hands. He tried to feel his face to see how badly he'd been hurt.

Dang them hands.

He felt himself free-falling. Was this a dream? No. *Face it, Delmont*, he told himself, *they taken off your hands, boy*.

He tasted of the flames. A sudden, searing blast of fire wrapped him in its arm.

And he knew that at least he would not have to live as a medically retired Force Recon Marine.

His granny'd read to him about the tunnel of white at the Rapture.

But Gunny Potts saw only black.

Dang you, Gran—

NINA CHASE ROSE to her knees soon after the shots from above died out. She stood on a rock the size of a doghouse in time to see the Night Hawk shake itself to pieces. The craft blew, sending her reeling off the stone. She rolled a ways down the hill, stopping herself by throwing out her arms and legs. Debris rained on the slopes around her. Now and then a bullet went off in the fire and raised sparks from the wreckage. She felt eerie, awed by the sudden silence after so much noise.

Men had died tonight. On both sides. Brave men all. For no coward could have climbed into a storm fire as those Iraqis had. And the men on top of that hill—Americans, and only four of them at that, if Bin Gahli was right—had held off the Iraqis like Fess Parker at the Alamo.

She had known such fighting men, in every sense. She had been friends with one group, and intimate with their captain, Jack Swayne.

She had wished to God that Jaffari had been right. That Swayne's team was out here. That he would show up, kill these psychos, come to her, hold her by the arm, tell her, "Show's over," and take her home. To hell with war. To hell with the career. And glory, and journalism prizes.

Just get me out of here. All I want to do is live. Hear me, Jack?

The helicopter fire changed her mind. This was the last place she wanted Swayne to be. Nobody could have lived through that crash.

Jack, she sighed. *Oh, Jack.*

SWAYNE WINCED AT a pain in his left side. He didn't recall getting hurt. Was it in the fall? Or had flying debris drilled him, parts of the Night Hawk sent flying by either the crash or the secondaries from boomers and twenty-millimeter rounds?

Not that it mattered. He had more to worry about than a side-ache. He made a radio call, "Team Spartan, report." And held his breath until the first response.

"Three," Night Runner said. "And I have Four with me here. He lost his headset and weapon in the crash. He's out cold, but has a pulse."

Swayne bit his lip. Friel had been hit. But no Gunny Potts.

"Spartan Two, report." Swayne held his breath. Silence.

"Spartan One, Eagle One."

Zavello. Surely he wasn't going to—

"Spartan One, this is Eagle. If it helps, I have no PER-LOBE signal for Spartan Two, Three, and Four."

Three locator beacons had quit. Hell with beacons. *Where was Potts?* By now he should have barreled down the slope, his Brat blazing. When he did, the other members of the team had better watch out that he did not land on them.

But nothing of the sort.

Swayne crawled up to the crest of the LZ to check out the Night Hawk. He looked over a pile of stones the size of bowling balls. Nothing.

Yes! Something. Movement in the inferno.

No. Just clouds of oily smoke lit by the licking tongues of fire. Just—

Swayne felt a stab of horror, a spasm that poked him in the injured ribs. Above the fire rose that same figure that had hovered over Abboud Dahni's death valley less than two hours ago. The Death Angel. It had spread its wings and risen into the smoke column. It had looked back at Swayne and winked. No, that wasn't right. It had looked past him to—

Swayne cursed himself. He had no time for such crap. There was no Death Angel. It had not carried off Potts.

Potts was still alive, dammit, alive and waiting for his Force Recon team to save him as he had saved their butts so many times before.

Yes. Maybe the blast had hurled Potts off the other side of the LZ. Maybe he had fallen back into the channel just below the hilltop.

Swayne radioed Night Runner. "Try a recon to the left. I'll check right."

"Wilco."

Swayne, a pain in his ribs on one side poking him like hot coals, sprinted cross-slope until he could peer around a clump of spiny bushes at the spot where he and the team had rallied before the final dash to the LZ.

Nothing.

Check that. Three Iraqis crept up the slope toward the fire.

A Friel-like urge to kill struck Swayne. Potts was dead. KIA. That thought as much as his finger pulled the trigger. One burst from his CAR-15 took them out, the splatter from their heads backlit a red-gold in the flames.

Swayne backed off and ran back to the far side of the LZ so he could not be cut off by any terrorists swarming the hillside to their flanks. He found Friel sitting up. He groaned from the gut like a drunk talking to the toilet bowl. And he held his head like a drunk too. But he was not drunk. The kid was in pain, his right ear the size and color of a ripe plum.

"My face is killing me," Friel said. "If I still got a face. Captain, do I got a face?"

"You have a fine face, Henry." Not to be abrupt, but Swayne had other concerns. "What about your legs? Can you walk? We've got to get out of this place." He probed his own ribs. He found no broken skin on his tender left side.

Friel checked out his arms and legs as if seeing them for the first time in his life, touching, prodding, flexing, bending. He pushed to his feet and bounced on his toes like a fighter before the bell.

"I'm fine," Friel said. "Four aces."

More like five aces, you little phony, Swayne thought. The kid was game, but didn't look the least bit fine. He kept staggering to starboard, like a punch-drunk palooka after his third standing eight-count. But Swayne couldn't cut him any more slack than the Iraqis would.

"Here," Swayne said, handing over his CAR-15. He took out his own 9-millimeter. Better that Friel, even a dazed Friel, had the firepower. If Friel could shoot, Swayne could do the thinking for both of them.

Night Runner materialized from the shadows. He didn't say a word, but his set jaw, mouth pulled down at the corners, told Swayne all he needed to know. He hadn't found Potts either.

Face it, he told himself. Face it, dammit. Potts had died. Potts—

No! He didn't have time to think about that. The team still had a mission. No way could they help the UNSCOM team if they did not save their own skins in the next few seconds.

With a twitch of his head, Swayne told Night Runner to lead the team away from this place, no longer a landing zone but a killing zone. He gave Friel a shove in the back to get him going. Swayne took up rear security duties. He shivered. This was Potts's normal spot on the march.

No! Face it. He's gone.

NINA STRAGGLED UP the hill, stepping over a scattered body here and a pool of black mud there, making her way behind the Iraqis, drawn to the flames like a mob to a burning Kmart.

Bin Gahli growled and spat in his way, and his men skittered to the margin of darkness around the fire.

She sat down on the ground, her legs crossed Indian-style, feeling the crash in the aftermath of the evening's nonstop adrenaline rush. Bin Gahli approached her, grinning.

"Dat helluva phi, TV lady Niner-Jays, dat be helluva boosht phi." He pounded his chest. "Merrycan heady popper-phi."

She translated: "American helicopter fire."

Weasel Face appeared and growled in Bin Gahli's off-ear. To keep his report from her? That brought up an acid-tasting laugh. The moron didn't know she couldn't speak Arabic or whatever they spoke. Hell, he could pass his secrets to her on billboards, and she couldn't tell the difference between them and a page full of Nike logo swoops going this way and that.

Not so Bin Gahli. He nodded at Jaffari's whispers and turned right around and crowed them into her face. "Whip dem Merry-can boosht somebeets bashtad."

"Oh. And how many men did you lose?"

He opened and closed one fist, three, no, four times and shrugged, both with his body and his canker of a face. As if to say, *What the hell?* He had his *Merrycan heady popper-phi.* Next to that twenty lives meant no more than a few fistfuls of sand.

As the three Marines trekked across the Iraqi night, Swayne tried to guess how many of the enemy they might have killed. A dozen? Two dozen? It wasn't enough. Not for the price of Potts's life. Not ten dozen. Not even ten thousand.

A part of him kept faith that Potts could not be dead, that somehow he had crawled away from the flames and perhaps was even now lying hurt, waiting for help. But no, that was thinking right out of Fantasy Land. The boomers had gone off in the flames. That made it a sure thing. The sound had come, not from over the crest of the hill, but from the wreckage. The blasts had sprayed molten metal fifty feet. It had put out the fire for a second. Then it had relit with a fury. No, Potts had died. Swayne found little comfort that the Arabs could not recover Potts's body and parade it through downtown Baghdad.

Unless. Could Potts have tossed those grenades into the fire from a distance? To create some kind of ruse?

Maybe. Then maybe they should go back. If they hit the Iraqis again. If they put the UNSCOM mission on hold just long enough to wipe out the terrorists and make a quick sweep. If—

Zavello's voice crackled in his ear. The colonel didn't have to say a word of his black report. Just by the tone of Zavello's voice alone, Swayne knew he'd have to give up the ghost of his last hope.

QUANTICO—1536 HOURS LOCAL

ZAVELLO SAT SLUMPED in his chair inside the OMCC, an array of photographs on the desk before him. He had never seen anything like it. Near-real-time IR photos. He hadn't even known that the CIA had such a capability. And the news devastated him too much to be pissed that they had not let him use it on other Force Recon missions, where it might have saved some lives.

None of it mattered now. The pictures proved that Spartan Two, Gunnery Sergeant Delmont Potts, a top-drawer Marine from Georgia, had died in the Night Hawk fire. Potts's PERLOBE beacon had ID'd him as the one guy still inside the helicopter as it crashed in the LZ. A series of four photos showed the bird lift and porpoise out of its hover. In the fifth picture a white flash erased the thermal return of Potts's body. That was the explosion. The time hack on the margin of the photo proved it was the moment the PERLOBE had blinked its last as well. There was nothing to do but report it to Swayne.

"Spartan One, this is Eagle. Spartan Two is lost. We have documentary evidence of one-hundred-percent certainty." Zavello had added the last because he knew that a commander in the field would cling to the last thread of optimism. The ninth photo showed Swayne's beacon marker and three thermal figures moving away from the battle scene along one of the preplanned escape routes. But the tenth showed they had not moved in five minutes. Zavello knew the ideas that would be running through Swayne's head. He had to tell the team not to fight its way back to the crash site. He ordered him to move out.

"To the best of our intelligence, you have been engaged by a force of twenty to thirty," he said. "We have thermal returns on that many souls, but are yet unable to tell whether the bodies are live or dead. It's unsafe for your team to go back and check it out. After the bodies chill down, we can update with new photo imagery."

Zavello downloaded a new heading and destination to the team. A compound twenty-five miles southeast of Baghdad called Salman Pak, thirty or so miles northeast of their position.

"Proceed with extreme caution toward Salman Pak while we continue researching the site." He promised details later and repeated himself on one point: "Do not linger at your present location. I repeat: Clear the area."

THE DESERT—0147 HOURS LOCAL

SWAYNE FELT NUMB from the first part of Zavello's report. Potts dead. Confirmed. He tried to suppress his grief at the loss. He had the mission to think of. The damned mission.

He knew why Zavello kept telling them to clear the area. Another deluge of Air Force hell had already been launched toward the LZ. They'd have the hot spot of the burnt Night Hawk to target. With luck, the bombs would catch the Iraqis that survived the fight.

He focused on the Iraqis. Considering their losses, he doubted the band would follow them. And if it did, the team had enough firepower to hold off an army. Then he remembered. Maybe not. They had lost the Brat and the smart gun. Maybe they couldn't afford a fight with too large a force after all.

On third thought, the badly mauled Iraqis would have to worry about an ambush in the dark. That might slow them down. Then too, they'd be sitting around licking their wounds when a new load of ordnance gave them more wounds than they could handle.

Hell, no! Swayne wouldn't allow himself to count on it. If ever he'd held sacred one tactical rule above all others, it was: Never, *never* expect an enemy to behave as you *need* him to behave so you can beat him. You must *force* him to act in ways you can use against him, but you can never sit around and pray he'll do the wrong thing.

In the movies, the soldier from Planet Zonk might step on the precise twig needed to trigger the good guy's Rube Goldberg invention that takes off the soldier's alien head. In real combat, any time an unwary good guy lay in wait for the bad guy to step on the trigger-twig, the enemy crept up behind and shot him in the back. No timely hesitation, no witty banter, no falling for a second trap. Just bang-bang, and the only good guy is a dead guy.

So. Swayne played out the worst case. The terrorist band would have the smarts to clear the LZ and follow them. And ASAP. They would take on the Marines on their own terrorist terms. The Iraqis could count. They'd know four men could only carry so many bullets into battle. They could figure how much ammo the team had spent. They'd try to press their advantage against the three left alive.

Meanwhile, the Iraqis had guns and bullets to burn. They'd be able to police the battlefield and come up with plenty of both from their dead and dying.

He checked the digital screen on his handheld GPS and saw that they were marching on course. How Night Runner could navigate that way—

A shock of sound hit them from behind. The rumble kept up for a full half minute. The strike at the crash site. The last vestige of Potts being swept away in a deluge of cleansing fire.

The outline of Potts's face showed up in the formations of rock against the blue-black horizon.

Potts. How was this team going to function without its most durable player?

Swayne heard a groan rise up from deep in his soul,

partly grief, partly preamble to a second sound: that voice
of treason that piped up on the heels of any setback. The
nagging, shrill, shrewish, demonic voice of his grandfather,
Senator Jamison Swayne. Every time things went south for
Swayne, he could count on it to creep into his mind. The
voice ridiculed him in moments of weakness, and ques-
tioned his every call. Now it asked: Could they do the job
without Potts? And did he even care?

BIN GAHLI SAT with a handset pressed to his ear, a bulky
device compared to the shirt-pocket radios Nina had seen
in the open U.S. inventory, not to mention the super-secret
gadgets she was not supposed to have seen.

One of Bin Gahli's deadly hoboes carried a low-tech
antenna wrapped in a towel. Antenna Man screwed one
four-foot section into another, into another, into another,
until it had reached a length of perhaps thirty feet.

After a short talk, Bin Gahli dropped the phone. Antenna
Man took the poles apart, rolled them into his towel, removed the battery, and packed the radio. Bin Gahli jabbered in his broken English, "Tungsten pap bird sodomy
sane—" something-something-else. She got the first part:
*UNSCOM captured, Saddam Hussein something-
something.*

Nina shrugged. *So what?* She had known that UNSCOM
might be directed to return to Baghdad from Amman, Jordan. Her D.C. sources had told her that much two days ago.
In fact, the superstar foreign correspondent of CNN herself,
Anorexic Ana, would be shadowing the U.N. convoy as it
left Jordan. Nina had been assigned to meet the group in
Baghdad. To do what, she didn't know, maybe gofer coffee
and smokes to Ana. She didn't try to guess why Saddam
would carjack the UNSCOM team and open the doors to
more abuse, sanctions, and bombings. A madman didn't
need reasons that made sense to anybody else.

Still, why—?

It struck her. Of course! Killing terrorists was no big
thing. The United States could plausibly deny having any-

thing to do with it. Saddam could accuse, accuse, accuse. The Administration could deny, deny, deny. The standoff might go on for months, then peter out for lack of interest.

Unless!

Unless Saddam was mad as a fox. What if he had kidnapped U.N. personnel, not in retaliation for the bombs dropped on Abboud Dahni? What if he used the UNSCOM team in just the way the U.N. wanted them used? What if they conducted an inspection? Not of likely storage sites for weapons of mass destruction, but the site of an actual mass destruction?

Suppose Saddam sent the UNSCOM team to the little valley where so many men had been killed? Suppose he then brought them here to this mangle of wreckage to establish that Americans had done the killings?

Caught in the act? Without U.N. approval? Hell, with even the Security Council kept in the dark? A unilateral terrorist strike by the leading antiterrorist nation? There'd be hell to pay.

The United Nations might close its myopic eyes to Air Force pilots blasting surface-to-air-missile sites in self-defense. But world opinion would shift like tectonic plates on banana peels if UNSCOM had to fess up that American military forces had pulled a sneak attack on the Iraqis.

That would put the Administration in a box.

They would have to stop the UNSCOM team from seeing this crash. They might even have to attack the U.N. convoy and try to blame it on the Iraqis. They'd pulled enough UNSCOM stunts already—intercepting Iraqi microwave signals with fake monitoring devices—to prove they were capable of such a stunt.

All she had to do was prove it. And get out of this hole alive so she could file a story.

No matter how she looked at it, the signs all pointed to glory. Superstar Nina might actually outshine Anorexic Ana.

She started composing some delicious off-the-cuff remarks for her first press conference. She took a little time to try out some ad-lib humility for her speech accepting the top-story-of-the-year award. She tried to come up with a news piece that had an I-smiled-in-the-face-of-death feel to it. She thought she might have just the thing.

Until the weasel character showed up. He handed something to Bin Gahli. A boot. A combat boot. Jack Swayne wore boots like that. Her heartbeat stumbled, as if all her journalism awards had fallen off the mantelpiece at once.

Jack? My Jack?

Nah! That boot could not fit Swayne. She knew his foot. No boot that huge had ever been on her bedroom floor.

She saw two splinters, a charred pair of sticks poking from the top of the boot. It took her two beats to realize what they were. Bones. The boot was still laced. It had a foot in it.

She turned away and fought to keep her stomach down.

She knew a Marine big enough for a boot like that. Part of Jack Swayne's group. The huge black noncom. Potts, wasn't it? What were the odds that the weasel's psychic powers had been right about a team of Marines with the identical makeup of Swayne's?

No way. That kind of thinking was what sold horoscopes. A few details that fit millions of people in dozens of countries. No way in hell could Jack Swayne's team be involved. It had not been Potts's foot that Bin Gahli wrapped in rags and draped over his back.

Even so, Nina couldn't help feeling a huge surge of relief when Bin Gahli told her, "Dat Jaffari. He say tree udder merry cans. Do dat way." He stuck out his arm, pointing across the smoldering ashes of the helicopter.

She felt a wash of relief.

Sure, Jack Swayne had not been here on this hill tonight. Of course not. Even if he had been here, he hadn't been the one to die in that fire. *Jack,* the only lover she'd ever fantasized about *after* taking him into her bed. He had taken off. *Jack! Alive!*

•   •   •

SWAYNE REALIZED THROUGH the fog in his head that the fog of the night had begun to lift. The first streaks of a red dawn colored the pewter sky above the far hills at the Iran border. Before it became full light, Night Runner stopped among a nest of boulders and leaned into the shadows. Friel, who had trudged along without complaining, made a show of setting up security on the back trail. He fingered the lump on the side of his head, more a dried kidney than an ear. Swayne joined Night Runner in the long shadows and signaled for Friel to join them and to cut off their mikes.

Friel shrugged. "IDM, sir," he said. "It don't matter. The explosion eighty-sixed my radio."

Swayne remembered that Night Runner had told him that long ago. No wonder he hadn't heard Friel. He'd probably been his usual self all along, complaining the night through, Swayne thought. If nobody could hear a Marine bitching in an empty forest, was it really bitching?

Swayne consulted his GPS. "We've put just shy of ten miles between ourselves and the enemy. Just shy of twenty-some miles to Salman Pak. We should find cover, take inventory, get some rest. Go the rest of the way at night. I'll check in with OMCC and see if they have any update on the UNSCOM team."

Swayne didn't like what he saw in his men: lethargy. Not even the brief stop for water at a tiny oasis had restored them. But what could he do to soften their grief, when his own spirit ached?

Rather than attempt a hollow "Win one for the Gipper" speech, Swayne simply said, "Lead the way, Sergeant Night Runner."

THE SERGEANT STOOD up, shook dust clouds off his clothes, and led them half a kilometer farther. Then he took a sharp turn to the left. Right away he caught the error. He should have gone right. Last night he had shown a tendency to turn off the trail to the left at ninety-degree angles. He slowed.

No? Yes?

"What?" asked Swayne.

"No sweat," he said, and stayed left.

He hated to vacillate. Yes, left. Take the initiative back by letting the rat-bastard tracker think he'd fallen victim to habit.

He led Friel and Swayne to a rimrock. Boulders the size of boxcars lay at its base, and the cliff above them arched outward, beyond the vertical in some places. Two shallow caves beneath the rimrock could shade them from the sun all day long and shield them from aerial observations.

Good choice. For now.

Friel collapsed into the shade at the mouth of one of the caves.

Swayne set the watch and took an inventory of rations, water, weapons, and ammunition. Worse than he'd thought. They had used up most of their basic load of grenades and ammo on the LZ. Even if it had not been an intense fight, they'd expected to be lifted out of Iraq. Hell with strict fire discipline. Better to be picked up with only one bullet left than to save a whole basic load and lose a man for all the thrift—

His stomach flip-flopped. He had lost a man, hadn't he?

They cleaned weapons, took stock of their wounds, and repacked gear. Only then did they eat. Friel nodded over a packet of vegetarian mush.

NIGHT RUNNER DID not even try to eat. He had no stomach for it. After a long silence, he said, "We should reposition."

Swayne stood up. "Where to?"

Night Runner gave a brief smile: *Thanks for not second-guessing, Boss.* He helped Friel to his feet and pointed to a less prominent, less comfortable spot a kilometer to the west.

As they settled into it, Night Runner could see Friel was less than pleased. Small boulders did not throw shade like the cliff. On the plus side, the cliff would have directed any blast downward. Even rifle fire would ricochet toward the base. Also, because the new spot lacked comfort, it wouldn't draw attention. Once Swayne and Friel had stretched out in the slim shadows among the rocks, Night Runner picked up his backpack, retraced his steps without a word of why, and . . .

"WHERE'S HE GOING?" Friel asked. By his tone, he didn't care.

Swayne shook his head. Poor Friel. The blast had singed his hair, turning his eyebrows to buff-colored nap. His skin glowed red. It shone from swelling. And that ear. Attached to the side of his head like a man-eating eggplant, growing as if it were sucking everything out of Friel's head. Any other time, Swayne would have laughed, likely at the urging of Friel himself. With Potts joining in—

Potts again. Swayne knew he had to put his mind to work on other matters. He tried to focus on a plan for tonight. But trying to put Potts out of his head only made him stick like a biker's tattoo.

Finally Zavello came on line. Swayne was glad for the scratchy voice, a diversion from the gunny's ghost. He gave Zavello a sitrep. They talked about scrapping Event 15 in favor of another team that had enough punch to make a move on Salman Pak.

Like any other Force Recon Marine, Swayne never knew when to quit. As long as a Marine had a will to fight, it ought to be enough. In theory. But a smart Marine didn't give his life for his country so lightly. In a hopeless situation, he saved his energy—and his life—to fight another day.

"Eagle," he said, "if you could drop in guns, ammo, and water, you wouldn't need another team. We could do this."

He heard Friel snort and turned to give him the evil eye. But Friel was still asleep—or faking it well enough. He could forgive the kid even a snide remark. He looked as if he'd been in a hatchet fight without a hatchet, to use Potts's words.

Potts again.

With effort he tuned in to Zavello alone, who was saying . . .

"This is Eagle. Evade the enemy until the situation develops further. On order, be ready to close on the compound. Maybe as backup, maybe as recon on behalf of another Force Recon team. Maybe to extract from Iraq so the Corps can't be linked to the Brutus mission."

A lot of maybes to Swayne's mind.

Zavello apologized for the lack of focus. He said he would be off the air for a minimum of six hours as his staff began putting together the dispositions of SCUM-SCUM and Iraqi conventional forces. He promised to be back later in the day, after the Spartans had gotten some rest. By then, he said, he expected to help them concoct either the attack strategy or an escape plan.

Swayne signed off. He couldn't blame the Z-man. He had even a tougher fight than the Spartans. He had to play politics.

Before long, Night Runner returned. He wanted to take first watch. Swayne let him. He drifted off to sleep, twitching like a dreaming puppy.

NIGHT RUNNER PULLED his three hours. But he did not wake up his relief. He had too much to think over, that Iraqi tracker at the center of it all.

At five hours into his watch, Night Runner still sat, staring into the desert—and rerunning last night. He kept rehashing his decisions, reworking his execution, looking for tactics that might have kept them out of the mess he'd put them in.

He couldn't get around one thing: if only he'd taken out the tracker and the terrorist leader when he had the chance. No amount of mental voodoo would undo that stubborn fact.

He fiddled with his rifle, picking absently at the electronics control panel door. It snapped open. Funny. He found the battery-low light blinking. That didn't figure. Those batteries should last a week. Unless—

Unless he was stupid enough to have left on the video recorder.

He checked.

He had. Mentally he gave himself a kick in the pants. The battery might have time to recover before dusk, but it would not make it through another night. Tonight, of all nights.

He remembered the scene he had recorded when he spotted the Iraqis coming out of the valley of death. Should he check it out? Should he risk using even another minute's worth of battery power?

Yes. He might learn something that would help the team. Maybe redeem his self-respect. He rewound the digital disk to its starting point. Cupping his hands around the tiny video screen, he squinted between his thumbs and watched the blue-and-white image.

Twenty-two seconds in, he froze.

"Son of a bitch," he muttered.

SWAYNE SPRANG INTO a combat-ready state as his eyes came open, rolling from his sleeping position against the stone. He found himself bound, blindfolded, and gagged. Somebody had sneaked up on him, hosed him down with a hair-drier besides. And glued his mouth shut. A pair of hands lifted the blindfold. When he opened his eyes, he found himself staring into Night Runner's face. The sergeant held a finger to his lips as he helped Swayne untangle from Runner's jacket.

"Sorry to alarm you, Boss," Night Runner said.

Swayne saw that Night Runner had arranged his jacket to shade him from the sun, which had moved too high into the sky to have been a mere three hours. The sergeant's T-shirt formed a second sunscreen to protect Friel.

"What's up?" Swayne asked, rasping his tongue against the roof of his dry mouth. "Did I hear you call out?"

Night Runner answered by handing over the video screen, not much larger than a postage stamp and tethered to the gun by its fiber-optics cord. Swayne took off his soft cap and used it to shade the video as it began running.

Swayne realized he was looking at the band of Iraqis that Night Runner had run across last night. He began counting to himself. Night Runner must have seen his lips moving. He said, "Altogether I count sixteen, but there may be more who didn't come into view. But that's not what I wanted you to see."

"Pause it," Swayne said. The image froze as Night Runner hit the tiny control panel with the tip of a 5.56-millimeter cartridge. "I recognize those two from a briefing a long time ago, closer to Desert Storm than Desert Fox. The one is—or was—an up-and-comer in the terrorist game. Only reason I remember him is that he is Saddam Hussein's ninth cousin or something."

"I remember too," said Night Runner. "Bin Gahli."

"That's it, Bin Gahli."

"But he's not what I want you to see."

Without taking his eyes off the screen, Swayne cocked his head. *Okay, I'll bite. What?*

The image began running again, and Swayne said, "Pause it. The skinny guy? Looks like a rat? Do you know him?"

"No," Runner said, thinking to himself: *But I would like to greet him with the tip of my bayonet.* "Bin Gahli might be the brains of that outfit, but the rat-face is the eyes and ears"—Night Runner remembered how he had betrayed himself last night—"and the nose. If anybody in Iraq is going to sniff us out, it will be this guy."

Swayne looked up in dismay. He had never heard Night Runner admit anybody could track him down. He had to confirm with his eyes what his ears had just told him. True enough. He saw concern in the brave's face. Even worry.

"But that's not what I want you to see," Night Runner said.

Swayne looked back into his hat. The camera lens swept the landscape, stopping on a second squad of Iraqis. Swayne started his count—*"Pause it!"* He looked up, shaking his head as if trying to reset his eyeballs. "What the hell was that?"

Night Runner grimaced. "Just a glimpse? Two or three frames?"

Swayne grunted.

"That's what I wanted you to see," said Night Runner.

Swayne's head twitched. The image flickered by. "Back up a little. Frame by frame—*there!*" Swayne pressed his face deeper into his cap.

Night Runner knew the feeling. He'd been there. All three frames might be fuzzy, but they were enough for Swayne to make a positive ID.

"Nina Chase."

The Iraqis had not blindfolded her or tied her hands. Was she on some kind of news-junket joy ride? Would there be film at eleven of the Night Hawk reduced to puddled metal in the desert? Could Potts be identified? Would his family find out how he had died, or even that he had died? From a goddamned television report?

By Nina? How could she?

Was she so naive? Didn't she know Bin Gahli would kill her as easily as crush a sand flea between his thumbnails?

He asked himself: *What was he going to do about it?*

Answer: *Nothing.*

He liked Nina a lot. But as a tactical entity she had no value. If she wanted to risk life and limb to get a story, fine. Surely she knew that at any given time, every special operations unit in the world, including rival terrorists, would go after Bin Gahli with everything from smart bombs to poisoned goat milk.

Yes, Swayne would be sad about losing her if she took a cruise missile in the kisser for CNN. But that would be her decision. No way could the Spartans pull her ass out of the fire. As a national interest, Nina would have a low priority. Make that no priority.

Forget Nina. Hell, she'd probably been deconstructed by the explosives that had rained down on the crash site.

• • •

AFTER TAKING THE hill, Bin Gahli found he had only seven men who could travel. Two of those had wounds. But the pair refused to be left behind.

Nina soon saw why. Bin Gahli took food, water, guns, and ammunition from the wounded for his healthy men.

Then he walked away. Not so much as a good-bye, good luck, or kiss-my-ass to the dead and dying. Just left them, some conscious enough to wail and moan. The bastard. He might at least have put them out of their misery. Instead of running out like a typical guy after a one-night stand.

As they marched into the night toward dawn, Nina tried to reason like a terrorist, but couldn't. *Good,* she told herself. She patted herself on the back. Dubious an honor as it was, at least she wasn't as ruthless as these sorry bastards. The sun would kill the men Bin Gahli had abandoned. But slowly, as they lay in flies and agony—

A shock wave broke off her thought. She hit the ground like everybody else. Bombs—she knew damned well from earlier tonight what bombs sounded like. And if you could hear them, you hadn't put enough damn distance between you and them. *Ahhh.* The Air Force had decided to rework the landscape. Erase the evidence of Americans—except for the foot Bin Gahli had carried off.

So. Bin Gahli hadn't left his men to die in the sun. He'd known the sun would never come up for the poor guys.

And he'd kept that foot-in-the-boot for evidence. UN-SCOM could use it as DNA evidence or some damn thing, she supposed.

She had to give the guy credit. He wasn't so dumb after all. If anything, she'd be better off playing a bit dumber herself.

When Bin Gahli called a halt to the march, she was startled at the setting. Here, in a hub of rubbled valleys with all the appeal of an ashtray, had sprung an oasis no bigger than a living room. All she had to do was take one giant step out of a landscape as inviting as the sunny side

of Mercury and set her foot into a lush speck of the world
with all the greenery of the Capitol Mall.

Like her captors she lay on the grass beneath a fig tree.
She took off her safari boots and went to the spring, hoping
to cool off her sizzling feet. But she felt a yank on her
collar and found herself flung backward on her butt. Found
herself staring into Bin Gahli's crash-test-dummy face, trying to interpret his spit-storm of English-Arabic blather by
reading his calf-liver lips. If the man realized how terrifying
he was, he would stop doing his deeds at night and scare
people to death by day. For his was the very face of terror.

Once she got over the shock of seeing him in full light,
she realized he was chewing her out for trying to dunk her
feet into the only fresh drinking water within miles.

He pointed. She looked. Bin Gahli's band performed
their ablutions by filling canteens in the pool and spilling
them over their feet.

She put on her best smart-aleck face. "All you had to
do was say so." But she didn't quite pull it off. Bin Gahli
scared her. The guy had killed his own fighting men after
all their bravery in going up that hill. She'd better find a
way to be useful. Instead of being a pain in the ass.

She put on a slump. Maybe she could fake being meek—
if only she knew what meek felt like. Maybe she should
shed a few tears. Guys always fell for tears.

She studied the terrorist's face, a carving in cow shit.
He studied her back. Almost as if looking for an excuse to
kill her.

No tears for you, she thought. Kill me if you want, but
I'd sooner have your baby than show you a drop of dew
in the eye.

Back at the spring, she lay on her belly, pushed back
the moss with one hand, and drank her fill. *Imagine!*
Through pond scum. The best drink of water she'd ever
had.

She found a patch of grass and lay down. Somehow the
trees chilled the blast furnace of the desert. In no time, she
fell asleep.

• • •

No matter how Swayne figured, they were in for hard times. On the plus side, their night stop at the oasis had given them time to drink their fill of water, refill their canteens, and refresh themselves. They had also eaten a few bites of the high-energy foods they carried. Now, as best he could tell, they had two days' worth of water. They might extend their rations twice that time.

They had the two assault rifles and four pistols between them—Friel always packed a small-caliber pistol in his boot top. And four boomers, concussion grenades. They could sting Bin Gahli well enough if he came close enough. Best of all, Swayne had the two best shooters in the Marine Corps. Either one could nail a target at five hundred meters.

What hurt more than anything else was that they had expended so much ammunition.

Friel had pooled the 5.56 supply and divided it with Night Runner. He gave sixty rounds to Night Runner and kept twenty-eight. Making the point that real snipers needed less ammo. Swayne saw the Friel arrogance as a hopeful sign. Maybe he'd recovered. An insufferable Henry was a healthy Henry.

By afternoon, a stiff breeze blew up. Swayne couldn't sleep with hot sand sifting into his nose. So he took the watch, then found that, dammit, he could not stay awake. He was glad when a burst of static in his ear broke the monotony.

Zavello's voice gave away his distress even before his words gave the news. Several convoys had been spotted by overhead satellites on the march in and out of Salman Pak. CIA experts suspected two possibilities, both bad.

First, Saddam might have ordered the U.N. inspection team dispersed throughout the region in armored vehicles. If so, no single snatch team would recover them. Leaving diplomacy to work—or *not* work. It seldom did with Saddam.

Second, the convoys had set up security around the compound to keep the Spartans out.

All that Zavello could say for sure was that one American, the one with the CIA PERLOBE implanted in his boot heel, had been detained at Salman Pak—or at least his boot had.

In that case, Swayne said, the Spartans should take a closer look at Salman Pak. He asked for a rundown on the site.

Zavello explained that Saddam had used Salman Pak to research the effects of biological weapons, including anthrax and botulism, on ethnic Kurds. Navy Tomahawks had struck the site during Desert Storm. Saddam had rebuilt it as a larger production facility. The Navy had restruck in Desert Fox. Saddam had re-expanded it afterward as Iraq's primary manufacturing plant and foremost testing ground.

Swayne pursed his lips at the irony. It looked like the Navy could best contain the growth of the Salman Pak compound by *not* bombing it.

Zavello next told him that two tank brigades of the Republican Guards had been placed on alert. One other brigade had set out on a march from a border outpost near Iran, less than forty miles away from Swayne's Force Recon team.

"Marching along little-used roads," Zavello said. "A convoy of thirty-three tanks and twice as many other armored vehicles."

Swayne could hear a voice in the background at Quantico. Zavello broke off his report. A moment later he came back on the air with more bad news: "With a convoy of twenty-two trucks, we think maybe a battalion-plus of straight-leg infantry. Stay out of sight, Marines. Will advise."

Swayne had to laugh after he'd signed off. *Will advise?* Zavello was going to come back with advice? Advice was the best Swayne's country could do for him? In that case he hoped it would be something better than the lame-brain suggestion to stay out of sight of an armored division-plus that was trying to hunt them down.

He shook his head, more than a little ashamed. He'd lost more than his gunny. He'd lost his sense of humor.

NINA HAD AWAKENED feeling chilly, the oasis as cold as her air-conditioned room back at the Watergate. *The Watergate*. Would she ever see it again?

She sat up and rubbed her arms before slipping into the Dan Rather jacket she'd used as a pillow. She saw Bin Gahli on a hillock outside the oasis shouting into his radio handset, Antenna Man holding up the pole. Bin Gahli's men adjusted packs, dusted rifles, cleaned loose ammunition, and reinserted it into magazines. A band getting ready for the march. She thought of the wounded crying out at the battle zone last night, their folded hands praying for succor as Bin Gahli turned his back on them and strode away.

She wasn't about to get left behind. She shook torrents of sand from her boots and laced them up.

Bin Gahli came back to the circle of greenery and said to her, "Dat boosht bepubbian gods."

"What about the Republican Guards?"

He tried to tell her. Nina didn't catch it all. Just enough to know that Bin Gahli hated the idea of Saddam's elite Guards taking credit for bagging the three Americans he had lost so many men to.

His pride. She doubted he'd grieve more for even the loss of the mother of all reptiles that had hatched him.

THE REPUBLICAN GUARD presence made Night Runner wonder. Had the team wasted an afternoon watching for Bin Gahli and his Tracker?

Maybe they weren't coming after all. Maybe they'd stayed on the LZ long enough to get plastered by the distant bomb bursts the team had heard while on the march. That was one possibility, and one he doubted. The strike had been too long in coming. Not even the college boys at an ROTC summer camp panty raid would be dumb enough to hang around that long.

More likely they weren't coming because they had no need to. Not since Night Runner had tipped them off. The Iraqis wouldn't even need a computer to figure their course and deduce possible destinations of the Marines. Night Runner had zigged and zagged during the night march. But he did not give enough thought to the larger evasion picture. A good analyst would trace the course changes on a map. After a few miles, he could lay down a ruler and draw a line that more or less averaged out all the twists and turns. Then he'd extend the line. *Bingo!*

All he'd need do was alert the military at any Iraqi outpost, city, or compound like Salman Pak near that line. Saddam could then focus his forces and meet the Marines at the gate.

Night Runner decided not to waste time bitching himself out. Better to plot a line of his own and remove all doubt that he'd acted the idiot. He lit up his handheld GPS and, using a series of keystrokes, laid down the precise track on the map segment they had followed during the night. Then, using graphic equations, he calculated their mathematical average, converting those directions of travel to a single vector.

By the time the solution appeared on screen as a bold arrow, Swayne had moved to his side. Night Runner couldn't very well slam the computer shut in the captain's face. He'd just have to eat his afterbirth.

Swayne went right to the core of the issue. "Bring up the downloads from OMCC and superimpose them on your readout."

Seconds later, everything the Iraqis had done made sense. The alerted units along the Iran-Iraq border had moved across their path, which now aimed to within a thousand meters of Salman Pak. Probably on information from Bin Gahli's Tracker.

So. Most of the Iraqis could block the team's path to Salman Pak. Only one brigade, reinforced with infantry, would need to search the open desert for them. In fact, the latest download from OMCC showed the brigade had fanned out its three combat battalions. They had begun to sweep the desert roads that crisscrossed the vector that Night Runner had conjured up with his math functions.

"That's what happens when you underestimate your enemy," said Night Runner, his black pupils crackling with anger at himself.

Swayne clenched his jaws. "Ever since Desert Storm we've always assumed their army was nothing more than a bunch of blockheads, and cowardly ones at that," he said. "I never guessed they had a terrorist with your skills."

Night Runner wasn't sharing the blame with his captain. "No," he said. "It's my bad."

"Fine," he said. "It's your fault. How are we going to fix it?"

Night Runner couldn't contain a smile. That Swayne. Never letting his rank or ego stand in the way of getting a job done.

Night Runner went to work at the tiny keyboard. Before long a series of hash marks covered the topographical depiction on his screen.

Swayne recognized them. "Terrain shade."

"Affirm. I recommend we plot this course." Night Runner traced a path through the hash marks with the roller ball. Keeping to low ground of the terrain shade would limit the odds of being spotted by ground forces. The route would take them toward Baghdad. "Let them predict we're going after Saddam's palace. Make them think it's an assassination. Nothing ruins a tyrant's sleep like the thought of a plot."

NINA WAS NO wilderness expert, but she could see fresh footprints on a beach as well as any Brownie scout. So it surprised her that Bin Gahli's weasel did not keep to the file of tracks when she saw them turning sharply left. Had he gone stupid? Addled in the heat?

She shifted her opinion of the little rat less than two hours later when a set of tracks—she assumed the same set—curved across their path, veering right. Jaffari kept to his straight line. Maybe the little vermin knew what he was doing after all.

As the last sliver of sun shimmered its way over the horizon, Bin Gahli's band took a break. They offered water, and she drank greedily from a skin that tasted of goat tallow. She didn't care. She thanked Bin Gahli for a dirty clawful of unleavened bread torn from a loaf and wrapped around a slab of jerky too salty, too rancid, and too tough to be anything but camel belly. But she ate it as if it were pheasant in apricot sauce.

The men also chowed down on a form of cheese the color and consistency of a deodorant stick. But it was anything but deodorant. More like its opposite, a true *anti*-deodorant. It smelled like week-old roadkill drenched in garlic oil, filling the air with a stench every bit the equal of last night's bombed-out valley. *That* was what gave the men their *eau d'dumpster* body odor. And that she would not eat.

Bin Gahli and his main man talked in grunts and slobbers, spitting crumbs at each other.

As they combed the last of the food out of their beards, and she picked at threads of camel meat caught in her teeth, Bin Gahli decided to tell her what was going on. As he did so, all smiles and grins, his breath more foul than ever, she began to rekindle the hope of getting out of Iraq alive. He wouldn't bother telling her all this news if he just planned to kill her. *Would he?*

She patched together what she could from his battered English: Jaffari had guessed at the *Merry-cans'* target. Bin Gahli had alerted Saddam, who would trap the infidels. The Republican Guard unit was to search the desert, and Bin Gahli was to prevent the infidels' escape by staying in place at the oasis.

The rest sounded simple enough. Bin Gahli had decided to do what any self-respecting terrorist would do. Something that Nina would do herself if she were a terrorist. He'd rejected his orders to stay put. He was on the move to hunt down the Americans and get all the glory for himself.

Jaffari had his own agenda. The Americans had evaded him for so long that his reputation had been tainted. Bin Gahli explained: "Dat Jaffari, boosht mad. Been fooled nebber. He killed his man. Always. *Never* always."

Bin Gahli had chopped up the telling, but she got the gist. Which sent a chill up her spine. Until last night, she had never met fighting men as deadly as Swayne's Marines. And now she wished she never had.

THEY ATE ON the move, Friel nibbling an energy bar for a solid hour, as if taking in calories one for one as he burned them.

Swayne began to worry about Friel once more. His arrogance had not flared up after handing out ammo. He'd spent the rest of the day sullen and morose. As if the essence of his smart-ass had died back there on that fiery LZ. Swayne wanted to hear a few gripes. Had Friel's cocky spirit been lost to the team forever?

Zavello reported that the Iraqi tank brigade had circled the wagons, giving Swayne's team free access to the night. He downloaded screens that showed the Guards brigade had moved south during the day, blocking the team's original line of travel. So far the Iraqis had not caught on to the new evasion strategy of Night Runner. A good sign. A very good sign.

Night Runner gave himself liberty to feel good. But not to excess. Just because the new trail might end-run the Iraqis did not mean the Tracker would be fooled. Night Runner asked himself: *Would I be fooled?* And answered: *Of course not.*

THE DAY TREK cost Bin Gahli's band one more fighter. The man's leg wound, wrapped in a seeping bandage, stopped him little more than a mile outside the oasis. The man fell behind at first, dragging the leg. Finally he dropped and could not get up. He called out to the group, but Bin Gahli paid no heed to the cry in the night.

An hour after hearing the last calls from the abandoned man, the weasel stopped the group in one place for a full five minutes. Nina sidled up to the bunch. Surely Jaffari had not lost the track. Even in this, the dimmest of moonlight, she could see it snaking across the sand ahead. But Jaffari and Bin Gahli traded burps and farts and struck off upslope toward the silhouette of a cliff to the left. When she saw the band spreading out on line, she started looking around for a place to land in case guns should start rattling again. None of the terrorists kept tabs on her any longer. She knew why. She wouldn't dare to take off into the wilderness. She was as afraid of being left behind as any of Bin Gahli's soldiers.

Jaffari halted, scribbled a finger at the ground, and swept his arm up toward the rock outcropping. She didn't see a thing. The Iraqis took him at his word, though, and kept their weapons at the ready as they sneaked forward, each man bent at the waist and knees.

She crept along behind the group, crouching behind boulders when she could, sinking to her knees at any pause. She couldn't quite get over the idea that the weasel was stalking ghosts. But she wasn't going to be stupid about it either. If he was wrong, no problem. But if the little turd was right, bullets would fly.

She caught up to the cluster near a shallow cave. Bin Gahli flashed the beam of a penlight into the enclave of rocks. She saw coals of a small fire that had been set to burn the litter of ration packets. It didn't require the Last Mohican to conclude that Americans had camped here. But how did the weasel know such things? Did he have senses that went beyond the normal range of humans? Like dogs able to hear high-pitched noises? Did—?

Whoa! She had extra senses of her own. She could smell trouble and this was it, in any language. The group milled around. She didn't have to understand the Iraqis' language to recognize confusion. The Marines had landed here, all right. But they'd un-landed. Apparently without a trace. The confusion turned to derision. Aimed at Jaffari, who was stumped, from the look of it.

Bin Gahli's rat made two sweeps along the base of the cliff, two half circles, his eyes following his light beam, looking for clues to the vanishing act. The penlight was a major clue by itself to the extent of his humiliation. Before he'd always used the barest light from the moon, as if he could see in the dark. Now he cast the beam like a magic wand. He held it high and he laid the light next to the ground to raise something from the tiny relief and long shadows. His third and widest pass took him out of sight.

While he was gone the mood changed with Bin Gahli's men. The humor had worn thin. Now they looked worried. She could read the concern on their scruffy faces: *If the Americans could fool their top scout, what kind of supermen were they?*

Nina almost broke out laughing when Jaffari returned, his face dour in the light of a match as the Iraqis lit up his and their pungent cigarettes—of dried animal dung, by the smell of them. If looks could inflict pain, Jaffari's glare would have taken her skin off in strips. That is, if he could have survived the ballistic missiles shooting out of Bin Gahli's eyes at the weasel. Jaffari, in disgrace, wanted to blame her for his failure. Just like a man. Too funny for words. But she knew that to laugh now was to die.

Jaffari threw down his half-smoked cat turd and took another, even wider turn around the slope, only to come back looking more defeated. Nina sat with her back against a stone. She hid her face on her knees, as if napping. She wanted no eye contact that might get her in trouble. If the Americans had indeed escaped, Bin Gahli would have no further use for her. He might rid himself of her as easily as the crap he constantly snorted from his nose. Even so, some part of her could not help being glad. Some part knew, just knew, the weasel had been following Swayne and his own top scout. And it gave her great joy to know that they had eluded this SOB.

But in no time, Jaffari redeemed himself. She peeked over her knees and watched him flash his penlight on the cliff wall. A little gasp stuck in her throat as she saw the beam lock onto a spot on the wall. A scuff mark. She sat up and watched Jaffari spit on his hands and, holding the penlight in his teeth, approach the wall. He went to work like a spider. Inserting his fingertips into cracks that did not exist until he put his hands to them, the man worked his way up toward the scuff mark. After a quick inspection he let out a squeal of delight and kept climbing. As he neared the top, his movements became animated. His elation brought on a deep sadness in Nina.

Bin Gahli watched Jaffari slither over the brink of the cliff, then spat. In a way that Nina could not divine, this was a command for two men to detach themselves from the group, one in each direction, to search along the cliff's base. Moments later a wheeze drifted back to Bin Gahli on the night air. The terrorist reacted to it, stomping along the wall until he came to a footpath winding like a broken spiral staircase up a split in the rimrock. Feeling whipped, she followed.

The group reassembled above, clustering around Jaffari. The weasel's penlight splashed back and forth across the flat terrain, one arm holding back the group, to prevent wandering feet from trampling the tracks so plain in the soft sand. Three tracks, in fact. They traveled ten feet directly away from the cliff's edge. Then, just like that, they ended. As if three rocket-men in combat boots had lifted off. Jaffari made urgent hand motions that kept everybody glued to their own footprints. Then he made one of his circular searches. When he returned, more hand signals, grunts, and gas eruptions followed. Bin Gahli took back his penlight and knelt, sweeping the beam close to the earth, creating long shadows to highlight the tiniest peaks and valleys in the sand.

When Jaffari called out, Bin Gahli stopped moving the light. What its beam revealed, Nina could not see. Until Jaffari pointed to a shadow longer than normal, a regular depression in the ground. Bin Gahli shone his flashlight into the depression, and even Nina could tell there had been a tire track. An aircraft tire track, obviously a helicopter, since it had dropped out of the sky to make a single print. At that, Bin Gahli flashed the light laterally to the spot where a second tire track should be if indeed a helicopter had landed here. And there it was, a second impression. Jaffari sagged in defeat. Bin Gahli stiffened in anger.

So. The Americans had stepped up into a helicopter. The incredulous Jaffari took back the penlight and shone it on the spot where a tail wheel would have rested. Once again Jaffari's bones flexed and Bin Gahli's grew more rigid.

Much argument followed, the Iraqis throwing caution to the wind and actually using words in place of grunts. Some pretty vicious words at that, judging by their explosive consonants, violent gestures, and more than a few *summbeets, booshts,* and *faroukews.* Finally, Bin Gahli dismissed Jaffari by turning his back, and Jaffari slumped away into the night. Nina could swear that she saw a tail hanging between his legs.

Nina stood stock-still. This was a critical time for her. She stared at the ground, not even daring to make eye contact that could prove fatal. An inner voice warned her, for once in her life, not to be a smart-ass. She felt Bin Gahli's eyes on her as he walked the edge of the cliff, pacing. Once he passed between her and the brink. She thought about it, and even felt her body weight shift as if to lunge at him.

But a guardian angel at her shoulder whispered a warning against trying anything so rash. A wrong move now would end in certain death. But not for Bin Gahli.

He would dodge clear, and she would go sailing into the night, falling fifty feet or more, if not killing herself, worse. Lying out here in the desert with broken bones and no way of surviving the injury simply meant a prolonged death. Bin Gahli might be pissed, but he hadn't gone bat-shit. He was testing her, the bastard, toying with her. Now that the Americans had foxed him, the sadistic bastard was going to get his jollies by messing with her mind.

Two could play head games, though, and she had world-class credentials in that very department.

He stood with his back to her, his toes protruding over the stone cornice. As she walked toward him, she sensed his body stiffen. At the last instant she moved to his right and sat down, dangling her legs over the cliff. He snorted and shifted to stand behind her, his shins against her shoulder blades. Casually, she leaned back and said, "Thanks."

She felt his body tense, relax, then tense again. The bastard was debating with himself. He could muscle her over the cliff just by squatting and thrusting his knees forward. But perhaps that was too easy for him. And what he did not know was that if that push should come, she was going to whirl and grab him by his suitcase-handle lips and drag him to oblivion with her. She wondered. Would his group of men leave him dying out in the desert, immobilized by a broken back, as easily as he had done to their mates? Probably—

A cry came from the direction Jaffari had wandered off. From the sound of it, the head game between her and Bin Gahli was over. Sure enough, Bin Gahli walked away, letting her slump onto her back, legs still dangling. Wearily, she dragged herself to her feet, more discouraged than tired, and rejoined the group. Jaffari's happy jabbering told her the bad news, though she didn't get a word of it: He had found the Americans' trail once more. Exactly how that added up, she couldn't figure. Why would they board a helicopter only to land somewhere within walking distance?

Bin Gahli had his humor back. He explained all to her as they started off into the night, again following the excited weasel-faced, snot-nosed, slack-jawed, mouth-breathing, son-of-a-bitching Jaffari. There had been no helicopter apparently, just a phony track, the sand swept clean in an arc around the phantom craft. Bin Gahli wasn't too arrogant to admire the work that had been done.

"Dat Merry can Bedwin not be boosht," Bin Gahli marveled, pointing at the weasel and mocking him. "Summbeets dam fine Bedwin bedder dat Jaffari."

Nina imagined that there could be no greater insult to a Bedouin than to have an American held up to him as a better Bedouin. Jaffari, his face longer than a giraffe's, slunk away. Nina fell in behind the group, more than once falling to her hands and knees trying to keep up. The group had lost time figuring out the Americans' clever ruse but—

The Indian called Runner came to mind. She remembered him as stone-faced, strong, smart enough to know that being an intellectual didn't require him to say he was. All she knew about him was that Swayne admired him— no, worshipped him. If anybody in that group of four Marines could be capable of creating such an elaborate tracking deception, it would have been a Native American. *Night Runner?* Her heart skipped twice, her pulse hitting overdrive. Was Swayne really out here? Her spirit called to him: *Jack?*

For the first time since high school, when her idealism had turned first to ice, then evaporated like dry ice, she allowed herself to entertain notions of chivalry. Was it ordained that Swayne had been dropped into this place, not only to wipe out Abboud Dahni and the rest of his savage deviants, but to rescue her? Did knights in shining armor actually exist?

Bin Gahli hissed, and the group came to a halt, smoking and joking until their leader blew a stream of snot into the sand. Then they plunged their cigarettes into the ashtray that was Iraq and dispersed like roaches under the spotlight. After Bin Gahli cleared the second of his cavernous, pitted nostrils, Antenna Man unfolded his segments, assembled his pole, and raised it into the air. As best she could, given the Turkish crescent of a moon, she watched Bin Gahli's face as the radio and mike were handed to him. And clearly, as best he could, he avoided looking her way.

The creepy son of a bitch was up to no good.

NIGHT RUNNER WISHED that he could be a fly on the cliff wall so he could know how well his fake Night Hawk had worked, if at all.

He had whisked the team's tracks to the base of the cliff with a broom of knotted grass. The Tracker would not be fooled by the whisk marks. He would expect them.

Then, Runner had climbed the tricky wall once, worked his way down, then climbed again to make three sets of marks. Once on top he made three sets of prints in three sizes. The first by dragging his foot slightly—for the captain's longer print. The second he made wider by grinding as if putting out a butt—to mimic Friel's broader foot. Both sets of prints looked fake, but what was to come would correct that. After making his own boot tracks, he dug two divots, scattered the waste sand, and pressed the broad side of his canteen into the hollow several times. This formed the tire tracks of a Night Hawk's landing gear. Bending the handle of his canteen cup into a curve and pressing this into the fake tire tracks allowed him to create a passable tread. He used the narrow edge of the canteen for the tail wheel. Once again, he didn't worry that the tread marks looked bogus.

Finally he sat down, took off his boots, and wrapped his feet in elastic bandages from his first-aid kit. With his boots tied together and strung around his neck, Night Runner removed the sheet of stiff plastic from the internal support frame of his combat pack. In training, Force Recon Marines had been taught they could use it in more than a dozen ways. They could lash it to a limb as a splint for broken bones. And they could roll it into a casing for a pipe bomb.

Night Runner simply made a fan. For two hours, he swiped the one-foot-by-two-foot sheet at the ground around the imaginary helicopter LZ. Working from the center, he made a series of broad circles, creating drifts of dust, blowing some areas clean. He dusted away the prints of his bandaged feet and fanned enough on the tire tracks and boot prints to finish his fakery.

Then, still in bandaged feet, he made new steps along the cliff wall and descended using the game trail. First sweeping out his footsteps with his whisk broom, then erasing even the grass marks by fanning the ground gently, in the direction of the prevailing wind. Finally, carefully, he erased every trace of his travel between the cliff face and the camp where he had left Swayne and Friel. He had studied that trail all day long, looking for fault. He found none.

If the Tracker, good as he was, did suspect the fake LZ—and he would have to be ultra-good to do so at night—it would still take more than a cursory search to pick up the Spartans' trail. For they had reversed course, and he'd used his fan technique for a full kilometer.

Worst case for the Marines, the Tracker would have lost only an hour. At the rate they now marched, they would have gained more than three miles on the Iraqis. Best case, the Tracker would buy the bogus LZ and head for the barn. But Night Runner wouldn't allow himself to think that. A flaw always showed itself, in even the best of deceptions.

Besides, Bin Gahli might get a helicopter from his cousin. By day, he and his Tracker could fly low-level, searching from the air in circles as easily as drawing them on a map. And in no time, they would have picked up tonight's trail. The average pilot might not. The casual observer would not. But an experienced tracker would be able to see tracks invisible to those others. He might not be able to follow them from the air, but he could be put down to read sign as easily as a child following a picture-book story.

Almost as he toyed with the idea of a helicopter, Night Runner heard the slap of rotors and drone of turbines.

SWAYNE KNEW HIS aircraft sounds. This one was Russian-made, loud as a tractor. A Hind. It could hold a dozen combat-loaded soldiers and half a ton of supplies as well. As he crouched in place, he worried about the detection devices it might carry.

Swayne called his men to huddle in the dark.

"If the Iraqis have infrared, we're in trouble," he said. Rather than lighted images, the IR would detect their body heat. The pilots could see them bunched in the open glowing like fireflies.

"Run for it?" asked Friel.

Swayne vetoed that with a grunt. "Not unless we're spotted. If it happens spread out and take them on from three angles. Aim for the crew—the armor would be too much to defeat in the dark."

The helicopter's thunder grew louder.

"They're coming at us," said Night Runner.

Swayne knew that sounds could play tricks in the desert, especially at night. But it would be foolhardy either to dismiss Night Runner's senses or rely on hope alone that the helicopter crew would not spot them. They had to act. ASAP.

"Lie down," Swayne directed. "Cover your faces."

He scooped sand and threw it over his men as they cupped their mouths in their hands to make breathing space.

He worked like a badger. He knew he needn't bury the men, only scatter enough sand on them to break up recognizable thermal and visual patterns.

Over the horizon, the sky glowed brighter as the sound grew louder. So much for IR detection. The crew had turned on the Hind's landing lights to scan the desert with bare eyes.

Even at that, the sand did its camo job on his two men. The dry sand broke up the outlines of their forms. Even where only a light dusting covered the black-gray mottle of their uniforms, the color blended with the gray of the desert.

Problem was, who would throw dirt on *him*? With only seconds to hide himself, Swayne belly-flopped. Sweeping his hands toward his thighs, he scooped up sand and threw it over his legs.

The vibrations of the helicopter tickled the back of his neck. The shadows made by the searchlight began racing across the wadi toward them. The Hind wouldn't miss them by more than a few meters.

Swayne buried his face, threw two scoops of grit over his head, and plunged his arms below the desert surface like ostrich heads. He closed his hands on two fistfuls of sand, as if gripping the earth by its handles.

The light bathed them. And it blinded him, even with his face on the ground, literally eating dirt. Swayne swore that he lay in plain sight. The Iraqis would spot them like ducks on a pond. Not only that, the sand around would gum up the actions of the Marines' only two assault rifles. He worried too about the clouds of dust he had raised. The tracks they had left. The disturbances in the sand. A glint of skin from the back of a neck. The only thing they hadn't done wrong was stand up and wave their arms. They were all but dead.

The helicopter crew could not fail to spot them.

They were going to be found back-shot.

Like ordinary cowards.

Nothing left to do but die.

The helicopter closed, sending shudders through Swayne's body. Shudders of sound, shudders of disturbed air, shudders at the fear of dying a coward's death.

So close now. One of the crew would see them. The rotor wash would dust them off.

He braced himself for a push-up. Hell with being shot in the back. Better to roll over, pull his pistol, and start shooting. At least die fighting. Like a Marine.

The feel of sand sifting down his neck, dirt pouring up his nose, the off-the-wall notion of drowning by suffocation in the desert—these things hit him where he lived. His nerves, already strung out on the thinnest of threads, reached the breaking point.

Damn! So this was fear.

He had fought his way out of tight places before. But there'd always been a fight. Not this. Not this helpless, naked—

He cursed aloud. The throbbing of the helicopter drowned out his voice. He stiffened. How could the damn thing get any louder? Was it going to set down on them?

It took every ounce of self-discipline for Swayne to lie still. He heard a voice. It gripped his spine. He did not want to give credit, but he knew he could trace the source to his grandfather, Senator Jamison Swayne. The old man had never given him any advice worth taking, but he had left the imprint of his iron will and nasty disposition on Swayne.

You wanna serve your country in uniform, son? the raspy Southern drawl hollered into his inner ear above the roar and rush of the Hind. *Get youseff a job at the Postal Office, heah?*

To spite the man, Swayne kept his grip on the desert. Nothing had changed in the sound of the pitch or yaw of the helicopter's rotor. He held his breath. He held his position. He held his emotions in check.

The lights swept by, leaving them in darkness once more. A second later the rotor wash rolled over them like a sigh.

Swayne lifted his face enough to take a cautious breath and croak, "Hold what you got. In case he circles back for a second look. If he passes over again, be ready to start shooting."

Night Runner snorted dust from his nose.

Friel grunted, a high-pitched squeal like a wart hog. "I felt butt-naked there," Friel said. "Sorry, Captain, I almost lost it. Almost jumped up screaming and shooting." He sobbed once and choked back tears that Swayne could not see but could sense in the electric atmosphere around the kid from Boston. "Only thing kept me in my skin? I remembered something the gunny used to say: 'Let barking dogs sleep,' he'd say. It made me laugh for a sec—" He buried his face in the crook of one arm.

"I'm sorry, sir," Friel gasped.

"Forget it, Henry," Swayne said, glad for the dark that hid Friel's shame. "I about lost it too. But we didn't, did we?"

Swayne felt Friel staring at him. Once again he was glad for the night. "Let's get going," he said to ease out of the moment.

They dusted themselves off and cleared their weapons of sand until the action worked on each. Night Runner brushed over their sand angels and led them on a new course.

Swayne took time to plot the course of the helicopter and extend it across his screen in the form of a new line on his already crisscrossed GPS display. One end of the line told him that the bird was on the way to the camp they had left. The other end pointed at Salman Pak. So. Bin Gahli had called for helicopter backup. That could be good. It might mean that the band had bought into Night Runner's fake helicopter extraction, had given up tracking them in favor of—

The GPS screen flickered. So did his heart. The GPS was too important to be left without. He uploaded the image on his screen to OMCC and asked Zavello by radio if the operations center analysts could ID where the Hind landed.

Zavello didn't balk in the least. Swayne couldn't help smiling at that, feeling the cracked mud around his mouth fall away. With every mission, Zavello was becoming a better boss.

Should the craft retrace its path, it might mean Nina was out of the desert. If she had been taken to Salman Pak, and since he was going there anyhow—

Forget it, he told himself. He wasn't about to try something reckless, ruinous, foolish, or fantastic. He sure as hell wasn't going to risk his team to rescue a civilian, for God's sake. Especially one so stupid as to put her trust in a demon like Bin Gahli. No, Swayne told himself, he was just curious about where she would be. That's all.

Curiosity. That's all it was, he assured himself.

Other than that she didn't amount to a hill of marbles to him, he told himself. Not a hill of marbles.

Half an hour later, after they had moved laterally more than a kilometer from the helicopter's flight path, they heard the rumble again. Better prepared this time, they pressed themselves against the base of a rimrock to hide. But the helicopter, flying on the reverse course, missed them by a mile. Literally.

Three hours later, they stopped to drink from their canteens and eat the last of their ration bars. By then Zavello had reported that the Hind had flown into Salman Pak for a rooftop drop of half a dozen souls. In less than a minute it had taken off for Baghdad without taking on anybody else.

The UNSCOM team might well be inside Salman Pak,

Zavello said. The CIA guessed that because Bin Gahli would've gone straight to Baghdad otherwise.

Swayne had to laugh. In past years Saddam had denied UNSCOM inspectors access to the compound eleven times. Now he might be holding them there against their will.

Swayne told Zavello that they had spotted Nina Chase with the terrorists. He waited for an eruption. None came.

Zavello told him that CNN had been broadcasting since late in yesterday's nonstop news cycle that a team of three had disappeared into the desert east of Baghdad. Showing lots of pictures of a rental car abandoned at a roadside. He mentioned with some glee that the network had hired some erstwhile Bedouins, obviously a band of Iraqi street muggers, who had made several cursory forays into the desert. "Did no better'n piss in the bushes," Zavello said.

The loss of a few reporters, including one Nina Chase, who hadn't been friendly to the Marine Corps in the past, bothered Zavello not at all. If she had been posted to her reward in journalism heaven ("And what a shit-for-brains oxymoron that is," he growled), so much the better. He had seen how CNN reporters could be taken in during Desert Storm, transmitting Saddam Hussein's propaganda and Stormin' Norman's bullshit with equanimity. He signed off without giving a second's serious thought to Nina Chase.

Leaving the subject of serious second thoughts and Nina Chase entirely to Swayne.

THE HELICOPTER HAD bounced and rumbled to a stop on the tarmac-like surface on the roof. Nina dismounted the flying death trap, ecstatic to find her feet on a regular solid surface. For the first time in days she felt as if she could take a step without being held back by sand sucking at her ankles.

But her joy was short-lived. A squad of Iraqi regulars all but ignored the terrorists and went for her. Four of them fought for a grip on her upper arms, dragged her into a stairwell next to the landing pad, and led her into the warehouse, copping feels as they went.

Dozens of light stands lit up the building's interior. A temporary city had been built in the middle of the warehouse, rows of bunks and portable toilets surrounded by a double fence line, topped with razor wire. In the inner compound stood a group of men, their fingers laced in the wire like refugees. Except that they seemed well enough cared for, clean-shaven, and sleek for the most part, they looked like prisoners of war in the films from Nazi Germany or its modern counterpart, Bosnia.

What's more, she knew one, possibly two of the men.

"I'll be damned," she said. "I suppose you UNSCOM guys didn't save a cot for me."

Although they were from a number of countries, they understood enough of her declaration to nod and smile cautiously, their eyes darting left and right to look at the guard posts at each corner of their compound, on elevated platforms surrounded by sandbags.

She heard enough English in the group to know that more than one man was offering to share his bed with her.

Still, she couldn't wait to be thrown in with them. Her escort guided her through gates in the wire and pushed her inside. She looked around for Bin Gahli.

Through the open door of the warehouse, she could see the terrorist and his ragtag band bolting down some of their solidified-bird-shit cheese and some kind of drink in foil packets. Bin Gahli still wore his shawl with the boot and foot wrapped in it. From the look of it, the guy wasn't going to let it out of his sight.

She didn't care. As long as he kept out of her sight. Nothing could make her happier than to be locked inside this enclosure. Just as long as Bin Gahli and his weasel stayed locked out.

SWAYNE'S GPS DIED the next time he tried to use it. When he opened its cover to examine his digital topo map, he realized that half a screen's worth had disappeared, and the rest faded fast. He didn't doubt that all the wear and tear had opened a crack in its casing, allowing sand to invade and short-circuit the device.

Swayne looked to Friel, who had fixed weapons and sights often enough. "Any idea how to fix one of these?"

Friel's swollen face twitched. "Did you shake it? Tap it? Wrap it with duct tape?"

"Henry?"

"It's out of my pay grade, Cap'n. If it can't be fixed with duct tape, it can't be fixed."

Night Runner's GPS took the data they needed for primary and alternate helicopter extraction LZs, which they would need whether Event 15 was canceled or not. Night Runner, who never trusted gadgets as much as maps, copied the information to paper. Then he outlined an evasion plan.

For the rest of the night, Night Runner directed the captain on a variety of headings. The team of Friel and Swayne would move forward perhaps a quarter mile. Lagging behind them, Night Runner used a combination of techniques including brushing, laying down false trails, wearing his Ace bandages across hard ground, and using the airbrush technique that he had invented to blow sand over their tracks. If the three of them could not be made to vanish altogether, then he might be able to create so many misleading hints of their presence that the Tracker's instincts might be worn down the way a bloodhound's nose could be overworked, leading to a fatigued sense of smell.

DAY 3—0319 HOURS LOCAL

TWO HOURS BEFORE dawn, he told Swayne and Friel to memorize the spot they stood on. "This is the LZ." When Friel moaned in the tone of a question, he said, "By walking right over it, we might well lead them not to consider it an LZ."

Just an hour before daylight, when the faintest of light could not be seen except by men who had spent that night in the utter darkness that only a desert can bestow, Night Runner realized the effort of hiding tracks might well have been a waste of his time. But a pleasant waste.

He flashed a smile at Swayne.

"Do you feel it?" he asked.

Friel shrugged. "What? You got a blowtorch on your face too?"

"The humidity?" Swayne offered.

"And warmth." Night Runner pointed a finger at the heavens. "Just look at the stars."

"What stars?" Friel said. "Ain't no damn stars. I seen more stars in the St. Paddy's parade than this."

"Exactly."

Swayne said, "Clouds. We're going to have a change in weather?"

"A severe change."

"Wind?" Swayne said. "That's not clouds up there, but dust aloft?"

"Affirm. The humidity is a sign of instability."

"Like we ain't been maxed out on freaking instability already," Friel said. "When?"

"I can't say for sure," Night Runner said. "Maybe midday. If we're lucky, sooner."

"Lucky." Friel moaned. "We get any luckier, Saddam Insane will be turning our skins into throw rugs." Friel sputtered a string of curse words. "Except for me. My hide's too beat up." He ended with: "I'm almost out of water."

"Stretch it as long as you can," Night Runner said. "Let's move so we can get some distance out of what's left of the night."

Half an hour later, Runner directed his tired mates to a sharply cut gully along the bank of a wadi. By the lay of the land, the gully would be open to the first warm rays of the sun. But as it rose and swept across the sky, it would offer them shade and conceal them for most of the day. The gully would protect them from the wind, when it came.

Night Runner left Swayne and Friel in the gully, telling them not to move dirt or overturn any stones that could be seen from the air. He then went back into the desert, carrying his boots, occasionally putting down the trace of a footprint by putting his hands inside the boot and pushing into the sand. Then he swept away all traces of every track he could. Wearing his Ace bandages on his feet, he returned by a roundabout route, fanning all his steps away with his sheet of plastic. Before the first long rays of sunlight had begun slashing across the landscape, he had fallen into an exhausted sleep, ordered by Swayne to rest as he and Friel split up the first watches of the day.

• • •

HIS NAP LASTED less than three hours. He sat upright, bouncing his head off the overhang of the gully wall. He squished the word out of his mouth as if trying to talk through a peanut butter sandwich.

"Helicopter?"

Swayne nodded. "We heard it just a second ago."

Night Runner fought to get his senses back. He dry-washed his face in the palms of his hands and fluttered his fingers through his hair, creating a shower of grit. He cleaned the dirt out of his ears so he might hear better, and dug at his itchy eyes until he could keep them open without blinking. Finally he put on his boots and checked his weapon. The nightscope batteries had died. So he took the scope off his rifle and stowed it in his pack. Then he slithered along bank toward the mouth of the gully to listen.

Back inside the twenty-foot-long fissure twenty minutes later he found Swayne and Friel.

Night Runner took a deep breath. "Hind, same as last night," he said. "Possibly the same bird. For the first ten or fifteen minutes, it was flying at altitude, maybe five hundred feet. Looking for sign, I'd guess."

Swayne shook his head. "They could see tracks that high up?"

"After you hoovered up behind us?" Friel said.

The muscles knotted in Night Runner's temples. "A few men could. One good man could. And that tracker is good. Probably lived in the desert all his life."

Swayne asked, "Then what?"

Night Runner spoke the words he didn't want to utter. "Started hovering. Maybe five miles off. They're on the deck now, following one or the other of the tracks we laid down."

Friel sagged. His chin dropped to his chest.

Swayne wiped off his 9-millimeter pistol, worked the action, and shook out sand that it had picked up since the last time he'd checked it ten minutes ago. "How long do we have?"

Night Runner scratched at his chin, plowing furrows into

the pancake makeup of the desert that had built up on his skin. "One hour, maybe two."

"So when do we get that lucky sandstorm to cover our butts?"

Night Runner couldn't answer Friel's question. He and Swayne worked out a battle plan. They agreed to put one of the assault rifles at the upper end of the gully. The other should look out onto the wadi. They would stay in the shadows and not start a fight unless the Iraqis found them.

Night Runner and Friel thumbed their meager supply of rounds from their magazines, dusted them off, and reloaded. Swayne moved into the opening at the lower end of the gully to make a report to Zavello.

After that, there was nothing left to do but wait. The team dispersed, each to his own thoughts, each feeling the occasional breeze kicking up the sand, each hoping high winds would spring up to ground the helicopter. Each had his hopes dashed when the wind died down, dropping another load of grit into their hiding place, and burying those hopes under another layer of sand.

LESS THAN AN hour later, the helicopter changed tactics again. Rather than hover over one trail or the other, it began casting back and forth along the vector that Night Runner had calculated. The vector that he had laid down to lead the Iraqis away from them. He let a smile toy with the corners of his mouth. His fakes and false starts had confused the Tracker. He had been reduced to an air search to find new sign.

Or else the forecast of wind had put a sense of urgency into the search—

Even as he thought about the blow that might hide them, new showers of dirt began falling off the gully walls onto the Spartans. First Night Runner thought a fickle wind had sprung up, perhaps at altitude. But no. An avalanche of clods tumbled off the wall. No wind could cause that.

"What the hell?" Friel called from his end of the gully. "Another plague? Am I a freakin' pharaoh or something?"

Night Runner locked eyes with the captain.

"Tanks," Swayne said.

"A ground search," said Night Runner. "They don't know where we are, but they think they can find us with an area sweep."

Zavello's tired voice broke in to confirm that armor had begun moving, crossing the desert on a mile-wide front. He advised Swayne to turn on their last GPS to receive a download. When he had done so, Swayne saw on Night Runner's screen that the west flank of the Iraqi column would roll over their hiding place in the gully.

SWAYNE DIDN'T BELIEVE in luck. He'd always made his breaks. And he had always prided himself on reading a situation to get the most out of it. He always came up with a plan to counter enemy moves. Now he felt as if the umpires had begun to hammer on him in one of those computer-generated tactical exercises. No matter how well teams did, umpires threw one impossible situation at them after another. The idea was to force them to think on the run and solve problems under fire. Such war games drove them to the brink of exhaustion and beyond. But it taught the Marines to fight and think at their limits of endurance.

Swayne knew how artificial such exercises were. Too many tricks and countermoves undid reality—only a computer with a spy feeding input to it could counter every move the team leader made. That many head games couldn't possibly be accumulated into an actual field experience.

Until now. It was as if the OMCC had enlisted Iraqis to screw with the Spartans in the desert. Just to—

Swayne shook his head. That he could even think such things worried him. The fatigue could do that to a man. A man had to resist it. Had to keep the reins in hand.

The earth vibrated. The tremors invaded their bodies at every contact point with the ground. When they spoke to each other, their voices trembled as if with fear. If they didn't focus, their eyes would fall into sympathetic resonance with the feeling and begin to fuzz over. Their lips tingled. Their hearing grew tinny.

Swayne debated whether to fight or flee. And whether the team would even have the initiative to choose.

He opened the chamber of his pistol a crack. For the tenth time, to be sure he had sent a round home. This time, he even pulled it back far enough to see the copper-coated slug sitting in its collar of brass. He was leaving nothing to chance. No fleeing. No bullets to the back.

They were going to fight. No way around it. Take out a few Iraqis—cheese-eaters, Friel called them. Finish the event right here and now.

FRIEL RAN THE numbers. Twenty-six bullets. Twenty-six dead Iraqis would make the world a tiny bit safer for cheese.

He had spent a lot of time in churches, growing up Irish and Catholic in Boston. A lot of kneel-time accumulated. His speed-rosaries laid end to end would circle the globe. More mouthing of the words than actual praying, though. Friel wasn't much of a pray-er, and had spent most of his kneel-time daydreaming. But if there ever was a time for praying, he expected it to be soon. He wondered about the gunny. Before that helicopter exploded in flames. Before the concussion grenades tore him apart. Before the fire had seared shut his lungs.

Did he have a moment to pray for his redemption? Friel hoped—

A rotating metal structure came into Friel's view, a rotor head that carried an almost invisible disc. A helicopter. Flying right at them. Coming out of nowhere, its sound lost in all the rumble and tremble of the earth, the blur of his vibrating eyes, the buzz in his ears.

He lay in the shade at the shallow part of the gully where it opened up onto the plateau above. Nobody should be able to see him from the air, especially nobody traveling at thirty to forty knots.

So.

He eased his rifle into position. The massive bird loomed over him, and he lowered his face to hide it behind the camouflage of his soft cap. But before his eyes went beneath the bill, he found himself looking directly into the astonished face of one of the pilots.

Friel decided. Prayer time. Not for himself, but for the Iraqi son of a bitch whose eyes now looked like a pair of bull's-eyes.

He yelled, "We've been spotted—" Hell. Might as well be honest about it. "—*I've* been spotted."

Not that it mattered. Wasn't nobody going to hear his ass anyhow. Not with all the racket. He'd sneaked onto the stage of rock concerts that weren't this noisy. Everything, even his thoughts, got lost in the roar of the helicopter blades and turbine exhaust passing over. Friel rolled into the open, sat up, and pointed his rifle up the ass of the helicopter's right engine.

NIGHT RUNNER FELT the loss of his senses more than anything—the worst loss possible.

He never heard Friel report the spotting. He knew well enough what had happened by the abrupt shift of attitude of the Hind, its nose banking up and right. The pilot had yanked it around to bring its guns to bear. He raised his rifle. He waited. He saw the pilot sitting on the right in the Soviet-vintage craft. He'd dropped the door glass on his side. His head swiveled about, trying to spot what he thought he'd seen. In panic. Night Runner liked that he could see the eyes, wide-open, darting about, desperate to shoot first. A man that scared could not aim straight, could not see straight, could not think straight. Advantage, Spartans.

He heard the crack of Friel's M-16. The helicopter flinched in the air as Night Runner laid the bead of his own rifle beneath the pilot's right ear.

The helicopter slewed right, barely in control, and Night Runner was aware of a grinding noise, a sudden popping, and a shower of sparks. The helicopter flinched again, but he did not. He kept the front post of his sights on the helmet where that ear would be. He squeezed off a burst of six. The impact whipped the head of that pilot across the cockpit, clearing his line of sights. Runner picked out a second helmet and fired a second burst as the Hind spun away.

The helicopter hit, slumping to its side on the ground, rolling over, the blades pounding the earth, the second turbine disintegrating, setting the craft on fire. Finally the helicopter had sheared its rotors on the deck of the wadi. A black stain oozed into the ground. Fuel. Any moment, Night Runner realized, the aircraft would ignite.

Faintly he heard Swayne telling the team to bail.

But Night Runner had to know. It didn't matter to him that the helicopter would catch fire. He didn't care that everybody in or near the bird would burn with it.

He had to know.

So he ran out of the gully, hearing Swayne shout. He formed his answer for later. *Sorry, Captain, I didn't hear you over all that racket*.

He dashed across the wadi and scaled the landing gear like a ladder. The Hind lay on its side. It whined like a child. Night Runner guessed that the power had not yet died to some of its electric motors. But they would die, like everything else in this bird. He climbed until he could look over the cargo deck into the cabin.

Four men lay in a tangle behind the cockpit. The one in a flight suit was a crew chief. The others wore the garb of the Iraqis that had followed the team.

Night Runner saw one man move and winced, ready to jump clear of the Hind in case the man pulled a gun. But no, that wouldn't happen. The Iraqi had been eviscerated. The movement Night Runner had shied from was a fearful heart exposed to the air, beating its last, quick, jerky beats.

He didn't care about hearts or blood or guts. He cared about faces. He checked them all. Only one of the men saw him, his ragged, bearded look changing from surprise to hope to recognition to acceptance, ending in anger. A bloody hand patted down the man's body. Night Runner came up with a vintage hand grenade of the pineapple variety from World War II. *Those Iraqis,* Night Runner thought as he jumped to the ground. Saddam could spending billions for weapons of mass destruction, while scrounging obsolete weapons from antiquity.

Night Runner hit the ground at a full run. He flew across the wadi, and dove into the safety of the gully as the helicopter blew, sending a column of black smoke and orange fireball into the sky.

"What the hell got into you, Sergeant?"

Night Runner blinked rapid-fire. The captain usually gave such looks of disgust to Friel. Or to staff weenies. Never to him.

Night Runner brought the lie to his lips. But he couldn't speak it to Swayne. He respected him too much. "Sorry, sir. I had to know."

"Is he there? The tracker?"

A tiny shake of the head.

Swayne cursed under his breath.

Friel danced around as if he had to pee. "No disrespect, but we don't need George C. Scott in those tanks, Cap'n. If the ragheads didn't know where we were before, they are going to be homing on that crash like white on rice."

Each of the three exchanged glances with each other, each thinking of the same thing: That was a Potts-ism, *white on rice,* and they thought of him now.

But only for a second. Night Runner took off to the north out of the gully. He went wide and fast in the hope they would outflank the Iraqi tank column. If the Guards homed on the crash site, it might miss the team.

But. He really didn't care about the damned tank brigade. What he wanted to know was, *Where is that damned Tracker?*

THE HELICOPTER EXPLODED as Bin Gahli put fire to the first of his second pack of cigarettes in the day's unbroken chain of smokes, as if trying to keep a perpetual flame going between his liver lips.

And difficult it was too, because of windy gusts building. A life on the sand told him what he didn't want to know: The most virulent of desert winds was on the way, the Death Wind, his namesake.

He saw the fireball of the Hind, its pillar of smoke, black and oily, rising perhaps two hundred feet into the air. A mixed blessing. The crash meant he'd found the Americans. But so had the Republican Guards, cruising the desert in their traveling pillboxes. The dense column of smoke flattened into a thin streak carried across the sky by the winds aloft. The dissipation of the smoke indicated high winds moving down from the heavens. He struck out toward the smoke signal, determined to find the Americans before either the regulars or the Death Wind caught them.

Bin Gahli had to laugh. Jaffari had fumed and fussed all morning as they flew about in the Hind earlier. The Bedouin demanded that the pilot set him down so he could pick up track of the Americans on the ground. For two hours they circled, looking for sign. Finding nothing. Bin Gahli told himself that the Americans had vanished in a helicopter last night after all. Jaffari had been wrong.

Until the ferret spotted and pointed out a dubious sign. A stone, overturned, its underside showing a different color than the surrounding landscape. Jaffari ordered the pilot to land, just to humor his tracker. Once on the ground, the Bedouin held up the stone in triumph, finding its original spot in the earth, placing it into position, arguing that only a man could have kicked it out of place.

Bin Gahli wasn't so sure. It could've been a badger looking for insects. Or the fennec, the tawny native fox with the big eyes and ears. Or one of the rare pygmy antelopes that inhabited the area. But Jaffari insisted, so Bin Gahli sent off the helicopter with three of his men, keeping two others besides Jaffari and himself to wander the wasteland. Wastefully, as it happened.

Jaffari would pick up a track, follow it for perhaps a

quarter mile, pointing out signs he thought should be obvious to anybody, signs that made no impression on Bin Gahli.

At first Bin Gahli had been impressed that Jaffari could make progress across the landscape. Eventually Bin Gahli could identify marks on his own, marks that truly could have been the scuffs and scrapes of humans that Jaffari said they were. But the trail too often disappeared, and Jaffari too frequently told him to stay put as he made one of his large circles looking for some tiny sign in a random smattering of signs.

And once, when they crossed their own trail, Bin Gahli laughed aloud. The shame showed in Jaffari's face. Nobody had ever beaten him at the games of the desert. He'd met his match, and either he or the American would have to die before long. Bin Gahli doubted that even he could stop Jaffari from killing the man once they found him. If they found him.

Standing out in the sun did not please Bin Gahli. Jaffari, no matter how determined he was to track down his man, had become ever more frustrated, sweating, cursing, even praying to the heavens for help.

Bin Gahli, for the first time since he had known him, began to doubt Jaffari's value. Maybe he wasn't so precious as he liked to brag. Bin Gahli raised the question aloud, to vex his man. And vex him he did. Jaffari flew into a rage and could not be made to track for a full half-hour.

But once that Hind crashed, Bin Gahli didn't need a tracker. Just the smacking of his lips put his other men on alert. The three of them set off on a direct line toward the smoke signal. Jaffari had nothing to do but follow. He wasn't used to that. He fumed, growing redder by the minute.

Bin Gahli hardly gave Jaffari's pride a second thought. He had bigger goats to roast. Those Americans. The Republican Guard brigade. And the greatest of all, the wind now tugging at his robes and wraps.

•   •   •

FRIEL, HIS EYES tearing, met Swayne's gaze and shook his head in despair. The very surface of the earth seemed to be peeling away, lifting and swirling, flying up in layers, and every cubic inch of it pelted Friel's tender face. The front halves of their monochrome cammies had been coated dust-gray as they walked into the wind. Their faces might well have been spray-painted with primer. The only color visible outside the spectrum of black and white was the red rimming their eyes and the various colors of their irises.

Friel didn't say anything. His eyes said all that needed to be said. That they had been sent to hell without first having undergone the formality of dying.

Swayne wanted to stop, to take a few moments to dig in their combat packs for some things from their desert kits. Night Runner vetoed the idea. He wanted to run up the miles between the team and the crashed Hind.

Fine. But Swayne was grateful when Night Runner waved at him to huddle out of the wind and into a shallow depression.

And poor enough cover it was too. The wind ripped by, carrying sheets of sand barely a foot above their heads. The tiny airfoil created on the lee side of the hole tricked the wind into dropping its load. A constant stream of grit sifted over them. Swayne and Night Runner shut off their mikes.

"We're too close to the tanks," Night Runner said, cupping his hands to direct his words. "I was hoping the visibility would be worse than this, that it would hide our movement. But it's not enough. We can't afford to keep moving."

Friel shook his head. "The only place I ever seen worse than this litter box was that blizzard in Montana," he yelled.

Night Runner scowled at the insult, but dismissed it just as quickly. The stakes were too high for wasting time in defense of his home state.

Swayne couldn't look at Friel's face for long. Blisters that had ballooned tightly with water this morning had burst—perhaps had been opened by the sandblasting. The fluid sopped up dirt from the air and streaked Friel's hand-some face with mud. Swayne could only guess how bad the kid felt. He admired him. For all Friel's bitching about nothing on other missions, he was enduring true agony like one helluva Marine. Potts would have been proud of him.

One at a time each man turned on his side so another one of them could dig into the light packs they carried for what was to have been a one-to-two-day mission. They took out face coverings that looked like ski masks, except of lighter fabric. At night they hid skin shine. Today they would protect their faces from the pelting sand. Over these, they placed goggles, tinted and vented to let in the air but not dirt particles. Over their mouths and under their masks each man adjusted a dome of porous brown paper that would filter the air. Before Friel had joined the team, Night Runner, Potts, and Swayne had been on windy desert missions. In the debriefs, they'd asked for these items in their hot-climate packs.

The main concern now was for their weapons. The sand would jam the action of any gun. Most of that usually could be dusted away in the field. But in this wind?

While Night Runner and Friel tried using their camel-hair brushes to dust down all moving parts—a battle impossible to win, considering the continual spray of sand dropping out of the sky—Swayne climbed forward on his belly to look over the edge of the depression.

When he recoiled, falling back into the hole, Night Runner looked at him knowingly, Friel in alarm.

"What?" asked Friel in a tone that said he didn't want to know.

Swayne raised all the fingers on one hand to them. "Tanks," he said. "On the move."

Five tanks. Friel shook his head. He kept his tongue, but Swayne could read his thoughts in the eyes downcast inside the lenses of his goggles: another plague.

Night Runner checked around the hole for a way out. "Nothing looks good," he said. "We'd have to expose ourselves. Behind us the nearest cover is almost a hundred meters away. Ahead?" He shook his head.

Friel asked, "Any chance they'd drive by without—?"

Swayne held up a hand.

"They stopped," Night Runner said, shielding his face from the swirling wind. "It would be pointless to keep driving around when they couldn't see. Better look again."

Swayne crawled up the short slope. When he backed down, he said, "Looks like the tanks pulled in close together to sit out the storm. I thought I heard—"

And now they all could hear it—the sound of smaller track vehicles moving around.

"Mech infantry," said Friel. "What's next? Frogs? Or snakes?"

Swayne said, "They'll be setting up ground security for the tanks."

Night Runner raised an eyebrow.

"Or else they'll search the area on foot for us," Swayne added. His mind went to work on every new wrinkle that he could think of. Had the unit stopped to orient itself? Was it just pinching into a tighter formation so individual vehicles would not be separated in the storm? Would they soon move out again? Could the team escape detection by holding tight? Would one of the tanks roll over them?

All his questions were rendered moot when a pair of armed Iraqi soldiers stood over the three Marines at the lip of their little dust bowl.

Swayne saw them first, each saluting his face against the wind with one hand, fumbling with the other at the front of his trousers.

He realized they had not seen him. *Of course, they had not seen him!* Would any two sane men dare piss on three Marines?

Night Runner and Friel, their heads turned away from the two Iraqis, stared through the lenses of their goggles into his eyes. For a second, Swayne was stymied. Their mikes were off—Friel's radio didn't work anyhow—and the dust filter prevented him from warning them by mouthing signals. He dared not move.

So he did the best he could, widening his eyes and flicking them to the right of his sockets. Night Runner mimed the sign to show he got it.

Friel flinched. So he had seen it too.

Swayne inched his hand toward his belly holster and the 9-mill. Slowly, slowly. As he did so, Night Runner and Friel leaned toward him.

"What are they doing?" Night Runner asked.

Swayne wasn't about to say what the Iraqis were doing. He doubted that Friel would sit still so an Iraqi could hose him down. All his focus now lay in getting his hand to his pistol. He knew three reasons why the Iraqis could not see them. First was their incidental camouflage. The Spartans were so well dusted that their forms melded with the desert. Second was the wind that made the Iraqis squint. Third was a human tendency not to see things that you were not looking for. And who would be looking for the possibility of certain death staring them in the face as they tended to urgent body needs?

At last his hand closed on the pistol. His thumb flicked off the safety. His mind reassured him that, yes, he had locked and loaded back in the gully. He called up a mental picture of copper and brass as proof. His thumb pulled back the hammer. In the next few seconds, one of the Iraqis would be dead. Whether the pistol's action would function properly and chamber a second round was open to question. If he couldn't get off that second shot, he would throw the pistol at the second startled Iraqi and cause him to duck.

As he pulled the pistol clear of its holster, he decided to shoot the one standing closest to Friel. That would leave the other to Night Runner, a hand-to-hand fighter second to none. He would choose Friel in a shooting situation. But when it came to knives and manual combat, nobody but Night Runner and Potts—

Swayne put the gunny out of his head, but not the anger at his death—caused by Iraqis like these. He raised the gun and fired, finishing the job the Iraqi had begun, emptying his bladder for him with a bullet hole. The man doubled over, not knowing what had hit him, knowing only that it hurt.

By then Swayne had shifted his aim and pulled the trigger again. *And yes!* The gun fired.

The first shot set his two men into action. Both sprang up, grabbing the Iraqis by their coats. They hauled them into the pit like sand lions after ants.

Swayne dove across the mass of men and peeked over the edge of the depression to see if any other soldiers had seen what had gone on. Nobody had. He was gratified to see that the wind had picked up, reducing visibility almost to nothing.

By the time he had ducked back into the hole, the Iraqis had been silenced, both by Night Runner's razor-sharp bayonet. Friel patted them down. He came up with two flasks of water and two tins of processed food.

Swayne gave a thumbs-up. Both men turned their goggles toward him. Friel scowled at him.

"What is it, Henry?"

"All due respect, sir. No Marine officer should ever let the enemy come that close to pissing on his men."

Swayne let it pass. Instead he responded to the question Night Runner asked with his eyes. He twirled a forefinger in the air and pointed across his chest by way of signaling that they had overstayed.

Night Runner held up one finger. He fished in his jacket and produced his GPS to get a bearing. He shook it, laid it gently against the palm of one hand, then rapped it on his knee. Then he shook his head, folded it up, and tucked it back into his jacket.

Friel's head wilted. Swayne swallowed hard. Losing their last GPS would blindfold most people. Sure, Night Runner was not most people. Still. How could anybody navigate if they could not see?

Not that it mattered. Navigation wasn't nearly as much a problem as that Iraqi mechanized unit, parked less than a hundred meters away.

Swayne turned on his mike. "Recommendations?"

"Moving laterally is a bad idea," said Runner into his own radio. "Too much exposure for too long. Moving away is the obvious thing, too obvious. They're looking for us out in front of them."

"So what?"

Night Runner pointed to the two dead Iraqi soldiers. "What if we put on these two helmets and threw on their jackets," he said. "What if we walked right through their formation while they're buttoned up?"

Friel, who could see the conversation going on between Night Runner and Swayne but could not hear it, leaned into the space between them and tapped on his ear. As Night Runner pulled back his dust mask and explained the situation, Swayne thought it over. The part he liked best had to do with getting behind the Iraqis. Like most regulars, all their attention would be to the front. They would feel safe that the Marines could not move about freely on ground they had just covered. The part he liked least also had to do with getting behind the Iraqis. Moving through those lines, even in this storm, was risky business.

Friel's body quaked. Swayne saw that he was chuckling as Runner spoke into his ear. He was relieved to see the first sign of a sense of humor returning to the Irishman since the chain of disasters had struck them. Friel liked the plan. Swayne could almost hear him crowing, *I like it. It's a game plan with balls*.

Swayne liked it because, even if they got caught behind the lines, the enemy *might* hesitate about shooting to the rear. Balls aside, this was a no-brainer. "Let's do it," he said, loud enough for Friel to hear.

Night Runner and Friel removed the coats from the two dead men and draped them over their shoulders like shawls, hiding their distinctive rifles. Swayne and Friel would wear Iraqi helmets. The disguise would not have to be total, just believable enough in the haze.

At the last moment, Friel peeled back his dust mask and spoke up, "Don't you think we ought to lose the goggles and masks?" he asked.

Night Runner nodded, dismayed at the near blunder.
"Good catch," said Swayne.

They pulled off the masks and goggles and made ready.
Swayne tried not to cringe when he saw the mask stick to
Friel's face, pulling off clumps of mud, taking patches of
skin. Friel's eyes went watery with the pain, but he kept
his mouth shut. What a kid.

Kid, hell. What a Marine!

Walking as boldly as if they had good sense, the three
of them stood up and marched out of the bowl on line.

They reached the tanks without incident. About what
Swayne figured. If Iraqi tank soldiers were anything like
U.S. tankers, they wouldn't even step down to the ground
to use the head—they'd just pee over the side.

Only as they passed between the tank fenders did
Swayne allow himself to breathe. At least for the moment,
the Iraqis couldn't fire on them with tank cannon. They
were too close even to swing the guns.

The air behind the tanks had been fouled by the hot
exhaust of diesel fumes. Swayne glanced left and right, and
saw that the infantry had parked in a rough semicircle on
the right flank of the tanks. Iraqis gathered on the dropped
ramps of their vehicles in squads. Getting their stuff together for a search. Noncoms and officers telling them how
many passes and medals they'd get if they came up with
the trophy of a team of Marines. Dead or alive.

Swayne's knees went brittle, but he kept walking, knowing that within seconds, drifts of blowing sand would hide
them. He hardly dared breathe. Less than a hundred meters
behind the tanks, he dared to look over his shoulder and
saw the most pleasant sight of the day—nothing.

Night Runner and Friel shucked their jackets. They put
on their masks and goggles again, and Night Runner led
them deeper into the dust clouds. They were going to pull
it off.

The roaring of the wind made Swayne want to shout to
release the tension in his chest. But, of course, he could

not. He kept his mouth shut, but granted himself a cry of jubilation in his throat.

His joy was short-lived. A voice shouted at them from behind the wall of dust to their left. An Iraqi voice. An *angry* Iraqi voice.

None of them spoke the language, but any man or woman who had ever served in uniform would know it by the tone: *What the hell are you three bozos doing out there? Get your malingering asses over here and get to work. Now.*

Swayne first thought to ignore the man and keep walking. What were the chances of somebody shooting blindly into the desert at three figures behind their own tank lines? Probably pretty good. So he waved and kept walking. But as he turned his back, he saw that beside the single figure, a platoon-sized bunch had materialized out of the storm. They all packed rifles. All of them were intent, many of them yakking back and forth at each other as they pointed. He guessed what they were saying: *You don't think that could be the Americans, do you? Nah, it couldn't be. Could it?*

Between gusts of dust behind the group, Swayne could make out the outlines of four, no, five heavy trucks. The battalion of infantry that Zavello had warned them about.

Swayne waved again at the group. He inclined his head toward Friel and Night Runner, and the three of them began waving over their shoulders. As they kept sidling away. As they felt the grip of fear.

"Get ready, boys," Swayne shouted over the din of the wind. "On my command. You shoot. I'll put out two boomers. You run like hell. I'll be right behind."

The figure who had done all the shouting now raised an arm and gave Swayne the hook, repeating himself in ever harsher tones.

Swayne saw Friel's and Runner's automatic weapons come to bear on the Iraqis. The formation took a unified step backward, as if responding to a command on the parade field. They looked to their weapons. Any second now, and all doubt would be removed.

"Take them," Swayne cried, unwilling to waste even half a second.

Before his voice had died in his throat, the guns beside him barked. Night Runner fired on automatic, Friel on semiauto. His ego demanded precise killing efficiency, taking out one man with each bullet.

Swayne's space-age hand grenades were hinged half-spheres that could be carried with their flat sides against his body. When deployed, the halves were clapped together and held by magnets for throwing. The fragmentation was not nearly as lethal as the concussion. By default, each was set to 3.5 seconds for detonation, and could be slung using a bayonet to gain some additional yardage. There was no time for any of that now. In fact, Swayne felt so pressed for time that he put his thumb to the slide lever on each of the grenades, setting them to the minimum detonation time of 2.8 seconds—just long enough for the average man to throw them out of suicide range. If he had a good arm. With that, he armed the boomers and tossed them.

Before the Iraqis had even lifted their rifles, Friel and Runner had taken out a dozen in their cluster. The remainder saw the two spheres hurled their way and dropped to the ground.

"Fire in the hole!" Swayne hollered.

Friel and Night Runner knew what to do.

All three Marines hurled themselves flat. They dropped their weapons, stuck fingers into their ears, and turned their faces away. They had no time for more than that.

The two explosions turned a simple firefight into a full-sized battle. No return fire came from the initial group, because Swayne's grenades had gone off, one in front of them and one behind, stunning them all, probably killing most of them by slamming the soft brain matter like Jell-O against the insides of their skulls.

The Marines knew they had no time to lie around whining about the stinging they had just been given by their own weaponry. Swayne turned to Night Runner, who handed him one more grenade. A glance told them that it had been set to six seconds, and Swayne had to laugh. Night Runner wanted nothing more to do with close-range boomers.

Swayne threw the other grenade. It fell short and rolled under the cab of a truck. As Iraqi soldiers piled out of their vehicles, falling over each other, weapons went off in all directions, many of them pointed up into the sky. The Iraqis who had not seen them must have thought they had been hit with an aerial attack.

And one careless tanker had swiveled the turret of his tank and opened fire with a 120-millimeter projectile. Either he didn't know that the truck convoy had moved up behind. Or he did not care. Either way his round struck the column about halfway back, buckling a troop truck like a broken pencil, spilling men in every direction, burning men, screaming men. The confused soldiers, who had been inside when the first engagement took place, turned their weapons and took on the only enemy they could identify, their own tanks. Just as Swayne's boomer went off, adding the color of more noise and shrapnel to the raging battle. The three Marines took off running.

They might have escaped unscathed. If a second convoy had not come out of the dust clouds, the drivers trained to turn a left and a right alternately off the track, stopping to deploy their fighting men from the herringbone pattern. The attention of most of those fighters was directed forward where all the noise, including screaming, rifle fire, and tank fire, had begun. But not all of them.

Somebody hollered in Arabic at the three Spartans, running for all they were worth away from the action. Swayne, Night Runner, and Friel turned all at once, each kneeling and bringing his weapon up, each opening fire at the same time, bringing down seven Iraqis who pointed rifles at them.

But the shooting drew attention to them too. Much unwelcome attention.

Friel tossed a grenade to Swayne. "Last one!" he hollered.

Swayne's heart leaped when the grenade hit his hands, and he checked the digital timer out of habit. "Henry, *it's armed!*"

"No, I don't think—well, maybe—"

It was. The unreadable hundredths digits in the window counted down toward two seconds.

Swayne flipped the grenade toward the Iraqis, keeping it close to the ground. "Hit the dirt!" he called out. Unnecessarily. For both Friel and Night Runner had already done so. Swayne dived over the sergeant, aware of bullets striking the ground all around them. He cursed that he could not find cover in this godforsaken land. Before he hit the ground, their last concussion grenade went off so close to them that it lifted him, deafened him, and blew the goggles off his head. Swayne rolled with the momentum of the blast.

As he bounced along, an illogical smile pulled at his face. As he hit the ground a second time, he realized he was falling faster. There was cover after all. He had been blown over a slope.

His smile didn't last long. He felt less and less lucky. As he continued to roll out of control. As the slope steepened. As the notion of Friel's plagues hit him. As a vision of that monster, the Death Angel, hovered over him.

Damn! No!

He would never give in to such thoughts. He splayed out his hands and legs to stop himself. The maneuver worked too, but did not prevent him from sliding. The ground, which had been sandy and soft all day long, sucking at his heels, trying to prevent him from walking, had suddenly grown as cruel as a granite Montana mountain.

He felt the ground tear at him. Every hard point on his body knocked against the sharpest edges of the slope. He felt a stone finger rip his backpack from his shoulders. His elbow smashed against a rock outcropping and paralyzed his grip. Finally, he fell six feet vertically, coming to rest upright, his feet not touching the ground. He found himself wedged in a crevice, the ground pinching him at the pelvis.

Swayne couldn't see, couldn't hear, couldn't feel anything except pulsations of pain. But at least he had stopped falling, and the battering had let up. Maybe he had fallen through a hole in the earth and plummeted straight into hell—

That monster again.

He struggled as much to stop a scream from escaping his mouth as to struggle free. No, dammit, this hell was Iraq and not a place after death.

A boot struck him in the side of the head. And Friel's unconscious body draped itself over his.

On the plain above them, war broke out. The swoosh of antitank rocket-propelled grenades answered the roar of tank cannon—Swayne knew them by their sound, having fired them in training. And his enemies had fired them at the Spartans often enough on earlier missions too. And—

He tried to look around but couldn't see.

He was blind too?

No. He patted down his face and adjusted the mask that had twisted itself around his head. He shifted his goggles off his left ear. He could see fine.

Well enough to see that his hands were bleeding. To see that more blood dripped from his face, and a trickle ran down his nose and into the mask. To see that his clothes had been shredded.

To see salvation.

Beyond Friel's body came Night Runner, crabbing downhill on his hands and feet.

"Runner!" Swayne called out through the drifting smoke, gunpowder, dust, and daze.

"Roger," Night Runner called back. "I see you."

Swayne realized something else had gone wrong. His hearing too? No, his earpiece had fallen out. He patted his face down and could not feel the mike that he transplanted into his ear for the duration of every mission. He found it at the back of his head. He righted it and placed the receiver back into his ear. No matter. The unit wasn't working, and he was hearing Night Runner's voice in the relative quiet of the gully.

"I shot up all my ammo," Night Runner said as if Swayne would court-martial him by afternoon.

"Forget about it," said Swayne. "My pistol is gone." Both of them looked around at once to see the worst case. They had their sharpshooter, but nothing a sharpshooter could shoot.

While Swayne tried to get his bearings, Night Runner worked quickly, pulling Friel off his captain and propping him against one slope in the bottom of the ravine.

Above, the firing slacked. Somebody had begun to take control of the chaos. The small-arms fire shifted. Rounds flew overhead, a sandstorm of slugs, to Swayne's mind. For the time being they were in no danger from gunfire. But by the time the Iraqis stopped fighting each other and started to search for the three guys that had started their civil war, they'd be furious.

"Help me out of here," he called to Night Runner, who did not hear him. So Swayne shouted louder, and Night Runner patted his headset. He shook his head. That was that: They had lost their last radio set.

Swayne went stiff and sucked in his gut to make himself smaller. Night Runner lifted him by the armpits out of the grasp of the earth. Together they half-dragged, half-carried Friel along the bottom of the gully until the walls opened wide enough to lower the lance corporal to the ground.

Night Runner held Friel by the shoulders, and Swayne grasped his face and shook it to awaken him. But Friel was out of it. The huge blood blister that was his ear had burst, drenching the kid as if half his head had been blown off.

Night Runner shook his head, and handed one of Friel's arms to Swayne. Together they pulled the kid to a standing position and draped him over Swayne's shoulders. Night Runner led the way along the bottom of the ravine for fifty meters, his boot knife out, and Swayne stumbled behind, Friel's toes dragging.

Through it all, the wind howled, some of the desert
blowing overhead, but most of it filtering down, creating a
Niagara Falls of sand.

After more than a hundred meters, Swayne staggered,
and Night Runner took Friel's weight off him.

"You rest," Night Runner advised. "I'll be back in a
minute."

Swayne sucked air, unable to find even a single spare
breath to ask where his sergeant was going.

NIGHT RUNNER RAN back to the spot where they had
stopped falling. He thought it useless to try hiding their
tracks. No trick would fool the Iraqis. The Marines had
tumbled down this slope. Bloody patches marked the paths
of both Swayne and Friel. Shreds of clothing hung every-
where. Swayne's pack, twenty meters above, had stuck on
a huge stone shaped like a shark tooth. Night Runner started
to work his way back up the hill to retrieve the pack, but
the sound of Iraqi voices changed his mind for him. He
turned around and danced his way down the slope into the
bottom of the ravine, ducking out of sight as the collection
of voices gathered at the rim. Then the chatter of voices
turned into the chatter of gunfire as the Iraqis fired into the
recess at the bottom of the ravine. A rocket-propelled grenade then exploded. Then another fusillade of small arms,
followed by half a dozen more explosions, hand grenades,
and more rockets.

Good, he thought, the more they disturbed the earth, the
greater the chances they'd cover the Marines' footprints.
The more fearful the Iraqis were, the longer they'd wait to
creep down the slope. The longer they waited, the more
wind-blown sand would bury the Spartans' trail.

Night Runner had never forgotten who the real enemy
was in Iraq. It wasn't Saddam Hussein, or that regular army
unit behind them, or even the Republican Guards. It wasn't
even Bin Gahli. No, it was the Tracker. As he ran, Night
Runner tried to visualize their position on the last digital
map he had seen on his GPS before it went haywire.

By the time he found Swayne, he had oriented himself. And he'd worked out a plan that might put them in the clear. He was relieved to see that Friel had come to his senses well enough to be able to stand on his own, with help. And that Swayne had gotten his second wind.

Before setting off, Night Runner collected a bundle of twigs to use as a crude broom to sweep their tracks. He pointed Swayne in the direction he wanted the team to take. Once his limping captain and reeling mate with the head of a suicide victim set off, he spent only a brief time in knocking down the ridges in their three sets of prints. Gradually the ravine widened out, exposing them to the wind. Night Runner stopped and looked behind. His heart soared like the red-tailed hawk to see sand blowing like snow in a Montana blizzard. It erased the last of their tracks in less than a minute by first filling in the scratch marks, then washing over them, blending and repainting the desert floor, piling layer upon layer of grit. Creating a trackless landscape.

Satisfied that the wind would free him of sweeping, Night Runner took the point, stretching a hand behind him for Friel to hold onto. He saw that the captain had taken Friel's other hand. The three of them struck out, the Blackfeet brave leading the blind. Night Runner changed directions often, gradually leading them into the teeth of the wind until he was sure they had outflanked the Iraqi unit.

They had no weapons, except for bayonets and knives and, he hoped, Friel's small-caliber pistol. They had no water. No food. No high-tech crutches.

But they had this windstorm. And that gave them an edge. The Tracker, no matter how good he was, could not follow them in this. No way, nohow.

When the storm let up, Night Runner knew he would be able to re-orient himself, by the stars if necessary, and navigate, either to Salman Pak—which no longer seemed likely now that they'd been disarmed—or to one of the helicopter pickup points. They were going to escape. The Tracker, no matter that he was the best tracker Night Runner had ever seen, could not stop them.

So how come he wasn't happy?

Was it because only losers sneaked away like a pack of coyotes driven from a kill by a ferocious lone cougar?

QUANTICO—0427 HOURS LOCAL

FOR TWO DAYS, ZAVELLO had taken his meals in his chair. He insisted on staying close to the radio except for the occasional run to the head. He wanted to be there. He would be the first to hear or see the electronic sign that the Force Recon team had survived. One by one the PERLOBE indications had died out. Gunnery Sergeant Potts's in the helicopter fire. Friel's at the same site, apparently from the blast of the exploding helicopter. The remaining two devices had apparently been captured or disabled in the encounter with the Iraqi tank unit. One PERLOBE had flashed its last location signal at the very moment radio communications had been lost. Zavello's analysts told him that the likely cause was an explosion. The second device had traveled no farther than a hundred meters from the battle site before it too was extinguished.

Zavello slept in his chair, too. Hours after the last battle one of the PERLOBEs flickered to life, sending a rush of adrenaline into Zavello's heart faster than any cardiac needle. But that device, Night Runner's PERLOBE disguised as a pen, began a forty-mile-an-hour trip toward Baghdad, and Zavello reckoned that an Iraqi soldier had picked it up off the battlefield and was taking it home as an American souvenir.

What he refused to consider was that Night Runner still had the PERLOBE. That the Iraqis had taken him prisoner. So he just bit his lip and waited, alternately hoping to hear that at least one of the team members had survived, and fearing an even worse fate if anyone had.

The helicopter extraction crew had made its best effort to approach the primary pickup point on the first night after the OMCC had lost contact with Swayne's team. But the wind had driven them back into Saudi Arabia. Lack of visibility was one thing. But the danger of flameout from wind-carried sands being sucked into the helicopter turbines was simply too great.

Standard procedure dictated that in the absence of communications, a team unable to make a connection at a primary extraction point would attempt to rendezvous at the secondary point exactly twenty-four hours later.

Although Zavello believed it pointless, he ordered the standby extraction to take place. If any of those Marines had survived a combat action against an entire armored brigade, and the thermal imagery from reconnaissance satellite had confirmed earlier indications that it was more—a brigade reinforced with infantry—Zavello might even start believing in God.

Had it not been for the probable loss of a team, Zavello would have been delighted by events going on just east of Baghdad. The Iraqis had kept up their search for the Spartans during the fierce storm—which meant that even if the sergeant had been taken prisoner, perhaps Swayne and Friel had gotten free. Radio intercepts revealed that mech infantry had swept the ground on foot for a good ten miles square. With platoons of tanks following, trying to stay in contact with the men fading in and out of the sand clouds.

And maintain contact they did. More than one Iraqi soldier stopping in place to rub his eyes or clear his nose had been struck from behind by a rolling track and crushed. In all, the Iraqis had killed or maimed sixteen of their own men in accidents in less than twelve hours. After the storm began to clear, analysts deduced from the undisciplined Iraqi radio chatter that forty-plus men had been lost in the storm. Not to mention two hundred, more or less, in fighting with the Marines and each other.

So the search turned to a recovery operation. Finally, two hours after dawn the day after the battle with the Marines, the windstorm gave up its last breath, and so did the Iraqis. Tanks and trucks formed into convoys and began moving out of the wasteland.

Before Zavello allowed himself to abandon the command center for a much-needed rest, he directed the staff duty officer to keep track of convoy movements, which he dubbed an "Iraqi-Chinese fire drill."

Saddam had placed on alert every mech unit within fifty miles of Salman Pak. Most of those were on the march. Zavello didn't need J-2 analysts or CIA slugs to tell him the destination. Salman Pak itself. He could see that for himself. What he wanted to know, and what nobody seemed capable of telling him, was why.

Sure, the Iraqis had the UNSCOM under wraps at the compound. But did this flurry of activity mean the Marines had lived through the fight and the storm? Did the Iraqis fear three men so much?

"I want to know," he demanded of his staff. "Dammit, somebody get me an answer. If those boys are alive, we have to give them a hand."

THE IRAQI DESERT—0657 HOURS LOCAL

AS THE IRAQI tanks rumbled away, the earth vibrated, creating tiny landslides again. Sand that had been blown into drifts, forming cornices over every gully and boulder in the region, began crumbling into heaps.

One irregularly shaped boulder seemed more affected by the vibrations than any other in the desert. Night Runner, sitting cross-legged in the open, his back to the night's prevailing wind, sand packed to his shoulder blades in back and drifted up to his shirt pockets in front, opened his eyes. Avalanches of dust slid off his face. Tentatively he lifted one arm from its burial place on his thigh and pulled the dust filter off his nose and mouth, exposing half-clean skin that looked starkly out of place in the gray cement-dust surroundings.

The air tasted fresh, cool, almost liquid. Night Runner tried his voice. It would only croak. He cleared his throat and told himself that the puff of dust had not come from his lungs but from the cement powder that had fallen off his brow and into the stream of his breath.

He called out the names of his team. Two nearby sand dunes cracked before his eyes. Emerging from the earth like the living dead from their graves, Swayne and Friel sat up.

Swayne was able to dust off his face somewhat, but Friel's seeping skin had collected yet another layer of mud.

"Are they gone?" Friel squeaked on his third try at speaking.

"For the most part," said Night Runner, breaking into a cough.

Swayne spent the first few minutes of his rebirth just trying to collect enough fresh air to compensate for more than twelve hours' inability to breathe properly.

He'd waited out the storm by putting his brain to work on a plan to get them out of Iraq. Salman Pak was no longer an option. First—

What was first again?

Yes. He must get his team out of the sun. They'd have to conserve themselves for an aggressive evasion. That was it. Yes, but—

How much effort had he spent in the last twelve hours of his life just on breathing? How much dust had he inhaled with air filtered through a handkerchief over a paper filter? How much energy had he wasted just on surviving the onslaught of the storm? And how much emotion did he have left after track vehicles had driven by within a few meters on two occasions in the last hours of the storm?

He checked around and found no evidence of those tracks.

Friel struggled to his feet, touching off a secondary dust storm around himself. "Give up a hand, Captain," he said, his voice wracked with pain. "I feel like I been the guest of honor at a blanket party."

SWAYNE TUGGED ON Friel's arm and got to his feet. He felt every one of his wounds cry out to him. And every one had dried into a stiff, sandy scab that now began to seep.

He found himself staring at Friel, though, and realized he'd no room to complain. He'd seen five-day-old photographs of battlefields before. Many of the bloated, blackened corpses didn't look as bad as the kid from Boston now did.

"Don't look at me like that, Cap'n. How am I supposed to feel when you look at me like a donkey's about to shit in your mess kit?"

"Sorry, Henry."

Friel touched the side of the scab that was his face. His hand came away with black slime. "It's okay, sir. I'm just glad I don't have to look at me. How long we been here? Was that battle just yesterday?"

Swayne nodded uncertainly, forcing his gaze away.

"Yes," said Night Runner.

"We'd better find some cover," Swayne said, "try to stay out of Bin Gahli's sights for the day, avoid his tracker, navigate the best we can to the secondary pickup point." Swayne dumped five pounds of sand from the pockets and folds in his clothing.

"Night Runner, we'll need your skills more than ever," Swayne added. "Do you feel up to finding the secondary extraction point?"

Night Runner smiled, the crow's-feet around his eyes cracking like a dry lake bed in his mask of dust. "Don't you remember?"

Swayne shook his head. "Remember what?"

"All that marching around in the sandstorm?" he said. "There was more to it than just evading that brigade."

Swayne turned a full circle, checking out the terrain. "I'll be damned."

Friel shrugged, dropping piles of sand enough to cover his boots. "What?"

Swayne laughed. "We're standing on the secondary LZ." He slapped his hands against his thighs, revealing the black in his cammies again. "So, from a concealment point of view, which is better? Stay in place so we don't make tracks? Or move off the spot, creating the trail that will lead the enemy away if they should find us? Then back-tracking to this spot at night. Following our own sign."

Night Runner didn't answer. Swayne guessed the ser-geant didn't favor either option. Something was on his mind, something that he was reluctant to talk about. Some-thing that Swayne could only guess at.

"Now is not the time to be silent, Night Runner," said Swayne. "If there's a third choice, I want to hear it."

It took a while, but Swayne could see that Night Runner had fought his internal debate and option three had won.

"I've been thinking," said the Blackfeet warrior. "This has been an invisible mission for us. All along we have tried to disengage from the enemy, but he has kept running us down and pounding away at us."

Friel made the sound of a spitting cat. "All that's left is a freakin' flood."

Night Runner said, "He has caused us to run and hide. And now we have perhaps twelve hours. We can stay here and continue to cower like rabbits and escape to fight an-other day."

He hesitated until Swayne prompted him. "But what?"

"I'm tired of running."

"You want to go after Bin Gahli's tracker." It was not a question.

Night Runner's mouth pulled down at the corners. *Wasn't it obvious?*

Swayne rubbed the grit into his forehead. "With what? We've lost all our weapons except—" He held out his hands to his sides, palms up. "All I have is a survival knife." He looked to each man.

"I got my baby-sticker too," Friel said. He patted the small of his back. "And my trusty .32-cal gopher-gun."

Night Runner rested his right hand on the handle of the bayonet on his hip. His left hand reached down and probed his boot top, indicating he had the two blades. His look said they were more than enough for a real warrior.

Swayne felt a leader's weight on his head more at this mo-ment than at any other time during this event. "We accom-

plished our mission. We've broken the backs of Brutus—
Abboud Dahni's terrorist group. The compound would be
a tough nut even if we hadn't lost all our firepower. Now
that we're on our own . . ." He hesitated as Night Runner
began nodding. "What? You think we ought to try to pull
the UNSCOM team out of Salman Pak?"

"In the absence of orders from higher," said the sergeant,
quoting chapter and verse of Corps scripture, "continue
with the mission."

"Not if it's a suicide mission," Swayne countered. "Once
we lost the capability to snatch the UNSCOM team, our
job became getting out of here alive."

"Or—"

"Or what?"

Night Runner closed his eyes for a long moment. When
he opened them again, Swayne could see an urgency that
surpassed any normal request a Marine might make of an
officer.

"Or else we close with and destroy the nearest enemy."

"Meaning Bin Gahli's tracker."

"Affirm. The Tracker."

So. Revenge for Potts it was, was it? Swayne shook his
head. *Could that be a legitimate mission? Should it be?*
When he didn't answer right away, Runner spoke up.

"Request permission to scout the area." He blinked
twice. "Sir."

The formality clinched it for Swayne. He couldn't let
his team get out of hand. "On one condition, Sergeant," he
said, giving back the formal address.

Night Runner raised his eyebrows.

Swayne said, "Your little recon has to be a two-man
mission. I'll be your support."

"Hell, you ain't leaving me behind," Friel snapped. "It's
got to be a reconnaissance in force or nothing." He bran-
dished the .32-caliber, which all but disappeared in the
palm of his hand. "And how are you going to do that without I bring along the artillery? You find this Bin Gahli, by

golly, and I'll dust his ass for him." He sniffed. "You can have the tracker puke, Runner."

BIN GAHLI AND his three men had waited out the sandstorm inside the gully where the Force Recon team had been hiding when they engaged the helicopter. Although they had been out of the direct, sandblasting effect of the wind, their night had afforded little comfort. Sifting rivers of sand had drifted into the gully all night long, forcing the men to reposition themselves every hour or less, climbing on top of the sand fill to avoid being buried outright. By the storm's end, the gully had been covered, and the men had been elevated to the level of the plain above the wadi.

Once during the storm, Bin Gahli had directed Antenna Man to poke the device out of the gully. Before the wind had snapped off and blown away the top twenty feet of the pole, Bin Gahli had learned that the Americans had been surrounded by the Iraqi brigade, which had opened up with cannon fire and machine guns. The Iraqi commander had reported the enemy had been eliminated.

But Bin Gahli had heard optimistic and even manufactured reports of victory from the field before, so he hadn't been persuaded.

The operations headquarters in Baghdad apparently had had the same misgivings. The general in the command center had demanded to know whether bodies could be produced. Bin Gahli had recognized the voice, one of his many cousins, and had appreciated the man's demand. But before he could hear the answer, his communications had been broken off, literally.

When the four Iraqis stood up and walked over the roof of the gully at first light, Bin Gahli knew at a glance that it would be pointless to ask Jaffari to track. The desert had been swept so clean, yesterday might as well have been creation day.

But he asked anyhow, just to see Jaffari squirm. Laughing, Bin Gahli set out on the heading he knew would take him back to the Salman Pak compound, where he might at least amuse himself with the American woman.

The UNSCOM team might be Saddam's, but he owned her. He would either take her for himself or give her to his men. Either way, after his band had no more use for her, she would be only too happy to beg for her death. And not with the bravado that she had displayed before. Next time she asked to be killed, she would be serious about it, serious enough to tell him—or give him—anything he wanted as a final, hopeless gesture. First he'd make her cry—she seemed determined not to. He like the challenge. Yes, make her cry. Then the rest.

JUST BEING ON the offensive elevated Night Runner's mood. He liked it well enough to sneak around and leave no sign in places where U.S. Marines had no business being. But he liked it better to have a target to close with and destroy.

Night Runner struck out on a wide, circular route, hoping to cut Bin Gahli's track. He had used his time well while the storm pummeled him last night. He had invaded the minds of the Iraqis. In the end he had concluded that they had three options: one, to march directly to the battle site with the brigade; two, to head for Baghdad; three, and most likely, to trek toward Salman Pak. If they had dropped off the woman reporter there, Bin Gahli might be going back for his CNN interview to claim credit for driving out the Americans.

Night Runner made a sweep to intercept them, no matter which option the Iraqis chose.

Within an hour of searching, he saw in reality what had come to him in last night's vision.

With hand signals, he directed Swayne and Friel to climb up beside him at the crest of a ridge. He pointed to a spot on the sunny side of a slope a kilometer away.

Swayne stared a long time, his hand shading his eyes, until finally he said, "I see it. A track crosses that sand dune."

Friel shook his head and kept staring until his face broke

into a smile. Literally, as chunks of mud fell away. "I see it now."

"Four men," said Night Runner. "Bin Gahli, the Tracker, and two of his soldiers."

More chunks of mud fell off Friel's face. "You can see all that in one set of tracks? A half mile away?"

Night Runner couldn't suppress a laugh. "No." He pointed into the distance. On the shimmering horizon, four dots faded in and out like a mirage.

Friel's body heaved as he hid his face in his hands. "I'm losing it, boys. I think maybe the heat's getting to me." A set of white teeth grimaced from the seeping sores. "I'm trying to pull my share, Cap'n. Honest."

Swayne patted him on the back, feeling the brittleness of the uniform fabric, which had been badly scorched in the fire. "Don't take it so hard, Henry. I didn't see them either."

Swayne and Night Runner agreed that the four Iraqis were a good two kilometers ahead, a little more than a mile. Night Runner told of his plan—he called it a plan. It had been revealed to him as a vision, but visions might be a little much for his fellow Marines.

They would follow the shaded areas of the terrain, those low spots that could not be seen by the Iraqis as the Marines closed on them. The Spartans would jog to catch up before Bin Gahli could get within range of a reaction force from Salman Pak. That was the simple part. The hard part was running under the conditions of blast-furnace heat. That could kill them as easily as any AK-47 slug.

Friel was worst off. He'd lost fluids from his wounds and burns.

But Friel vowed that he was up to it. Swayne only shrugged. Night Runner didn't doubt their willingness, only their capacity. They were Marines, all right, but they were not Indian warriors.

Night Runner cared about their welfare. But he worried more that they might hold him up.

•　•　•

THEY INTERCEPTED THE track less than an hour later. Night Runner left his gasping mates slumped against the shady slope of a wadi as he climbed to a vantage point.

Peering around the base of a boulder, Night Runner smiled. They had closed to within three hundred meters of the last visible track of the Iraqis. That was where the track dropped into low ground. It did not reappear on the opposite slope, an additional two hundred meters away. This meant his quarry was about four hundred meters away, give or take. He stared, using his "ten-thousand-meter gaze." Friel had given it the name after looking into his eyes when Night Runner was using the master tracker's technique of staring, wide-eyed, at no particular point in the distance for a long time. The technique let him scan a landscape without moving his head or eyes. With it he could see the flitting of a bird at a thousand meters, or the twitch of a beetle's antennae just ten meters away. Both would register.

Runner took in the situation. Directly ahead, ten miles away, a great outcropping appeared, made visible not by its coloring but by the geometric regularity of its angles. That was Bin Gahli's destination, Salman Pak. Closer in, at about five miles, a convoy of trucks traveled from left to right across the panorama of desert. Night Runner probed his memory banks for the last topographic screen that had appeared on his GPS. Definitely a road, he remembered. He could confirm it later on his map. But he knew he wouldn't need to.

At a kilometer, a fennec returned to its den. Later than normal, its belly distended from a late meal. At two hundred meters a lizard flashed from one shady spot to another, its belly held high, as if two inches from the desert floor was so much cooler than the surface of the sand itself. At twenty meters, a platoon of ants engaged in mob labor, dragging the carcass of a fly into a burrow at the base of a stone the size of a paperweight.

Night Runner saw all this as he lay staring as if entranced. But no terrorists came into view.

He slid back off the hill. The rest of last night's vision. Would it play out as well as the first of it?

BIN GAHLI COULD march for hours across the desert even at the apex of the day. He called it his camel stride, a long-legged pace, not so fast as to fight against the pull of the sand, but quick enough to eat up the desert miles. By mid-afternoon, he expected to arrive at Salman Pak. If they ran across a military vehicle to commandeer, sooner.

He felt Jaffari at his side and knew something was wrong—walking in file was best to take on the desert, and they had traded places among themselves all day.

"What is it, ferret?"

"We are being followed."

"Why do you whisper? Are they so close they can hear us talk about them?"

"No."

"Then stop whining. Have you seen them?"

"You know I don't have to see an American to know he is there."

"Yet you know it is an American. Why couldn't it be one of the Iraqi soldiers, perhaps one of those separated from his unit in the battle against the Americans?"

Jaffari snorted and dropped back into file as if he could not, or would not, bear such insults.

Bin Gahli halted the column after he had dropped into one of the dozen or so wadis they had left to cross before coming to the road. Time to soothe Jaffari's ruffled feelings.

"How many Americans?" he asked, putting an arm on his man's shoulder.

Jaffari wouldn't look at him. "Are you merely trying to vex me?"

"It wouldn't do for us to carry on a conference in plain sight back there, now would it?" Bin Gahli said. "I want to take home an American just as badly as you. Wouldn't Saddam be grateful if he could parade one or two American soldiers through the streets of Baghdad so that the citizens affected by the bombing could have a go at them?"

Jaffari grunted.

Bin Gahli grabbed him by the front of his jacket and shook him. "But first we have to catch them, now don't we? Quickly now, how are we going to do that?"

NIGHT RUNNER PUT Swayne and Friel onto the tracks of the Iraqis. He told them to follow. "But slowly, so you don't catch up. No faster than their walk. And keep your eyes open to the front. Always looking to see that the tracks continue ahead at least a hundred meters. If you see a sign of any change, such as separating from the file into two tracks or stopping to mill around in a place not suitable for a break, head for the nearest cover and wait for me."

He then told them that he would parallel the trail, moving ahead. Friel offered him the .32-caliber. Night Runner declined without saying why. Namely, that he felt much less a Marine now than he had been two days ago, and much more a Blackfeet warrior. These men, his friends and fellow Marines, but white men anyhow, would not understand. Because they could not.

So he left them running at a jog that he could sustain across the Montana plains all day. Here, perhaps no more than a couple hours, but he would need much less than that.

Before he had gone ahead more than ten minutes, he ran across a set of new tracks. At first glance, he tried to deny them. They hadn't been in last night's vision, so they could not exist. But he did not fool himself for long. Visions were visions, and tracks were tracks. He leapt over a sand dune, rolled, and came up with his bayonet drawn, ready for combat. But whoever had made the track had not lain in wait for him.

Then he saw why. Somebody lost and confused had made the tracks. A soldier, by the tread pattern. He had walked in one direction, climbing to high ground, turning in a circle, probably to get his bearings, then taken off in another direction. The footprints were irregularly spaced, indicating the man had been staggering. Long drag marks led to each step and pointed out the toes as well, indicating extreme exhaustion.

An Iraqi soldier lost in the sandstorm. Trying to find his way back to his unit. All the while getting farther away. He would be no factor—Night Runner bent over and looked closely at the track. The heavier weight on one foot-print, indicated by the way the soil was breaking up on his right foot, showed that he still carried his rifle, probably slung over the shoulder. Even so, as a fighting man, he was finished. Runner wondered that he had not yet thrown away the rifle. Only fear of getting a lashing for having lost it prevented that. Once he became hungry enough, scared enough, thirsty enough, and addled enough, the rifle would go.

Meanwhile, Night Runner had work to do. He picked up the pace again, now jogging slower, beginning a slow arc turn toward his enemy. The turn he made was into the wind, naturally. He would never again make the mistake he had made on that first night three nights ago, allowing himself to be scented.

ALL SWAYNE'S ATTENTION was on the track of Bin Gahli's band at his feet. He had followed a trail before. While hunting javelina in Texas last year. And elk in Canada, during the winter trek back into the United States in the last event scenario. This was different. Now, instead of Night Runner, *he* had to track. Not that finding the trail was so hard. But he had to make sure he and Friel did not blunder into the terrorist band. Night Runner had warned him—as if he'd had to—about Bin Gahli's tracker. The thought that an en-emy might have their own version of Night Runner chilled Swayne to the core, even on a day as hot as this.

With Friel on his heels, half-dazed by the heat and lack of water, Swayne absorbed himself in both the tracks and the dangers he knew lay at the end of those tracks. So he did not see the Iraqi soldier coming at him from the left, and they smashed together like two cars in a collision test. Both hit the ground like crash dummies.

The Iraqi spoke first, scolding in a tone of, *Why don't you watch where you're going, buster?*

Swayne rolled away from the soldier, realizing what had happened, pulling his survival knife, preparing to lunge at the soldier.

FRIEL THOUGHT THAT Night Runner had played a joke on them, springing an ambush as a Marine instructor would do in Force Recon training to admonish them for dropping their guard and becoming lax in security.

He shook his head, expecting Night Runner's strong, dark features to materialize. Instead the dark and gaunt features of an Iraqi soldier morphed into view. Friel blinked several times, expecting the vision to correct itself. It did not, and when the Iraqi started speaking in his own tongue, he realized it never would.

When the sorry Mook bastard unslung his AK-47 assault rifle, charged the bolt, feeding a round into the chamber, and began lowering the barrel on Swayne, Friel knew they'd both be dead in seconds.

What crap! Runner had told them not to do this, and they'd done it, damnit.

The Iraqi began firing at Swayne before he had leveled his rifle. The sharp report of the rifle on automatic fire stung Friel's eardrums and masked the sound of two ladyfinger firecrackers going off. The .32-caliber pistol spat twice, and a pair of red-black geysers spouted from the Iraqi's temple, just behind his right eye.

Friel cursed himself for missing so badly—he had been aiming for the ear. Then the black-handled survival knife of the captain bounced off the soldier's chest and fell harmlessly to the ground, and Friel knew what had happened: The Iraqi had jerked his head back when Swayne made to throw the knife. His bullets hadn't been aimed high after all.

Friel didn't dare laugh until he knew that the captain had survived, but then he saw Swayne standing with a dismayed look on his face.

● ● ●

ONLY DUMB LUCK had saved his life, and Swayne knew it. If the soldier had lowered the rifle first and begun firing, he probably would have stitched Swayne up from the groin to the face. But while trying to bring down the rifle, the Iraqi had pulled the trigger, and the AK-47's notable tendency to rise as it was being fired on automatic had delayed him just enough for Friel to pull his pistol and fire.

Friel. There he stood, covering his face. His body shook. What was going on with him? Was he losing his nerve? Battle fatigue? PSD, as they called it these days?

"Don't take it so hard, Henry. I'm okay. You're okay. That's what counts."

Friel gasped, "I ain't taking it hard, Cap'n. I'm laughing. But it hurts my face *real* bad."

Swayne joined him in a gut-buster. The release felt good. It got rid of the invigorating giddiness of being shot at and missed.

After a half minute of laughing, Swayne tried to sober up.

"You ever consider re-upping with the circus, Cap'n?" Friel wanted to know. "A knife-throwing talent like that is wasted in the Marine Corps."

It broke them up again.

It took a while, but they finally got a grip on their composure.

"I can die happy now," said Friel, drying something that might have been tears off his face. "I've seen something better'n any Hollywood flick. 'The Two Stooges.'" Friel doubled over again.

Swayne flashed a phony smile to show he was being a good sport.

Finally Friel sobered up. "I won't tell anybody, Cap'n. I promise."

"The hell you won't." Swayne pried the AK-47 out of the Iraqi soldier's hands carefully, so as not to touch off any more precious rounds of ammunition. Switching it to semiautomatic—all Force Recon Marines were trained in the weapons of all their allies and enemies—he handed it off to Friel.

"Get up into a firing position on higher ground. Before you go, give me your pistol." The urgency in his voice spurred Friel to immediate action, the humor of the moment all but gone. Swayne recovered his survival knife, patted down the soldier for more ammunition, weapons, or water, and finding none, crept up to lie beside Friel.

"We can assume that anybody within a five-mile radius heard the gun go off," Swayne said. "They'll be checking it out. The first Iraqi that shows his face, take it off."

"I know you're not joking anymore, Cap'n. But do you know what you're asking is like a joke?"

Swayne knew. To expect Friel to take out a target, at two hundred meters or more, using a rifle he had never fired before, was too great a demand for anybody. But nothing less would do.

"If you have a better idea, I want to hear it."

Friel ejected the assault rifle's magazine and handed it to Swayne. "I'm guessing you didn't find any more clips on the cheese-eater."

"Probably tossed away all his excess weight long ago."

"I'd appreciate it if you'd give me a bullet count in this clip then."

As Swayne unloaded and reloaded, Friel kept his eyes on a scan of the landscape. "See that white stone about a hundred meters off?" he said. "Follow my line of sight."

Swayne looked where Friel aimed the rifle. "Tally on the stone."

"How many beans in the clip?" Friel asked.

"Nine."

At that, Friel fired the round in the chamber, raising a geyser of sand three inches above and slightly to the right of the stone.

"Zeroed," Friel said as they slid down the hill together a few feet and repositioned ten meters to the right. As Friel reinserted the magazine and recharged the weapon, Swayne's brain went to work in overdrive. How could they help Night Runner now that Bin Gahli and his men had been alerted? Only one thing seemed illogical enough to be logical, and waiting in this spot doing nothing was not it. If he did not act soon, Night Runner would be left out to dry.

ONLY MEN WHO had been under fire before could have moved as quickly as Bin Gahli's band when they heard the Iraqi rifle discharge on automatic.

As if a grenade had gone off in their midst, they dove in all directions, their weapons pointing outward. Once satisfied that they weren't under siege, Bin Gahli and Jaffari put their heads together.

"Perhaps twenty bullets fired," Bin Gahli said. "Followed by a single shot. Maybe a finishing shot?"

"Plus two more from a second weapon, a very small weapon," Jaffari added.

Bin Gahli shook his head. He hadn't heard the small-caliber shots, but didn't doubt their existence. Together he and Jaffari crawled into a position where they could look over their back trail. What they saw gave them nothing more than astonishment. A lone man running after them.

Bin Gahli wondered aloud, "Do you suppose one of our soldiers took out the Americans?"

"Get down," Jaffari said, ducking below the line of sight. As he did, the third man in his band took a peek.

"He said to get down, you fool," Bin Gahli growled.

The terrorist did as he was told, and abruptly. Too abruptly. A hole blossomed in his forehead, and the back of his head sprayed blood down the sand dune. Bin Gahli crowded lower, looking into the eyes of Jaffari and nodding in appreciation for the warning he had sounded. The noise of the rifle report reached them.

"And then there were three," Bin Gahli said. "Three of us against two of them, do you think?"

Jaffari shrugged. "Maybe two, maybe three. Maybe just one."

Bin Gahli called out to the last foot soldier in his shrinking army. Again he and Jaffari locked eyes. Their man did not answer.

LIKE HIS ENEMIES, Night Runner had hit the ground when the automatic rifle went off. Once on the ground he kept moving, snaking on his belly, not granting himself a wasted concern for Swayne and Friel—he'd gotten too close to the enemy himself. Close enough to hear the rattling of metal, the familiar sounds of a rifle sling as the weapon was taken from the shoulder and taken off safety. Although his running had put him into oxygen debt, he forced himself to breathe slowly and quietly.

Carefully, carefully he peeked over a dune and surveyed the depression, getting his bearings. He saw only one man, his back to Night Runner, peering around the cover of a boulder to check out the wadi ahead of the terrorist's original direction of travel. Night Runner heard voices to his left, and surmised the remaining terrorists had sought cover in that direction.

Moving sideways like a crab, he put his eyes to work looking for anything in this path that would betray him by making a sound. Carefully he displaced some twigs, even as he continued slithering. In seconds he had come up to within hand-to-hand combat range of the soldier, not six feet away.

The sound he heard next was unmistakable, the slap of a slug hitting flash and bone, pulverizing body parts. The

Iraqi soldier heard it too and turned his head to see what was going on to his left rear. He never saw Night Runner, never made a sound as the blade struck him twice. First, the piercing, paralyzing stab to the right kidney. Second, as his back arched unnaturally, a hand in his hair, yanking back his head, and the hot feeling of the knife drawn across his throat. He dropped his rifle and clutched at his neck as if he might stop the bleeding, although he was all but dead, his only sound the gushing and bubbling from his open trachea.

The man's rifle fell too far away for Night Runner to grab it without exposing himself to the other terrorists. Besides, something in his newfound nature suggested to him that having one of the white man's weapons would be something of a sacrilege. He'd just engaged in an ancestral form of combat, a sacramental bloodletting of his enemy by a warrior armed with nothing but a knife.

BIN GAHLI DIRECTED Jaffari to pick up one dead man's weapons while he ran, firing, to where he had last seen his only surviving soldier. He found him lying sprawled, the desert sands sopping up the last of his blood. In rage more than anything else, Bin Gahli fired one magazine empty from his AK-47 in the direction in which he saw tracks disappearing out of sight. He took his man's weapon, emptied it, broke it over a stone, and picked up all the loose ammunition.

He and Jaffari struck off toward Salman Pak, now at a run, neither of them willing to accept even odds or worse.

Along the way Bin Gahli threw off the burden that he'd been carrying ever since they'd taken out the American helicopter. Not so much because of its extra weight. He didn't like the idea of it as a talisman of bad luck. Nothing had gone right for him since he'd carried off the huge foot in the boot.

SWAYNE KEPT OUT of sight as much as he could, running along the wadi. Only when he heard the gunfire from Bin

Gahli's position did he stop his foolhardy rush. He found cover. Catching his breath, feeling the effects of the sun and lack of water, he tried to calculate. What had gone on? What should he do next? Why had he been so stupid?

Less than a minute had gone by when he felt a hand on his shoulder and flinched, throwing his body aside, bringing the .32-caliber to bear. On Night Runner's face.

He cursed. "How did you do that? A warning next time, please." Swayne wiped the embarrassment off his face, and looked deeply into Night Runner's face. The sergeant had changed. He had always kept himself aloof, never un-friendly, but never gregarious, never speaking unless he had something to say. Swayne had always chalked it up to the differences in their cultures. And now he thought that Night Runner had withdrawn even deeper into his Indianhood, putting still more distance between them.

Once his heartbeat had returned to normal, Swayne said, "Friel cut the odds down." He pointed to the bloodstains on Night Runner's wrist. "How about you?"

"Two left. Bin Gahli and his tracker." Mentally, Night Runner had erased the capital T. He no longer considered himself the Bedouin's inferior. Now the rodent-faced man had become his quarry.

Swayne shook his head. He didn't care how good Bin Gahli's tracker was. He was grateful that Night Runner was on his side.

Moments later, Friel caught up, gasping. Swayne noticed that his eyes were puffy, almost swollen shut. But as the lance corporal crumpled into the space between Night Runner and his captain, he simply looked up and said, "Where to?"

Swayne said, "I heard you got your man, Henry. Good shooting."

Friel blinked, his face swollen but blank, as if to say: *Good shooting? What the hell else?*

Night Runner stood up, bayonet in hand, and began stalking toward the spot where the two remaining Iraqis had disappeared over the horizon.

Swayne did not want to push Friel any further beyond his endurance. Any more exposure to the sun, and those burns on his face, lacking eyelashes as he did, would mean that they'd lose Friel's sharp eye for good. The kid wouldn't be around for Event 16 when it came up.

"Sergeant Night Runner," he called. "Hold it."

Night Runner turned back toward him, a stunned look on his face. He locked eyes with Swayne. "So formal, Captain Swayne?"

Swayne looked away. "I'm not so sure the Sergeant Night Runner here is the same Night Runner who took off a few days ago from Quantico with us."

Night Runner's mouth came open to protest, but he held his tongue. "Maybe you're right. I'm letting my ego get in the way."

The notion of Night Runner as egotist nearly caused Swayne another outburst of laughter. "You can't expect to kill all the terrorists in the world on one mission," he said. "We didn't get Bin Gahli but we got Abboud Dahni. And most of Bin Gahli's band."

Abashed, Night Runner disagreed in posture if not in words, and Swayne could see that the only terrorist in the world that now mattered to Night Runner was that tracker.

Night Runner, ever the perfect Marine, showed that he was not going to sulk because he couldn't get his way. He flapped a hand in the direction of the dead terrorists and said, "We should check out those two bodies. See if they have any water. Maybe food."

Friel stirred. "I could go for that."

The team did not relax before checking out the bodies, though. Swayne parked Friel on a vantage point where he could watch out over most of the area, covering his and Night Runner's movements with the eight rounds left in his AK-47. Night Runner swept right of the trail, going a kilometer beyond the location where they had struck Bin Gahli. Swayne completed a similar loop, moving to the left of the trail. A half hour later, they joined up.

"They're moving quickly," Night Runner reported. "Not

worried about being followed. More concerned about putting distance between us and them." He looked into Swayne's eyes, awaiting a reaction to his unspoken entreaty.

Swayne understood what Night Runner wanted that reaction to be. He wanted permission to take off, and quickly. He wanted to engage Bin Gahli—no, Bin Gahli's tracker. Swayne shook his head.

No words were needed between the pair. Night Runner sagged, but only a little, and pointed, indicating Swayne should lead the way back to Friel. Another wave of his hand indicated he would follow, keeping an eye out so that Bin Gahli could neither circle around or backtrack—never again would he make any assumptions about this enemy.

When the team had reassembled, Night Runner dropped a heavy bundle wrapped in cloth. He gave Swayne the answer to the questions in their eyes by showing them Potts's boot.

The moment was a dark one. Swayne and Runner, the ranking men on the team, wanted to bury the last of their friend and mate. But the lance corporal countermanded them. "I ain't leaving the gunny," he said. "You can leave us both, but you ain't leaving all we got of him in this goddam box of kitty litter." Neither the sergeant nor captain dared argue with the man who had the rifle and who had taken so many blows to the head.

Night Runner led them away from the killing ground so they would not be vulnerable to a helicopter assault after Bin Gahli had gotten clear of the wasteland and made contact with Iraqi regulars. Friel, whose condition could best be described as guarded, both mentally and physically, kept up. Even with the extra weight he lugged over his shoulder.

The search of Iraqi bodies had produced no more than a half-pint of water, and Swayne and Night Runner ordered Friel to consume it, because he was losing so much of his fluids through the burns on his face. Friel protested, but only briefly before gulping the water greedily.

Night Runner had also found a foul-smelling white

cheese. Friel refused it. "Eat a cheese-eater's sack lunch? Not only am I not going to eat it, I don't want it within arm's reach of my nose." He screwed up his face. "Make that a half mile."

Night Runner shrugged. "You're not hungry enough."

Swayne and Night Runner shared the cheese, Swayne finding it difficult to swallow because of its fragrance, its salty, grainy texture, and the lack of water to cleanse the bilious aftertaste from his palate. But once he had finished, Swayne found it perked him up, as if he had swallowed an energy pellet that sent rays of strength through him like nuclear fuel rods at his core. Now, if only he had water. If he could slake his thirst, he might even be able to put himself into a frame of mind to grant Night Runner's wish to go after Bin Gahli.

Meanwhile, Night Runner began digging into the wall of the gully. Friel, his face a mud-mask, took a breath, as if he might make one of his smart-aleck remarks. Instead, he released a noisy sigh, lay his head on one arm, and went to sleep. The other arm cradled the grisly boot.

Swayne could see Night Runner was not digging for water. Each time he put the tip of his bayonet to the bank, he would dig less than an inch before breaking into a tunnel the diameter of a quarter. The end of each tunnel was a thumb-sized, leathery sac hanging from the roof of a tiny compartment. In half an hour, Runner had collected thirty of the miniature coin purses. Without explanation he separated them into three piles. From his pile he took one of the larger sacs, pinched it between the thumb and the finger of one hand, and touched the blade of his bayonet to it. At the touch, the leather split, giving birth to a black, slimy entity with only slightly more substance than a slug.

Swayne knew it was the pupa of some insect, but he didn't want to know which.

Night Runner told him anyway. "It's the chrysalis of a desert moth," he said. "Every four or five years it rains out here, and the dampness causes them to hatch. Meanwhile, the little critters store their own water." He popped one into his mouth, chewed twice, and swallowed. "Good source of protein too." He licked his lips. "Tastes great," he said. "Less filling too," he added without enthusiasm.

In survival training, Swayne had eaten all sorts of exotic foods, many of them unmentionable. As always, the issue was the one Night Runner had put to Friel: *Are you hungry enough?*

Swayne decided he was. And thirsty enough too. Quickly, trying not think about it, except as cracking peanuts and wolfing them down, he devoured his pile without chewing. He lay down, hoping to sleep. The more he tried to divert his imagination from the idea that every gurgle in his gut was a moth trying to climb out of his belly, the more vivid the image became.

SWAYNE AWOKE. As far as he knew, it could have been an hour later or a week. The only thing certain was that he didn't want to be asleep, didn't want to dream. Every unpleasant fantasy in his life had joined forces with every one of his unpleasant realities. He had traveled to Vietnam to find his father's remains, only to fall into the same ambush that had killed him. Moths the size of pterodactyls had come into the desert to avenge the deaths of their unborn. And his grandfather the senator had visited his dreams to narrate his undoing.

He felt Night Runner staring at him. "Better get some rest, Runner. I'll take the watch."

"I'm not tired," said Night Runner. He blinked, as if remembering his manners. "Sir. Thanks for offering."

Swayne heard his own thoughts forming into words in his mouth, even before they were spoken. Entirely against his nature, he did not suppress them, did not even evaluate and re-evaluate them. He just spoke his thoughts, giving free rein to his emotions.

"How not tired are you?" he asked.

Night Runner inclined his head toward Swayne. He formed a question by raising one eyebrow.

"Not tired enough to go after Bin Gahli?" Swayne said.

Night Runner blinked. Then he smiled.

Answer enough for Swayne. He stood and stretched, surprised at how refreshed he felt from his restless rest and meal of soft-shelled bugs.

Friel, so used to awakening at any noise in the field, also stirred and sat up. "Time to go?" he yawned more than asked, flakes of mud and dried ooze falling off his face.

"You're not going anywhere, Henry," Swayne said. The astonished expressions on both Night Runner and Friel dissolved into understanding as they listened to Swayne's plan.

When he had finished, Friel said, "Good plan, sir."

Swayne gave him back one of his own Friel looks: *Good plan? What else?*

Somewhere under the mud, Friel blushed. "Sorry. I mean, you always come up with good plans. Except for the part where I don't get to go with you guys."

"I hear you," Swayne said. "But somebody has to meet the extraction bird and tell the pilots where to pick us up."

Friel looked at the ground a while, then up at Swayne, his eyes a pair of red-rimmed oases on a dried lake bed. He pulled the boot next to him. "You can count on me, Cap'n." He turned to Night Runner. "Sergeant?"

"Yeah?"

"Good luck on getting that guy."

"Thanks, Henry."

After handshakes all around, they separated, Friel backtracking toward the LZ, the spot where they had shaken off the effects of the sandstorm this morning, Night Runner, Swayne, and their lengthening shadows jogging toward Salman Pak.

Swayne wondered if Friel would last the day. His body had gone ever farther south since the crash. Now his mind seemed headed toward the equator as well.

THREE KILOMETERS FROM Salman Pak, Night Runner flapped his hand behind his back and dropped to one knee. Swayne tensed, bent low, and turned to the rear. He pointed into the night, Friel's .32-caliber pistol in his left hand, his survival knife in his right.

By now their shadows had blended into the twilight. Night Runner, dusty as the desert, dropped in and out of Swayne's vision like a piece of holographic art. Night Runner darted left, then right, back and forth. He played stop-and-go like a finch in a thicket.

When he crouched below the horizon, Swayne lost him. He said to the shadow in the spot where he'd last seen him, "What's up?"

The answer came from behind him. "Stay here, sir."

Swayne whirled. He saw a flutter of black melt into the dark. But when he took his eyes off it for a second to check their back trail again, Night Runner had disappeared. Swayne blinked at the spot where the warrior was not. What had happened on this event?

Runner had changed since—well, almost from the time they'd directed their smart bombs into that valley. He'd become even more of an Indian. And today, he'd made another leap back into his ancient warrior culture. Swayne knew of course that he could not go there with his sergeant. But tonight the man had run off and left him in a time warp. Swayne stayed in the here and now, while Runner shot back to another age.

Swayne kept up his watch. He pushed the button on every one of his senses so that he might detect what had put Night Runner on alert. Finally, after he had moved forward to where Night Runner had stopped, he could see what Night Runner had seen. The flickering of a fire half a kilometer away. A bare glow on the line of travel to Salman Pak. He was no tracker, but any fool could see the reason for alarm. A fire? Might as well throw a marching band into the mix at this stage of the stalking contest. A fire, for Pete's sake? It made as much sense as play-action on fourth and forty, down by six TDs in the Super Bowl.

Swayne felt out of place. He had as much business in this scrape between Runner and his nemesis as a referee in a pro wrestling match. Two giants had joined a mortal combat of primitive stealth. Swayne meant nothing to either of them. The best he could do, if he did anything, was stay out of the way.

All at once he felt vulnerable. He'd been staring at the fire's glow as he worked out his status.

Cripes! Staring at the fire! Exactly as the tracker planned. The Bedouin had created a ruse for Swayne to see. And sucked him in with it. He turned his back to the fire to check the most likely avenues of approach. He forced his mind to work on defenses left open to him. Another chill ran through him. The terrorist must have had all those defenses in mind before he ever put a match to his kindling.

Runner's tracker had already made half a dozen moves in this chess game. He was so far ahead of Swayne already that the only thing left to do was dig a foxhole and fight it out. *Damn!*

Swayne had taken on forces larger than this. He'd fought his way out of trouble with entire battalions—hell, just a day ago.

But this tracker! He had skills so—

No. He got a grip. He must keep his wits. He put his mind to work.

Yes. His mind. His best weapon. He ran through the options. *Work it out, Jack, damn you! How would the Bedouin think?*

He ran through the choices. As the Bedouin might run through them.

A lesser unit than the Spartans might fix on the fire and try to sneak closer to get a better look. This tracker would not expect that from what he had already seen of Night Runner. Scratch it.

A better unit would try to skirt wide, bypassing the fire, and go on to Salman Pak without being detected. The terrorist might expect that course of action. The Marines knew the UNSCOM team was there, and Bin Gahli must know they knew. Swayne thought it a good possibility.

But flawed. Bin Gahli and his tracker could do only two things, both dicey. They could either split up and watch both the northern and southern passages. Or they could guess at one or the other and remain together either north or south. He doubted that one of them would try to take on three Marines. Or risk losing track of them.

Swayne's skin crawled at the third possibility. The tracker would know all the spots for looking at his fire. He could wait along the line of travel for Swayne and his team to do what he had already done: stop in place to evaluate the situation. Taking a page from Night Runner's book, Swayne darted left, throwing himself on the ground, trying to work his body into the sand like a flounder on the sea bottom. Except that something beneath him, something familiar, got in the way.

He slid to the side and found that he had landed on Night Runner's camo jacket.

What the hell was going on?

NIGHT RUNNER HAD peeled off all his clothes by now. He'd stripped his jacket back where he had left Swayne. His shirt and T-shirt lay ten meters upwind of that. Ten meters beyond that his pants, socks, skivvies, and boots. A little way further upwind, he had stopped, dug into the soft sand, and showered himself with dirt like one of the elephants on the nature shows. This tactic had a twofold effect: The dust camouflaged him, and masked his scent as well, at least for a while.

After that he ran laterally a good fifty meters before circling downwind. Patches of dirt crust and sharp gravel hurt his bare feet. He cursed himself for the pain. He'd grown soft.

He vowed to toughen his body once this event was over. From now on he was going to be more the warrior, and so a better Marine.

That would be fine. But it was for later. For now he had to think like the terrorist.

Runner guessed that the tracker would backtrack to wait for the Marines to bypass him before seeing the fire. He wouldn't try a simple ambush. The Americans would be too alert. Until they spotted his fake camp. Then they'd focus far off. They'd think their enemy had stopped. They'd feel a false sense of security because they knew where the Iraqis had set up. That was what the bastard was up to.

But the Marines had a few things in their favor too.

For one, Night Runner had not followed Bin Gahli's trail directly. He'd felt too vulnerable to ambush. So the Bedouin could not know for certain the trail the Marines would travel.

For another thing, Runner had not allowed the ground to channel him. When a wadi tried to force him one way, he climbed out of the dry bed and took a new tack against the grain of the land. The Iraqis could not predict how he and Swayne would get to Salman Pak.

For a final thing, Runner knew the tracker would wait downwind, using his sense of smell. As far as the Iraqi knew, the Marines had not caught onto his nose as a weapon.

After Runner had dashed a good hundred meters with the wind, he counted off a hundred more to be safe. Then he turned crosswind. Now he moved slowly. And so quietly—the soles of his bare feet kept so well in touch with the ground, he could take back any step that might make noise. He inhaled through his nose, exhaled through his mouth. Testing the wind. *Was this smell-thing legit?* Or was he playing at a kid's game while the Bedouin and Bin Gahli ate a full meal and drank their fill of water at Salman Pak? Had they left the fire to trick the Marines into a fool's mission, to gain time for Saddam to disperse the UNSCOM team?

Night Runner forced the doubts out of his mind. He'd be stupid only if he didn't treat the Bedouin with respect. And, of course, this was good technique. Hadn't he sneaked up on camps by trailing the smoke in the woods? Hadn't he found lost horses on the Marias River bottoms by creeping up their sharp scents? Hadn't he found herds of elk by tracing wafts of their perfumed urine?

Yes to all of those.

Why not a man?

No reason. How could he not find one smelly-assed terrorist whose desert upbringing didn't let him waste water on daily showers?

Within seconds of telling himself he could do it, Night Runner did. He picked up the stinging scents of sweaty men. The most familiar, least offensive smell was his own—from the clothes he'd dumped. Then Swayne's. Finally, a sharp smell tinged with pungent spices of a diet like the salty, garlic-flavored cheese he and Swayne had shared. And the acrid tars and smoke residue of cigarettes.

He had the bastard.

Night Runner locked onto the tracker with nasal radar. He turned into the smells, tracking the wind. He moved more quickly than he would have liked. But move quickly he must. The tracker was now sneaking up on his captain.

SWAYNE KNEW ANY soldier who did not feel fear was either an idiot or psychopath, prone to do stupid things. He had known fear many times. He had kept it under control. First by accepting it. Then by facing it down with reason. And action. And he had learned to rely on fear to instill the proper note of caution in every tactical move. Most of his fears in the past, though, had been personal.

Until now.

Now, he was alone in a wilderness. Now a stalker was after him. Now his enemy was as stealthy as Night Runner. And as vicious as any hyena.

But Swayne kept a lid on it. He kept his eyes darting from one spot to another, holding his gaze until the center of it began to give way, then moving it again. He put down the urge to get up and run.

Then he wondered if he was worse off to stay still.

He was fast enough, wasn't he? A sprinter who'd finished in the top three of every race he'd ever been in. Why not run? Not in panic, but as a defense. Like the antelope. Was a prey animal better off standing in place? Or fleeing? The Iraqi might be clever enough to stalk him. But could he run like a cheetah and catch him? Was—?

His scan hit on an odd shadow. Odd because it had changed shape. Perhaps only by six inches, but it had moved.

Swayne turned his body away. He turned his head, but not his eyes. To see if he could trick the shadow into giving itself away.

There!

The shadow moved again. Toward him. No, it had been moving all along. It had crept toward him. It zigzagged from larger shadow to larger shadow. Not a hyena, but a lion. A lion with its belly pressed into the savanna. Thirty feet and closing. He gripped the .32. It felt so small. So useless.

He shifted his body. Then cursed himself for losing sight of the shadow. Somehow it had vanished from the last spot where he had a fix on it.

There!

He picked it up again. This time a shadow within a shadow. But moving still. Now at twenty feet. It stopped.

He raised his pistol. No point in playing games. Not at this range. If the terrorist had a rifle, he probably would've used it by now.

It vanished again.

He waved the pistol and turned his body. The Bedouin should have shot him by now. Why—?

But no. The stalker would not want to alert Night Runner. By now he could tell any average Force Recon Marine from a Robert Night Runner Force Recon Marine.

Only the thought of Runner kept Swayne's trigger finger from probing every shadow in the night with a bullet. Only panic could make a man lose it like that.

He grappled with fear, threw up logic, and came up with a plan.

They had rehearsed sign-countersigns. In most combats they had little need of them. Their high-tech toys all but eliminated battlefield identity problems.

The technique wasn't new or even very clever. But it

had always worked for U.S. forces because of their pop culture. Swayne laid his aim on the most likely of three shadows to attack him. He called out his sign. "Forrest Gump's mother."

Night Runner, if it was Night Runner in his pistol sight, would know the reply, but not one Arab in ten million would.

Swayne saw the shadow morph into a more compact form, a form about to spring. He squeezed the slack from the .32-caliber's trigger.

"SALLY FIELD," NIGHT Runner said. And rewrote the combat equation.

As a kid he'd hidden himself beside game trails waiting for hours until bands of deer would pass by. He would put out a finger and scratch them from shoulder to flank as if his nail were a twig. As a teen, he had tracked a cock pheasant through the thickets undetected, reached out with both hands, and picked up the bird, which was so astonished that it did not struggle or even flap until he tossed it into the air to release it. As a young man getting ready to go to boot camp after quitting college, he had stalked a black bear sow grazing in the high meadows one summer and slapped her plump rump. Until he struck her, she did not know she was being followed. Startled, she had run off, looking over her shoulder, and had run into a ponderosa pine, knocking herself silly.

He vowed to someday pull the same stunt with a grizzly bear. After plotting the perfect escape.

This night he had stalked an even more dangerous, more wary creature. Bin Gahli's tracker. He had followed his scent rather than his tracks until the smell became so powerful that Night Runner's nose dripped.

He had seen the man pull a short, curved sword from his belt and creep to within five meters of the captain before Swayne raised his pistol and gave the sign. *That Swayne. Always so cool in a pinch.*

Night Runner found himself two meters short of where he could make a sure attack. If he leapt without giving the reply, Swayne would shoot at the motion. If he called out as he closed in, the terrorist would have time to turn and slash with his sword. If he kept silent, Swayne might begin shooting anyhow, taking potshots at all the shadows. So Night Runner lay flat on the ground. At just the moment when he might have reached out and slapped his grizzly bear on the ass. Or more to the point, bury his bayonet blade in the spot at the base of the tracker's skull.

When he spoke the countersign, Bin Gahli's tracker sprang into the air like a gymnast off a trampoline. Night Runner would have laughed, as he did when the frightened black bear collided with the tree. Except that this quarry was more dangerous than even a grizzly. Night Runner expected an attack. He would meet it head-on.

But no. The tracker ran off, no longer a grizzly, but a black bear.

As Runner loped after the man, he came to know what had gone through the tracker's head. This was more than fear. More than panic.

Runner had sneaked up as nobody had ever done to the tracker. He had closed to a short lance-toss. He had spoken Sally Field's name so close to the man's shoulder. He had blown holes in the man's self-confidence. He had destroyed not only the man's composure, but the man himself.

The tracker now ran in a full-blown state of terror.

Night Runner kept him in sight. He tensed himself to sidestep. He dared not err now. He had won this fight, down to the final stroke. But he must not strike wide. He must not get too cocky. Must not give away the victory.

He doubted the Iraqi could keep up the pace for long. He might be strong, might have the endurance for plodding through the desert all day long. But by the smell of him, Night Runner knew the man was also a smoker, lacking the deep lung capacity for mid-distances, races which Night Runner had won in high school and college.

Even worse, the more the coward ran, the more the panic

would eat up his reserves of strength. He was all but done.

The man knew he was the prey and no longer the stalker. He must also know he was at his hour.

Once he spun around in full stride, and almost fell, slashing his lethal sword into the space behind him.

But Night Runner had taken a parallel track two full meters behind and to the right of the man's right shoulder.

Night Runner ran naked. He knew he would, once and for all, earn the warrior's name that had been given him in his adolescence. He saw himself as the descendant of that Blackfeet brave Heavy Runner. He imagined himself going into hand-to-hand combat wearing only a breechclout. Or, as now, nothing.

And using an ancient Indian way that the white man claimed as his own, visualization, he had seen himself in a vision. He had watched his victory many times last night and today. Any second now, he would play out that vision. He alone would emerge from this running battlefield. In just moments there would no longer be any question as to who was the best tracker, the most effective fighter, the most ruthless warrior alive.

FOR ONE FLEETING second, Swayne felt a twinge of anger at Night Runner. Had he tried to sneak up on him? If so, Swayne had almost shot him and he'd give him hell for—

Then, he saw the two shadows bolt into the night, and he knew. What was he thinking? Of course he knew. Runner wouldn't pull a stunt like that. The very idea of it had just been his fear talking.

Swayne did not waste time debating his options. It would do little good for him to run after that pair on this landscape. At night? That'd be nuts. And he would not do well to stay where he was either. What if Bin Gahli still lay out there?

For lack of any better idea, he backtracked a half mile. Away from the fire and Salman Pak felt safest. He did not keep to a line, though, and six times made quick and random turns. Finally he settled into a spot that would allow him to watch his back trail in case Bin Gahli showed up.

Then he waited, his pistol at the ready. He worked out a new sign-countersign. Once *Sally Field* had been spoken, the enemy had it too. If Night Runner should not be the one coming back to find him—

Forget that, he told himself. Night Runner would be back. That was all there was to it.

NIGHT RUNNER'S SPIRITS flew higher with every new and fearful stride of the tracker. The Iraqi was not the master of battle that he'd imagined after all. He did make mistakes, even fatal ones—soon to be fatal.

Runner went into the frightened man's head. He knew his very thoughts. He had misjudged Night Runner. He had been so sure of sneaking up on his man that he did not even consider that Night Runner had left his own smell behind in his clothes. Or that anybody could track a Bedouin by scent. Worse, he had not kept in shape for war. He had not trained to sustain a chase such as this. He'd thought he would always be the chaser. He was too arrogant to consider that he might ever be the chasee.

And now he lagged. His breath came in gasps. His gait broke after only a quarter mile. Now he did little better than stagger. And his mind, now in full panic with his body, had shut down in its ability to think clear thoughts and act clever. He telegraphed his moves now.

The tracker turned and sliced the night again with his sword.

But Night Runner had seen it coming two steps before, when the man tried to reset his footwork in a kind of two-step dance move. When the sword flashed by, Night Runner roared, throwing out his arms, as if he would leap like a cougar. And he did leap. But not ahead. He ducked to his left rather than at the man, diving under the arc of the swing. He tucked his head, rolled, and came up on his feet in a low crouch.

The tracker did a double-take, cutting at where his attacker should have been first, then slashing belatedly in the direction Night Runner went. But Runner had dived clear of that spot too. Long before. The third awkward slash tripped up the tracker and sent him sprawling on his back. He rolled, tucked, and gained his feet. Cutting the space all around him in yet another frightened sweep of his blade.

No Night Runner. The tracker faced a bush in the shadows of the moonlight.

Night Runner crouched and called to the man from the rear. The tracker spun, lost his balance, carved the empty air, and gasped in his frenzy.

Runner stayed put. He should not toy with this bastard, but make short work of him.

He faked a second leap. The tracker didn't buy it this time, but stepped into the move and threw a sharp uppercut with his scimitar. If Runner had pulled the same stunt as before, he would have taken the edge full through the gut.

But he'd learned never to repeat a move with this fox of the desert. This time he held his ground. He threw sand instead of his body.

The tracker, eyes wide open to meet the attack, took the grit full in the face. He moaned and slapped at his eyes. Not in pain so much, thought Night Runner. But in that spasm of fear that comes from knowing the fight is ended. The tracker turned a full circle, blindly flailing with his sword.

Night Runner waited until the blade had passed by, then stepped in, delivering a hard slap with his left hand, cupping it to the man's right ear in full force, exploding his eardrum.

Then he leaped back, hearing the snick of the knife blade cutting the air where he had been.

The tracker, now off balance, staggered to his right. Night Runner waited until he saw the man's weight shift to his right leg, then flicked out his left foot, delivering a kick like a soccer player volleying the ball out of the air. His instep struck the outside of the man's right knee. The kick blew out the tracker's knee. The leg buckled, and he went down, groaning in pain and wheezing for air. A pathetic package of fright.

Night Runner visualized his end game. The man's eyes were shut in agony. But he would struggle to keep them open, desperate to fend off a killing blow. Night Runner leaped straight up, kicking out in turn with both feet, not at the man, but to fling more sand into his face.

Once he landed, Night Runner stepped back and waited for the final act. Blinded, the tracker swung his sword in a wide arc. Night Runner stepped inside the arc with one foot and threw his own knee into the tracker's nose. The man would never use it well again, even if he lived through the night. Which he would not. His lifetime now was measured in seconds, not nights.

Flat on his back, the tracker slashed away.

Runner had long ago left the killing radius. He knew the tears, the sand, the wrecked eardrum, and the blood in the smashed nose had all but disarmed his enemy. The Blackfeet warrior had stolen all his enemy's senses. The only weapon left to the man was that remarkable sword. Runner kicked the damaged knee again, and skipped back. When the tracker swiped down at him, he hacked into his own leg above the knee.

Some sword.

Night Runner marveled at that blade. One stroke and off with his own leg.

The tracker had had it. And he knew it. He groaned and called out something in his language. Night Runner did not know the words, only the tone. Resignation, the Arabic version of "uncle." The man lay still, arm—and sword—at his side.

Night Runner stepped on the wrist and put all his weight on it, pinning the hand and the weapon to the ground. The tracker did not struggle. Instead, he lifted his chin like a gladiator offering his throat, accepting his defeat and death with honor.

Through the sole of his foot, Runner felt the body tense and knew he dared not buy the surrender. He leaped back—

As the tracker's other hand swept up at him, a dagger jabbing the air where Runner's groin had been.

Runner kicked out. The dagger went spinning into the night. In one motion, he stepped on the wrist again, knelt, and delivered a killing stroke, burying his bayonet up to his fist in the soft triangle beneath the sternum. For good measure he carved an arc of his own—inside the tracker's thorax, visualizing heart and lungs being severed from their trunks of circulation, the large veins and arteries emptying in seconds into the chest cavity. It was like killing him twice.

For he would have bled to death on his own. From the lost leg.

But he could not be left to die on his own. He could not depart this world in peace. He would not be allowed to fall asleep. He had to be killed.

And even twice was not enough. Not for Night Runner.

This man was one of those who'd killed Potts.

Not even killing him ten times over was enough.

AT FIRST, SWAYNE thought he heard a shriek of pain. Then he realized the call was a cry of victory. Whose victory he did not know until five of the longest minutes of his life had passed.

Once again, he saw the shadows move.

Swayne called out over the .32-cal at the end of his arm, "Mark McGwire's record."

"Four better than Sammy Sosa, nine better than Roger Maris, ten better than Ruth," said Night Runner, moving himself and his shadow silently into Swayne's space. The space behind him.

Swayne shuddered. *How did the man do that?*

He turned and saw that Night Runner carried his boots and clothes. "The tracker?"

"Done."

"Bin Gahli?"

"I found his trail. He's off to Salman Pak."

Swayne went silent. He could not see the face, but he could sense the change in Night Runner. Something had changed within his very character. Swayne might ask about that later. Or he might not. Not that it mattered. He doubted Night Runner would ever tell him what it was.

Better to keep to the business at hand for now. So he shared his thoughts about how they might infiltrate Salman Pak.

His thoughts about Nina he kept to himself.

IN NINA'S EXPERIENCE all of male-kind could be reduced to a handful of generalizations. Generalization One: If a man failed to make eye contact with you, he was as good as out the door. That was the feeling she had had when Bin Gahli returned to the compound looking tired and harried. She had stood at the inner compound's fence and watched him, but he had never once looked her way. He'd hissed and pissed in Arabic at the Iraqi regular army officer in charge. Then he'd stalked off in the direction of a field kitchen at the back of the warehouse to fill his hideous face.

Okay, so he was history. Perfectly fine with her. Never had she been so grateful for the loss of a man. Not only that, Weasel Face had not returned with Bin Gahli. She wondered. Could he have fallen victim to the Americans? Or was that too much to ask for?

Two hours later, as she tossed on a cot, she heard Bin Gahli's voice again. She did not need an interpreter to tell her that he was quarreling with the same Iraqi officer. Soon their voices approached the fence. She peeked out from behind cracked eyelids. Big trouble. Bin Gahli glared at her, more venom in his face than she'd ever seen in the desert.

Generalization Two: When a man stopped avoiding your gaze and began staring, he was coming after you. All at once she knew the meaning of the phrase *murder in his eyes*.

At the outer gate to the tiny prisoner-of-war compound the Iraqi officer barked a command, and the pair of guards stepped into Bin Gahli's way. Big mistake. Bin Gahli flicked a huge left fist into one's solar plexus, a right to the other's jaw. Before they could hit the floor, he grabbed both by the back of their collars and smeared their faces—and their blood—into a roll of razor wire. Then he jettisoned them to the concrete. Bad for them, thought Nina. But nothing like the bundle of bad she was in for.

The Iraqi regular, apparently an officer of some rank, protested. Not adamantly enough for Nina. Bin Gahli turned his lethal gaze onto the officer. The man paled, turned to mumbling. Finally his words petered out.

Bin Gahli held out his hand. The Iraqi officer handed over a ring of keys. In seconds, Bin Gahli had Nina by the throat, backing her up against the wire, tearing at her clothes.

"Wassamatter?" she gasped through her constricted throat.

"The matter," he said in perfect English, "is that I am now going to deliver on my promise. First to ravish you." He laughed like a character out of an old Dracula movie. "I rather like the word *ravish*, don't you?"

She was too astonished to reply. And too much engaged in trying to recall all the nasty things she had said to him while under the impression that his understanding of English was so poor.

"You never needed a translator."

"Rather obvious, wouldn't you say?"

"Then why?"

"I kept you around because I thought it funny when you insulted me. Nobody does that to me anymore. Not since I developed my reputation. I quite enjoyed it."

She gargled, "No more? I could really rip you, you know. I haven't said much about your hideous face yet."

He tightened his grip on her throat. "No. I'll ravish you first. Then I'm going to kill you."

"For insulting you?" she gagged. "I could apologize, you know."

He pulled her up onto her toes, touching his pitted nose to hers. "Not even your best, most sincere regret would change the fact that you are an American, my mortal enemy. So I would still kill you."

She laughed.

He relaxed his grip a little.

"What?" she said.

"You're not crying."

It struck her at last. He *wanted* her to cry. He *needed* her to cry. Nobody ever stood up to this creep. Until he made her cry, she might live. God, it might be painful. But at least it would be life.

She laughed as wickedly as she could.

He retightened his grip. "What do you find so humorous?"

"The Americans," she gasped. "The Marines. They kicked your ass all over the desert, didn't they?" When he didn't respond, except by tightening the vise of his hand even more, she added, "And Jaffari. He's dead by now, isn't he?"

"Hardly," Bin Gahli said without conviction. "I've left him to set an ambush for your three Marines."

"Still three left then," she gagged. "Have they wiped out the rest of your Girl Scout troop?"

Furious, he shook her by the throat.

Her face red for lack of air, she raised an eyebrow at him. "Yes. They did get the weasel, didn't they?"

"No."

"Then where is he? Shouldn't he be back by now?"

"No."

She saw the eyes flicker. She knew what that meant. It was a lie. The weasel was overdue.

"No. He's dead. And they'll get you too. You're through, you butt-ugly son of a bitch."

Still holding her in the grip of one iron hand, he tore with the other hand at her Dan Rather jacket. The bastard was going to ravish her, as he put it, in front of United Nation's UNSCOM team. He could do that, she supposed. But not even that would make her cry.

Out of the corner of one eye, she saw a movement. One of the UNSCOM team members crossed the little prison.

"Stay out of this, Englishman," Bin Gahli muttered without taking his eyes off her.

An Englishman was to be her white knight? God save the queen.

"Right uncivil that. Might we discuss this?" the Brit said.

"Discuss?" she squeaked. In another minute, Nina knew she was going to be unconscious for lack of air. "No discussion," she whimpered, although barely a sound escaped her throat.

"No discussion," Bin Gahli echoed.

"Surely you would negotiate—"

"Piss off." Bin Gahli turned his hideous gaze from Nina to the would-be white knight.

Who shuffled away to lose himself in the cluster of U.N. observers. So much for a United Nations rescue. Where were the Americans in that group? she wondered. Was it a rule of the United Nations that once you put on the blue helmet you turned into a coward? Were there no white knights left—

A general commotion started up near the main entrance to the warehouse. Nina's vision had started to close in on her, but her hearing was still good enough over the sound of her pulse thumping in her ears that she knew a helicopter was about to land on the roof. Hope held back the fog of unconsciousness. *Marines! The Marines have landed.*

Her white knight had come to rescue her after all. Jack Swayne and his band of patriotic killers had dropped out of the sky. They would kick ass on these bastards. And plant a lethal boot in Bin Gahli's ass. After that, she planned to dump on these UNSCOM boys, telling the world about their cowardice. And maybe have Swayne's group kick their asses too for good measure.

She heard shouting over the rush of white noise in her ears. Bin Gahli released her throat, and she fell to the concrete gasping.

The Marines were coming! Her white knights, the Marines were coming after all!

She flattened out on the cement. Gunfire would rip Bin

Gahli in two, but she'd be safe. Bin Gahli—

The shouting died down. All she heard was the clatter of boot heels across the concrete. Metal on cement. *The Marines wore boots with metal taps?*

She stood up, shaking her head to clear her vision.

And there he was. The man who had saved her life. None other than Saddam Hussein, the scourge of the Great Satan America himself.

"Son of a bitch," she said.

Bin Gahli turned to her and lifted one corner of his fat mouth by way of a smile. "Would you like me to translate for you?"

She stifled a heartsick laugh at the irony.

Bin Gahli and Saddam launched into a sputtering, hacking conversation. She couldn't help notice how short Saddam was. Five feet six inches, tops. She glanced at his boots, then looked away so nobody would notice that she had noticed. For Pete's sake, the man wore elevator combat boots with heels easily two inches thick and soles to match. The leader of the world's leading terrorist nation wore shoes right out of Pee-Wee Herman's Great Adventure? If the man ever fell off them, he would break a hip.

After they had jabbered for a while, Bin Gahli looked Nina's way and mugged a look of disappointment.

"The great and glorious Saddam won't let me kill you," he said.

She felt her world had crumbled. Sure, on the plus side, who wouldn't want her life spared? But the UNSCOM team had livers the color of Grey Poupon. And her white knight's soul was black as a beetle.

Bin Gahli shrugged. "I can't rape you either. The president is going to fly you back to Baghdad with him."

She shook her head, her puzzled expression asking the question she was too stunned to speak: *But why?*

"So you, as a respected member of the press, the world's second-oldest profession, can tell world about his boundless compassion and merciful nature," Bin Gahli said, making no effort to hide his cynicism.

"Ahhh," Nina said. Finally, she understood. "And his terms for the release of the UNSCOM team."

"That too," Bin Gahli said. "After they inspect the helicopter wreckage."

"And? I hear an *and* in there."

"And to announce the engagement between you and me." Bin Gahli smiled, baring jagged, discolored teeth she'd not seen in such close-up before. At a distance they'd looked like whale teeth. Up close the Arab's gaping mouth reminded Nina of the side of the barn in winter back at the family homestead in Vermont. The side where all the farm dogs peed on each other's markings, leaving putrid, yellow icicles.

The smile was as vile as the man. Lacking in either humor or warmth. Fueled instead by the man's evil intentions, chiefly what he would do to her once she'd served his cousin's purposes. She'd never pictured herself as an Islamic wife, and doubted she'd ever be one. At least not for long. If Bin Gahli didn't kill her, she'd do the job herself.

If anything could make her cry—

No, goddammit. Not even that.

OUTSIDE THE COMPOUND Swayne and Night Runner had measured the time, two minutes, between sentries, who traveled in fours between the first two outer fences. Between the second and third fence, guards walked in pairs, but with leashed dogs, and traveling in the opposite direction, also two minutes apart. Swayne and Night Runner agreed that this was an unusually strong security force at a high state of alert. That was before the first Land Rover patrol made its circuit outside the wire, driving by with its tactical lights shielded from the air.

Night Runner turned his face to give Swayne a *What the hell is going on?* expression.

Swayne shook his head and murmured, "I know. It's almost too much security, even if the UNSCOM team is inside. It's a dead giveaway to satellite intelligence. They must know that after all they've been pounded since Desert Storm."

"Unless it's a move to make the world think the team's inside."

Swayne bit his lip. *Which was it?*

To the left, down the road five miles toward Baghdad, a tank battalion had straddled the highway. To the east, in the direction of the Iran border, tanks and infantry had done the same thing. North of the compound, somewhere out of sight, the noise of generators and vehicles moving suggested another military unit on standby. Perhaps a surface-to-air-missile battery to provide air-defense support for Salman Pak. But suddenly all the generators at the site went silent.

"There is one other thing," said Swayne.

"The Pope is making a visit?"

"Think about it. Only the Pope would get that much protection. Unless—"

"You don't suppose—"

A pair of helicopters sped in at low level from the northwest. They landed inside the compound, on the roof of the huge warehouse. From their position Swayne and Night Runner could see a squad of heavily armed men—*big* heavily armed men—run from each bird to secure the roof. The helicopters then took off and took up flying a racetrack pattern over the spot that Swayne had guessed was the missile site. Finally, a lone helicopter approached high and slow. It too landed on the roof. A party of five dismounted.

The sentries moving around the perimeter speeded up. Dogs began yapping around the compound as if picking up on the nervous energy of their handlers.

"Somebody very important is on that building," Swayne said. "Those guards are scared, very scared."

Night Runner said, "If it isn't the Pope—"

"El Presidente himself. Saddam Hussein."

Night Runner whistled silently. "We're never going to get in there. Those bastards on the roof would kill their own mothers if they tried to get near Saddam."

Swayne lit the dial on his wristwatch, the only electronic device that still worked for him. The only other pieces of technology that had survived this event were Friel's .32 and a penlight. "Twenty minutes until the pickup bird reaches Friel's position," he said. "After that, ten minutes until he comes for us."

"Yes, but before we can do anything useful, we need to figure out what *they're* doing." Runner turned to Swayne. "Don't we?"

Swayne got the message. Night Runner expected him to come up with a plan. He lowered his head and rubbed hard at his temples. "I'm thinking, I'm thinking."

Night Runner waited quietly.

"Say it is Hussein," Swayne said. "That's why they shut down the missile site, and that's why the helicopters are flying over it right this minute—so some joker with a taste for revenge or power can't fire it up and take out the dictator's bird."

"Figures," Night Runner said. "But what about the tanks?"

"Because of our little firefight yesterday"—was it only yesterday and not a month ago that so much had happened to them?—"they must be worried that we know where they are keeping the UNSCOM team. They'd like to move the team to a different hiding place, but they're worried about doing it without a heavy escort. Trouble is, because Saddam is making an inspection visit, they're not allowed to bring a field unit carrying live ammo within five miles of his paranoid person."

Night Runner chuckled. "I wonder if they know that they're up against two measly guys on the verge of exhaustion, armed with a couple shivs, a pellet pistol, and an AK with eight stinking bullets."

"Two measly Force Recon Marines," Swayne corrected. "And one of them a Blackfeet warrior."

By way of appreciation, Runner simply touched Swayne's shoulder.

Swayne outlined a hasty plan, thankful for the darkness.

Because he couldn't see Night Runner's face, he wouldn't be shaken by the inevitable incredulity. And more importantly, he wouldn't betray his own misgivings to the sergeant.

FRIEL FOUGHT OFF a feeling of abandonment. He kept telling himself that his part in the mission was vital to the team. Force Recon Marines, being such a small unit anyhow, almost never separated themselves to perform individual actions. On the rare occasions when they did split, such actions never lasted long. Gunny Potts should be here on this LZ with him. If the team had not lost all commo, Friel would be with the captain and the sergeant.

Yeah-buddy, he told himself. They had not really bailed on his ass. And his job was to see that the bonehead pilots didn't bail on anybody either. If they tried—hell, if they even thunk it out loud—he'd kick—

He heard it!

The extraction bird. At first it sounded to Friel like the buzz of a flying beetle, the sound harmonizing with the swish of rotor wind. Friel had heard the sounds often enough. A stealth-equipped chopper.

He pulled a once-over on himself. Sure enough, he looked like a geek at the shore, covered with sand from the neck down, a bundle wrapped in cloth on his chest.

And he waited like a happy-as-a-pig-in-shit, oiled-down hunk at the sunny shore. Except for the lack of the ocean, the beach, the sun, and the oil. And, oh, yeah, the *happy* shit.

THE LAND ROVER'S crew of two, a driver and the sergeant of the guard riding shotgun, could be forgiven for not seeing the signs that Night Runner had left. For he had brushed them out after crossing the path that had turned into liquid dust from the incessant circling of guard vehicles around Salman Pak. Anybody could have overlooked the irregular dirt pile that lay against the base of the outer security fence.

And it was only human for the driver to slam on his

brakes at the apparition that materialized in the beam of his blackout drive light. A monster rose out of the rivers of dust. As if the devil had dug his way out of hell. Then, as if to prove it was not merely a ghost, the monster threw heaps of sand onto the windshield, blocking their vision. The vehicle rocked as the creature leapt onto the hood of the Land Rover.

Still, the driver could have saved his and his companion's lives. He could have gunned the Rover.

But he hesitated because he couldn't see out the windshield. He might have laid on the horn too, to attract attention. He could have drawn his pistol and fired through the windshield.

He did none of these. Just sat, wide-eyed and immobilized.

True, for no more than two seconds.

But long enough for Night Runner to spring from his disguise as the dirt pile at the base of the fence.

Long enough for him to run up to the Rover and tap on the driver's window with his left hand, even as he threw his right, putting all his weight behind it. The driver swiveled his head.

As the blade of Night Runner's bayonet drove through the glass, into the driver's left eye. The window shattered, and Night Runner's thrust kept going until the blade pierced the back of the man's skull.

Meanwhile, the sergeant riding shotgun turned in his seat as the monster on the hood dropped to the ground and jerked open the passenger door.

SWAYNE FOUND HIMSELF face-to-face with an Iraqi in panic. All the man wanted to do was get out of the truck. Maybe run away. Maybe start screaming. He opened his mouth and sucked his lungs full of air. Swayne, fearful that the walking sentries might be within earshot, gave the man a quick left-right combination. His left buried the spike of the AK bayonet in the man's right lung. His right smashed the Iraqi in the mouth.

The Iraqi sergeant was fatally astonished, but Swayne was nearly as surprised. His right hand must have picked up a magical quality in the time he had spent in the desert. For when he struck the sergeant's face, the Iraqi lost his head. Literally. The face adorned with the ubiquitous Saddam-Stalin brush mustache flew from the man's shoulders into the rear of the vehicle. Swayne was too stunned by the sight of it even to think about the pain to his knuckles. Or even to get out of the way of the spray of blood and air coming from the man's severed neck, a powerful exhalation that should have been a call for help.

"Let's go, Captain," Night Runner said, already sitting in the driver's seat, brandishing a crescent-shaped sword. The steel glistened with gore. "Did I mention the tracker's sword? Some blade, huh? I swear I barely touched the guy with it."

Swayne came to his senses and dragged the headless corpse out of the Land Rover. He dropped it into the twenty inches of dust in the roadbed. The body sank out of sight.

Night Runner began idling forward even before Swayne had jumped in. Swayne checked his watch. "Fifteen seconds," he said. "Could have been faster if I hadn't gone ga-ga there."

Night Runner reached out his window and dusted off a spot so he could see where he was driving. "I was more than a little ga-ga myself. I swear. If my people had had this kind of a weapon—" He shut his mouth on the rest of his thought. And changed the subject. "I don't think we've been spotted."

Swayne searched the Rover for weapons. In the back, along with the head, he came up with a new AK-47, fully loaded, which he propped up on the floorboards next to Night Runner's knee. For himself, he checked the action and load on a sawed-down shotgun. It was a Kmart-variety Mossberg 12-gauge pump, loaded with six three-inch shells—Federal brand, ironically enough.

After filling his jacket pockets from a box of Federals—

double-aught buckshot—he knelt on the seat to search for more stuff.

That head. He wanted to throw it out, but worried that he might not get it far enough from the road. Nothing tipped off an enemy to a sneak attack like littering the area with enemy heads.

He came across a set of Jason-brand sporting binoculars and a Sony portable CD player powered by the very batteries the pink bunny was always hawking on television.

He held them up for Runner to see. "Who the hell is selling all this stuff to Saddam in the middle of a so-called embargo?"

Before either could answer his question, he found the answer to a three-day-long prayer. He didn't say anything, just moaned in relief as the Land Rover reached the halfway point in its circuit around the compound.

Night Runner said, "Water?"

"The mother lode."

They each greedily pulled at one of the quart-sized foil packets of water. Rivers of mud swelled up at the corners of their mouths and drained into their collars. Swayne burped and handed off a second packet, pointing at the logo on it: the International Red Crescent.

"So much for aid to the Iraqi on the street."

Night Runner grunted. Then he convulsed, spewing a fountain out the window of the Land Rover. Undaunted, he gulped a second quart.

A radio speaker crackled on the dash of the Land Rover as it approached the main gate of the compound. Night Runner and Swayne looked into each other's eyes.

"I don't know either," Swayne said, answering the question on Night Runner's mud-splashed face. "Whatever you do, don't stop."

Swayne had thought at first they might get into the compound by easing through the gate in the Land Rover. Not now. A full platoon of Iraqi soldiers stood in a cluster at the sally port.

As they drove by, one of the soldiers made the motion of picking up a telephone and putting it to his ear.

Night Runner leaned forward and banged his fist on the dash, making a motion of his own—to tell the Iraqi they were having radio problems.

"Don't look back," Swayne cautioned. "He's giving you the signal to come over. If you don't see it, you can't come." He began pounding on the dash as well, sneaking the glance over his shoulder in time to see a finger gesture.

"We're clear," Swayne said.

"But can we afford to come around again?" Night Runner asked.

"No." Swayne wiped the mud off his chin with a sleeve, leaving more filth on his face than he'd cleaned away. He checked his watch for the dozenth time in the last ten minutes. "If something doesn't give inside that building by the time we come around again, we're just going to have to abandon the U.N. and head for the hills."

"Yeah," said Night Runner, "and what a shame that would be."

NINA HAD JUST learned that Bin Gahli might not be so agreeable after all to letting his cousin Saddam use her as the news outlet for the Iraqi propaganda machine.

She took the news with more than a grain of fear. "And what about our marriage?" she asked Bin Gahli, her throat throbbing at the effort of speaking.

He snorted, exposing the piss icicles of his most sardonic smile yet. "Ours will be the briefest of engagements." He took her by the arm and led her to the stairway. Saddam followed, flanked by the two biggest bodyguards Nina had ever seen. "We're going for a helicopter ride," Bin Gahli said. "Unfortunately for you, it will end in tragedy."

Nina hesitated on the steps, but Bin Gahli dragged her upward. She regained her composure as they reached the roof. "So," she said, "I'm going to make an escape attempt from a thousand feet?"

"Something like that."

"You can kill me," she said.

"Indeed I can."

"But you'll never make me cry."

His hideous eyes widened, incredulous, as if she'd just stolen his most precious secret. Then they narrowed to dark, evil, glittering slits.

"We'll see about that."

The helicopter turbines began to whine. So did Nina, but she cut off the sound so she would not humiliate herself. Once again, for the third time in as many days, she admonished herself to die with dignity.

FRIEL COULD NOT relax until he was sure the Night Hawk, now on final approach, would not flatten his ass. When he saw the craft touch down forty meters away, its outline a shade blacker than the night sky, he rolled over, raising a dust storm, stood up, and ran bent beneath the blades to the cabin door.

It gave him a brief thrill when the crew chief slid open the cargo doors and stepped outside to look around. Because Friel was already standing next to the helicopter. He climbed aboard, set down his bundle carefully, and reached back out to tap the crew chief on the shoulder. The man shrugged to show he couldn't see anybody. But when he came face-to-face with Friel's mask of sores and mud, he leapt backward, tripped, and fell on his butt.

Friel didn't have time to enjoy. How often could anybody say he had defeated the night-vision capability, including space-age thermal IR detectors, of the most sophisticated night-fighting helicopter on earth? And stowed himself away besides? But he had Iraqis to fry.

He grabbed a headset off the transmission bulkhead and spoke over the intercom, passing along the magnetic heading that Night Runner had given him.

That done he turned to the still-astonished crew chief and leaned close so the man could get the full effect of his scabbed-over face and wild eyes.

"If you gimme a drink a water, I promise not to kiss your ass."

• • •

As Night Runner slowed the Land Rover, Swayne climbed into the backseat, kicked the Iraqi head out of the way, and trained his binoculars on the rooftop. "Bingo Saddam," he said.

"Nina Chase?" Night Runner asked.

"Her too," Swayne said with no joy. "And Bin Gahli. It doesn't look good."

"How so?"

"She just gave him a knee to the family jewels."

"And?"

Swayne took the binos away from his eyes, deciding he did not want to watch. "He picked her up and threw her into the aircraft." Swayne gulped. "He's working her over."

"Saddam?"

"He's amused. The son of a bitch."

Night Runner turned around to make eye contact with Swayne. "Want to try to take out the helicopter as it lifts off?"

Swayne didn't answer right away. He had killed, or been responsible for killing, any number of people, some of them women, not all of them by accident. But all in the line of duty. He had never, never once, killed somebody he knew personally, let alone a woman he had known in that other way.

He weighed the costs. He put his mind to looking for an equation that might save Nina's life. Nobody in the world would complain, probably not even his superiors, if Saddam died in a crash brought on by Force Recon Marines. People who knew of his deeds would applaud the death of Bin Gahli as well. The loss of Nina Chase, a CNN television reporter who had yet to air her first story, would not even make a footnote in history. Of the people who knew her, Swayne couldn't think of a single one who actually would admit to liking her.

Except for one. Who would now decide whether her life was worth the price of Saddam's and Bin Gahli's.

If that weren't enough, even as the helicopter's rotors began to pop as they screwed into the air, a huge beam of light as wide and as long as a football field lit up the Iraqi wasteland to the west of the compound. The huge hangar doors slid wide-open, releasing the white light of the interior.

Three Land Rovers similar to the one they had commandeered left the building in convoy. The white paint had been sprayed over—from the look of it, by hand with cans of flat primer. But the letters U.N. were visible underneath when the lights of the warehouse hit them just right. Swayne shook his head. The intel geek that had briefed this mission so long ago had told them UNSCOM was driving GMC Suburbans. Guy must have owned GM stock.

"What are you smiling about?" Night Runner asked.

"Nothing."

"What's our move?"

The very question on Swayne's mind. Crunch time, he thought. Time to make one of those decisions he was so poorly paid to make.

WHEN FRIEL FELT the Night Hawk bank left, he knew they had arrived at the loitering spot that Swayne had picked more than a mile short of Salman Pak. They set the bird down behind the last line of ridges to shield the craft from radar. He saw the copilot lean forward and punch a clock on the panel. Ten minutes. They were to loiter no longer than that. If they didn't get a signal to pick up Swayne and the chief by then, the Night Hawk was to get the hell out of Iraq.

Friel didn't think he could go with that. Yes, Swayne had told him that he and Night Runner could walk out of Iraq, as they had out of Canada last year. Still. Friel wasn't about to bail on them. If he had to hijack these Mooks—

He looked around the cabin. The way these flyboys looked at him, he might as well have been one of those bags of bugs that Night Runner had left for him to eat—which he had not. If he tried to mix it up with this group, they would kill him. Or he would kill them.

Maybe they'd put him out with some water and a rifle.

He thought about how he looked. Hell, yes, they'd put him out. And be glad as granny about it.

Listen to my ass, he thought. *Talking just like the gunny.*

He saw the crew chief, horrified, looking at him. He smiled his best winning smile. The crew chief backed away and almost fell out the open door of the Night Hawk. Screw him.

The gunny. He patted his bundle. Wouldn't the crew chief just shit if he opened that bundle? But he couldn't do that. Couldn't disgrace his gunny. He had to get the foot to where he could give it a decent burial. Out of Iraq.

Goddamn Iraq. No way was the Corps ever going to get him back in this country again. *Semper never.*

AT FIRST NINA regretted kicking Bin Gahli in the balls. Each time he had slapped her face—backhand, forehand, backhand—she'd regretted it a little more. When he punched her in the sternum, she considered asking for forgiveness. But once they were in the aircraft, she lying across the cabin floor, he lying across her, groaning and rubbing at his personality, she could not have been happier. If she could get free again she would finish the business of crushing his Easter eggs.

She caught a glimpse of Saddam leering at her, the head of state only too happy to have a front-row seat for violence. Rome came to mind. Tyrants of Rome. The things they did after they'd pushed decency to its limit and beyond. Tyrants in power as long as Saddam rated no better than Jeffrey Dahmer on a throne with a chain saw for a scepter.

Even so, Saddam had no idea what was at stake in this struggle. Not a contest for wealth or spy information or sex or money or national pride. None of those trivial things. But a battle for her very spirit.

She felt the aircraft skew, then lift off the ground and slide forward into the cool night air. Bin Gahli's sandaled feet stuck out, forcing the crew to leave the door open. If she could get free, she would make the leap herself. Anything but give in to this mutant with the mouth of a dragon who would eventually throw her out anyhow.

She stiffened, clenching her legs together, her arms against her sides, her hands formed into fists, her mouth and eyes clamped shut. The end would come, and she would welcome it. The only trouble was that it might not come soon enough for her.

And where was her white knight? Her Jack Swayne? Her savior, her lover, her life? The Marines, if indeed the Marines had landed, had done their work. They'd plastered Abboud Dahni and bugged out. Leaving her to her fate.

She made the sound of spitting that only she could hear. White knight indeed. What a crock!

Had it not been for Bin Gahli, she would truly have cried.

ONCE SWAYNE MADE up his mind, he had to leave the execution—the literal execution—to Night Runner, armed with the AK-47. Swayne's shotgun would never reach the helicopter, and if it did, its ball bearings wouldn't have the velocity left to do any damage.

Swayne gave the word. Night Runner did not hesitate, even for a second. He stopped the Land Rover, stepped out, checked the chamber of the AK-47, lifted the rifle, and fired. On auto. He kept up the chatter until the tail rotor of the helicopter spun itself to bits.

The aircraft went out of control. The tail boom went right. The nose tucked. The craft rolled on its belly axis, setting up to crash-land on its rotor head.

Swayne could only guess at the terror going on inside the bird. People were tossed against the bulkheads and whipped into the night sky. He thought he saw a body ejected from the first craft sail into the rotor of the second.

When the two helicopters collided, it was like throwing two buzz saws together. The main rotor system of the lead helicopter sliced into the fuselage of the trailing bird.

And both aircraft, which had been trying to land in formation on the roof of the warehouse, burst into flames, spewing fuel, enveloping Saddam Hussein's Republican

Guard security force and the compound in flames.

The explosion attracted the attention of every pair of eyes within ten miles. Except for two.

Aboard the presidential aircraft, Saddam Hussein lay beside Nina. The pilots slewed left and dived, an evasive maneuver, the possibility of assassination never far from their minds. Holding his groin, Bin Gahli leaned against the center console between the two pilots, looking out the open door to watch the pair of security force aircraft burning as one, scorching their way through the roof of the warehouse at Salman Pak.

Commanders of the tank units east and west of Salman Pak put their units on full alert.

The presidential pilots did not turn for Baghdad. That was too predictable. They set a random course for the wilderness areas of Iraq. Until they could be sure the Iraqi Air Force hadn't joined in a coup attempt and would not intercept them on the way back to the capital.

THE MARINES PILOTING the Night Hawk helicopter didn't waste time telling how much they didn't like sitting naked in the desert. All the stealth technology in the world couldn't hide them from sight now that the landscape had been turned into a garden party lit by one gigantic Iraqi torch. The two flyboys decided they ought to leave early.

"Bullshit!" Friel said, pointing at the clock. "You've got seven minutes, and you're not leaving my people on the ground." He did not speak it as a threat. More an appeal. One Marine brother to another.

"Roger," said the abashed pilot, "we'll move a few miles to the east, then circle and come back. Don't worry, Corporal, we'll be here on time. But you had better hope your people are here, too. If they're not—"

He didn't finish the sentence. Didn't have to. Henry Friel knew the score.

Not that he'd go along when the chips began to fly. Friel kept his mouth shut. He might go along with leaving his people. He might not.

Nah. Not.

No way was he and Potts gonna let these Mooks leave their peeps.

NIGHT RUNNER FLOORED the Land Rover even before the fireball erupted. From here on out, Swayne thought, things were up to luck as much as skill and brains.

Their luck held. In that every Iraqi in the area turned to gawk at the fire. That ruined their night vision and gave the team an edge that would last long after the flames died down.

Their luck solidified. In that after the initial blast, the Iraqis driving the three UNSCOM Land Rovers sped up. That took them away out of range of the Iraqi soldiers at the compound gate.

Their luck improved. In that the Rover drivers kept their speed down, so Night Runner could catch up.

Still that luck held. In that Night Runner could drive parallel to the three-car convoy, doubling it on the far side. All the Iraqi guards and drivers were looking back at the fire when Night Runner turned to come at the lead vehicle from the opposite side.

Their Rover struck the lead vehicle, traveling fast enough to stun the occupants, but not so fast they would kill any of the UNSCOM team who might be inside.

Their dice remained hot.

Runner and Swayne both jumped clear of the wreck. Night Runner threw his package onto the hood of the second vehicle in the convoy. He fired his AK-47 at the Iraqis in the lead vehicle. One burst took out the driver and guard in the front seat. Even as they died, he shifted his eyes to I.D. passengers. All Iraqis. In seconds, all dead.

There'd be no pardon for killing a truck full of U.N. men. Only terrorists could get away with that.

Swayne's luck held as well. Night Runner's package had drawn the attention of everybody in the second vehicle in the convoy. And why wouldn't it? The severed head of the Iraqi sergeant bounced on the hood and came to rest, its vacant, wide eyes staring into the Land Rover.

By the time the Iraqis in the second Rover got over the shock, they had a new problem. Shotgun fire, one blast each from Swayne's 12-gauge.

At that point, the Force Recon charm began to run out. The second Land Rover crashed into the first. Swayne saw that the two cars had been smashed up. Neither would be any help in an escape.

The men in the third vehicle piled out and ran into the desert. Some had guns, some did not. Night Runner leaned over the hood of the first vehicle and brought his rifle to bear on the Iraqi driver of the third vehicle, standing outside his truck. One round put him away. The rest of the men, though, he did not know about.

Until Swayne yelled, "Everybody hit the ground!"

Runner repeated the command in French.

Six men in the second Land Rover fought each other to get closest to the deck. Six men in the desert dove to the ground.

One other man looked around, confused.

Still, Swayne could not tell. Did he have a weapon?

Finally, he began to crouch, turning as he did so, and Swayne saw the machine pistol coming around to bear on him.

Two blasts from his shotgun settled the issue. Shooting high, Swayne took him once in the head and once in the neck.

His assault rifle at the ready, Night Runner ran back to the third vehicle in line, shouting, "We're Americans! United States Marine Corps!"

"Back into the Land Rover," Swayne yelled.

Already, it might be too late. He heard diesel trucks roar across the compound. In the distance, he heard the squeal and clatter of tanks.

The men lying in the desert kept their grip on the sand.

Until Runner called, "We're pulling out in ten seconds whether you're in the vehicle or not."

They got that. These two really were Marines. Here to save them rather than execute them. They jogged toward the Land Rover. The UNSCOM team inside the second Rover didn't move. Swayne pulled open the door. "Anybody speak English in here?"

"Oui," said a meek voice. "A leetle."

"Tell your people to get out of here and into that third car."

The man spoke to his mates in French.

Swayne jogged back to the third vehicle. Four of the UNSCOM team from the second vehicle joined him.

Swayne looked back toward the second vehicle. "Why aren't the other two coming?" he asked.

An Englishman said, "They're Frenchmen. They—"

"Enough said!" Swayne barked. "We're out of here, Sergeant."

All Night Runner needed to hear. He juiced the Land Rover, and they were off.

There was no room inside for Swayne. It was packed with UNSCOM guys draped over each other. So Swayne grasped the side-view mirror and leaped onto the hood. As they drove toward the Night Hawk pickup site, Swayne fired his shotgun at shadows running at them. The buckshot might not do any damage at such a long range. But the shadows hit the ground just the same.

Three tanks pulled into line outside the compound and took the wrecked Rovers under fire. Before long all three were pillars of fire.

Swayne shook his head.

"French toast," said Runner.

As the Rover bounced along, Swayne worked out a new plan—hell, he'd not thought about getting this far, let alone to the Night Hawk. As far as he could tell, nobody was following. Until the Iraqis sorted out the bodies in the night, chaos would buy time for the good guys.

Finally, Night Runner let the Rover coast to a stop. He stepped out, reloaded his AK-47, pointed up a steep cliff, and looked to Swayne.

"Half a kilometer to the LZ," Night Runner said. The look on his face, barely lit by the glow in the sky, showed his chief fear. Swayne felt it too. If Zavello assumed they were all dead because of the daylong break in commo, there would be no pickup bird.

If not, they'd have to make a new set of plans. The UNSCOM team would have to give up to the Iraqis again. And live with the results of all the killings by the Spartans.

Swayne and Night Runner—and Friel, should they link up with him again—had no such options. For they would never surrender.

"Everybody out," Swayne said. Nobody moved. When he looked closer, he could see fear on all the faces. It hit him. As far as any of them knew, this was the UNSCOM cemetery.

Swayne softened his tone. "Men, there's a helicopter waiting for us less than a mile away. We should hurry."

The news got them moving. Ten men piled out of the Land Rover, untangling themselves, hardly anybody cursing at anybody else.

Considering the circumstances, thought Swayne, not bad.

DAY 3—1407 HOURS LOCAL

ZAVELLO HAD COME TO LIFE back at the OMCC. After days of gloom and doom, the single PERLOBE that had been planted among the Americans in the UNSCOM team had come to life. It had left the compound.

At first Zavello suspected the worst. That the UNSCOM team was being sent to different hiding places.

Then the PERLOBE had taken a path that defied all explanations. Off-road, into the outback of Iraq at high speed.

Zavello could only hope.

When the PERLOBE changed direction again, it moved much more slowly, as if its bearer was moving on foot. Zavello's heart leaped in his chest. Still, he dared not say anything, although others in the command center had begun to cluster around the computer monitor that he had been glued to for all this time.

Finally, Zavello muttered the happiest obscenities of his life. "It's headed toward the pickup point the Night Hawk called back to us. There's no way that a SCUM-SCUM or an Iraqi could know where that pickup point is. Only somebody on Swayne's team could know that."

Murmurs rose up behind him.

"Listen up," Zavello barked. "Don't anybody jinx this by saying a word. And give me that handset."

THE DESERT—0008 HOURS LOCAL

FRIEL WATCHED THE SECOND HAND SWEEP past the ten-minute mark. The copilot turned to look at him, then looked away quickly, cringing.

Friel didn't care what he looked like.

The pilot keyed his radio mike and kept it open a full ten seconds before giving his report, breaking radio silence. "Eagle, this is Night Hawk Two-Three. One soul on board. Departing LZ at this time."

Friel reached behind his back to pull out the .32-caliber pistol—but no, he had handed it over to the cap. The stupid idea of hijacking a Marine chopper didn't get any more brilliant with age, but he wasn't about to leave his team behind. Not unless they were dead.

He pulled his boot knife. He would give them one last chance to change their minds. Then he was going to take over the helicopter. He keyed the intercom of his microphone.

"Negative on the departure!"

Friel, his mouth open, his first word yet unsaid, couldn't believe that somebody had spoken his thoughts for him. A familiar voice.

"This is Eagle. Hold what you have. I have a PERLOBE return moving toward the LZ."

Colonel Zavello! No Marine enlisted man ever gets close to a Marine colonel, especially Colonel Satan, Friel thought. But if he could throw his arms around the one-eyed screamer of a full-flapping chicken colonel right now, he would hug and kiss him like a Boston hooker, lots of enthusiasm, no tongue.

He gave it a second thought.

Okay. Maybe just the hug.

QUANTICO—1409 HOURS LOCAL

WHEN ZAVELLO HEARD REPORT that ten members of UNSCOM had climbed aboard, along with two more Force Recon Marines, he closed his eye in relief. He fought back a tear.

His staff whacked backs all over the command center as Zavello fought to maintain his composure. It wouldn't do for anybody in the OMCC to suspect he was human.

He pulled off his headset. He put his wraparound sun shades over his satin eye patch. Then he closed his eye for real, thinking that he might stay in the chair for another eight hours. To get the first restful sleep he had had in days. A tear, hell. Only thing wrong with him was he needed some sleep. Swayne's team had worn his nerves to nubs. When they got back he was going to chew ass till Good Friday if they—

Zavello's exec let loose with an obscenity.

Zavello opened his eye, blinked at the GPS scope, and even wiped a hand across the screen.

But it was no mistake. That wasn't a gnat crawling across the scope.

That was a PERLOBE dot. A helicopter's. Instead of turning toward the south-southwest, to make its egress somewhere near the Saudi-Kuwaiti border, the dot turned due east. His Night Hawk, with the results of Event Scenario 15 safely on board—not counting the loss of one Marine (forget the Frogs Swayne had told him about in his quick report)—now flew right at Baghdad. To intercept a radar blip come out of the Iraqi interior.

SALMAN PAK—0031 HOURS LOCAL

"WE'RE NOT GOING TO GET AWAY WITH THIS, you know," the pilot said, even as he banked the Night Hawk to the right and laid it over onto its nose to get it to top speed.

"Better turn off your radios. Just a few minutes lost commo is all I need," Swayne said.

The pilot couldn't wait to shut off all his sets. Swayne could see he'd met Zavello already.

The copilot dimmed all the cabin lights. A screen on the console between the two pilots stayed bright. A strobe passed over the screen every second or so. A dot winked as it eased toward the center of the scope. Swayne didn't have to ask what it was.

The pilot told him anyway. "Air-to-air radar. That's Saddam's bird."

"We going to catch up?"

"Yep. Then what?"

"We'll just have to play it by ear."

"You better put those guys on the deck. Wouldn't look good to have a whole planeload of U.N. eyes. You know, in case you did a thing not so great."

Friel and Night Runner shoved the UNSCOM team to the deck. Swayne heard Friel shout, "Ack-ack!" To get them to move.

Swayne saw a form take shape in the sky, set off by the lights of Baghdad. Before long he could see into Saddam's craft.

The cabin lights blazed. The dictator sat between two clones. He smiled down at the deck of his craft, his eyes bugging like a nun's at a porno flick.

Swayne felt a nudge. Night Runner handed him the AK-47. Friel winked. This was Swayne's call alone.

The crew chief slid open the door wide enough for Swayne to poke the muzzle of the AK-47 an inch into the wind.

The nearest thug had leaned forward. Swayne could not get a clear shot at Saddam. Yet. He'd need just a glimpse. Or maybe a burst through the head of that bodyguard in his line of fire would do the job well enough. Two, maybe three thugs with one burst. He went through the litany—

One deep inhale—
Release and hold—
Take out the slack—
And feel the pulse—
Between the beats—

NINA DIDN'T CARE about what Bin Gahli might do to her. If only he'd get it over with. The knee to his groin had cut off his sexual fury. But it had raised his anger to a toxic level. He had a way of hitting her with pulled punches. The blows did not strike hard and fast enough to cut her skin. But the energy of each punch shot through muscle and bone into her internal organs. Her head throbbed. Her lungs stung. Her belly ached. If only he would get off her. She would go for her knife, the one in the buckle of her belt, and open him up like a tin of sardines.

He'd kill her, of course. She'd be glad to die. It'd be less painful than what he was doing to her now.

She should shed a tear. Get it over with.

She flinched when Bin Gahli reached over her head, but was relieved to find that he merely wanted to slide open the cabin door of the aircraft. He slid off her legs and grasped her by the ankles.

He was about to grant her wish. About to pull her out the door. She'd beaten the bastard. He'd given up trying to make her cry. He was taking the loser's way out.

She changed her mind. She didn't want to die.

She clawed her way across the helicopter's floor. So Bin Gahli opened the other door and began to push her out the opposite door.

She faked cramps, not much of a stretch. She wrapped her arms around her belly and found the knife handle.

As Bin Gahli slid her toward the opening.

Saddam called out. Nina guessed he wanted to know what the hell was going on. Cruelty was one thing, but was the bastard blind and stupid as well? Did it take a Rhodes scholar to see that Bin Gahli was about to give her the heave-ho? Or was Saddam trying to save her life? Like that'd happen.

Nina felt the seconds go by all too slowly.

At one, her hair flew into the slipstream of the helicopter. And she pulled at her knife.

At two, she could see but not hear Saddam give orders that had no effect on Bin Gahli. Through the slits of her swollen eyes, she found the scab of his face.

At three, she looked lower, to the neck, and in one swift motion, she slashed at his throat, the two-inch blade aimed for the jugular.

On four, Bin Gahli threw back his head.

Her knife all but missed, making no more than a scratch down his jaw. She knew she would not have time for a second swipe. Face it. She'd won the battle of tears but lost the war for her life.

So. On five, she rolled, got to her knees, and dove for the open door.

A BURST OF—

Swayne's finger froze when he saw the cabin door slide open. He saw Bin Gahli ramrodding Nina toward the opening, but he tried not to look at that. He needed to focus on the rifle sights. Still, Saddam's head did not come clear.

He broke his focus. Nina. In the fight of her life. He glimpsed her battered face, visible across the chasm of thirty or forty feet. The sight tied a knot in his gut.

He swung the rifle toward Bin Gahli.

Hell with her. He could now do a favor for the Free World.

He swung the rifle back at Saddam.

At the very second the Englishman disobeyed orders to lie on the floor with his head covered. Suddenly the Brit sat up and shouted, "What the bloody hell are you doing?"

Loud enough for Swayne to hear through his ear cups and over the noise.

The only thing that could have stopped Swayne from killing Saddam Hussein was a U.N. eyewitness. He dared not put his country and the Marine Corps on the spot, no matter what he felt.

So he adjusted his aim once more and shot Bin Gahli in the left eye. The terrorist's head whipped backward—as Nina stabbed at him with some kind of blade that'd be useless even for paring potatoes.

Bin Gahli pitched over on his side near the far door. The wind tore at his wraps or sheets or whatever they called them. And Bin Gahli slid out of the craft and sailed into the night.

Swayne's mind went into overdrive. Maybe he could talk his way out of the murder. Sure. He'd needed to try saving the CNN reporter's life. Incidentally, the CNN reporter that he had often enough lain in bed with.

As the Night Hawk broke right, he saw Nina get to her knees and make her blind leap.

His heart locked up in mid-beat.

He had not saved her life after all.

Nothing could have made him feel worse than the death of Nina.

Until the Brit reached up, peeled back the ear cup of Swayne's headset, and said, "Why the bloody hell didn't you take out that madman Saddam when you had the shot?"

One lifetime, two singular chances. Both now lost forever.

Never had Swayne come so close to puking while not under the influence of a hangover.

EPILOGUE

For Lance Corporal Henry Friel. Something had died within him, and a grief of many faces haunted the aftermath of Event Scenarios 14 and 15.

Foremost among those faces shone that of Gunnery Sergeant Delmont Potts. As it happened to him so often, Friel did not realize how much he valued something until it was gone. He felt the loss more keenly, of course, because the gunny had sacrificed his own life in saving Friel's.

They'd had their funeral. Full honors. But Friel knew he'd never get over one thing: the closed, partially filled casket.

Friel had also lost some of his good looks, partly to the burns now healing with the help of painful skin grafts from his thighs, partly to the depression that accompanied that pain, and partly to seeing his excessively pink face in the mirror far too many times a day. More than anything to the years of aging he'd experienced in less than a week.

Although he might not admit it, perhaps the worst of all was the loss of something even more grievous, the loss of innocence. He'd thought he had given that up at age twelve when he'd discovered his mother in bed with his uncle. But in that instant when Potts had grabbed him by the collar and thrown him clear of the burning helicopter, he'd realized that, well, hell, yes, innocence could exist. Even as, in the next instant, Potts was lost, taking with him Friel's belief in its value.

Of all the names that Friel had been called, stupid was not among them. He possessed enough self-awareness to know that he was a callous, cynical smart-ass, even for a Force Recon Marine. And he knew enough shade-tree psychology to realize he would return to being a smart-ass once a period of grieving had passed. Although the end was not in sight, his grieving would eventually be over. His face would heal. His body would recover.

But not his soul. Friel prayed more fervently than he'd ever done in all that daydreaming kneel-time back at St. Ignatius: *Dear God, if there is a God, save my soul, if I have a soul.*

FOR SERGEANT ROBERT Night Runner. Something had come to life within him, the spirit of Heavy Runner.

As difficult as it was, most of the mission had been routine. Except for the personal combat with Bin Gahli's tracker, whose name was Jaffari, as he had learned in the mission debriefing.

From the moment Night Runner had seen Jaffari in his video scope, everything else had become all but irrelevant. Saddam. UNSCOM. The United States. The United States Marine Corps. And as much as he loved the man, even Potts.

The tracker had become the thing, the only thing, everything. Night Runner had become a Blackfeet warrior, undertaking a personal mission against a Bedouin warrior. Nothing in his life had ever been so fundamental. And his undertaking of that kind of personal warfare had led him to an understanding of his heritage like nothing else.

And for one moment, rather than him possessing the heritage, the heritage had possessed him.

That night he and Jaffari had fought with knives. Night

Runner had won the combat. He could feel the final irregular, lurching heartbeats growing more feeble at the tip of his bayonet. Before Jaffari's spirit could depart the body, Night Runner knew that he must send him to the other world bearing the proof that he had been dispatched by a member of the Piegan tribe of the Blackfeet Nation. Without thinking, as thousands of his ancestors had not given it thought, he withdrew his blade. First he tore off Jaffari's turban. Then, after one quick, circular slash, he tore off Jaffari's scalp, held it to the heavens, and shrieked his warrior's victory cry.

His kill, then, was not so much for Potts, but for himself.

The white man would never understand that this was no war crime, but a ritual that all of his kind had accepted in their own rules of warfare long before they knew that white people ever existed, let alone the Geneva Conventions. So Night Runner would never talk about it to anybody. Except in the sweat lodge. If Heavy Runner should come to him for a sweat and a chat.

But he would not stop thinking about it. And he could not stop smiling about it either.

For Nina Chase, who had willed herself dead, and even tried to commit suicide. The experience in Iraq was a wash. Something lost, something gained, all even in the end.

It had appeared that no man was going to save her from Bin Gahli, and that thought had crushed the last vestige of her own innocence like a combat boot grinding a cigar stump in the dirt.

But Saddam Hussein, killer of millions, had saved her life for the second time in as many hours, grabbing her by the ankles before her body could fly into the night. Once again, her white knight, the darkest of knights.

In gratitude, she had prostituted herself before the world. As a CNN reporter, she had confirmed that Saddam had released the UNSCOM team on his own and had destroyed the Salman Pak compound, including all of its biological weapons of mass destruction. Unfortunately, two French members of the United Nations team observing this act of peace had been struck by flying debris in the explosion and had died.

After Saddam had released her, she had become quite the celebrity, doing one news show after another. She had tried to persuade her bosses that it would be better to recant her report. But they had countered that she could not provide proof, so it was better to let the whole situation ride, to take advantage of all the free publicity a CNN reporter was getting. Not to mention the certainty of journalism awards to come.

Let it ride, her bosses said. So it rode.

All she had left was the tiny victory she could never tell anybody about because they just wouldn't get it: She'd never cried.

FOR CAPTAIN JACK Swayne. Scenarios 14 and 15 would never end. Not as long as he could summon the memory of Gunny Potts.

Oh, he had shed one of his demons. When Bin Gahli flew out of Saddam's helicopter, his arms spread, his dark form swallowed up by the night, Swayne had killed more than a terrorist. He'd killed that Death Angel that had tried to possess him.

But that did not spare him the pain of losing the gunny. Even as he lay on the beach beside Nina Chase, Potts was in his mind.

Swayne's aftermath of Iraq had flip-flopped from grief to disbelief to relief somewhere between post-mission debriefings. He had talked to the Marine Corps headquarters reps, the CIA, and a twit from the National Security Adviser's office. He was about to undergo a second round when he saw Nina's report on television. His jaw dropped, his spirits rose, and his briefings grew shorter by half.

After more than a few near misses, they found each other and grappled like newlyweds at her apartment. Then at his. When she had finished her celebrity appearances, they flew to San Francisco, missed a flight because of more grappling, then made connections to Hawaii.

For days they wrestled, the lovemaking needy, insatiable. They took from each other rather than giving, both knowing that they would have lost each other forever if she had fallen from that helicopter in Iraq. Until finally, they were exhausted and began giving rather than taking, staying out of sight until the bruises on her skin had yellowed to a shade that could be covered with makeup.

Until at last they lay on the beach, letting the salve of the tropical sun heal their aching bodies and bruised spirits.

After a long silence one day, her eyes closed, her head under a towel, she told him what had happened inside that helicopter. She told him that Saddam had shot Bin Gahli in the head before grabbing her ankles. He was surprised. Not so much at her confusion about who shot whom. But that she seemed to be asking him to contradict her.

"I want to know, Jack."

"Know what?" All the while hoping she would not ask a question he could not answer truthfully.

"Do you have any way of knowing what I went through in Iraq? Finding out there's no such thing as a white knight?" It was not a waif whining at him in self-pity, but a clever woman asking a reasonable question in a straight-arrow fashion. But with an ulterior motive. That Nina.

But nevertheless asking a question he could not answer. So he tried an evasion.

"It must have been awful for you."

She sighed, clearly disappointed, but willing to let the issue drop. She'd always respected him enough to let things like this drop. If she hadn't she'd have repelled him.

He wondered. Was she disappointed that he would not admit to being in Iraq to save her life? Or that he had not, in fact, been there?

He pulled the towel away, grasped her hair, and pulled gently, lifting her head so he could look into her irises, dusky and gray as twilight, a sliver of red remaining in the white of her battered left eye. One tear in each eye. He dabbed the tears with a corner of the towel.

"He never made me cry, Jack."

"Huh?"

"When he was doing all those things? I never cried. You think I'm stupid to say so?"

"No. I think I understand. It took guts not to cry."

"Thanks," she said.

"Don't lose hope, Nina."

"In what?"

"In white knights. In guardian angels. In saints wearing halos, or Marines wearing helmets."

She sniffed. A smile played on her lips. "And what else?"

"When all else fails," he said, "don't lose faith in that buckle-knife of yours."

Her mouth flapped open in astonishment. She had never told anybody about that knife, fearful of the stir it would cause if her fellow journalists found out she'd packed a weapon into a story.

He winked at her. "You never know when you'll have to cut some terrorist's throat."